FINNISH BU . _

by
Geraint Roberts
First impression 2021
©Geraint Roberts

Cover design: Gareth Jones from a painting by Rita
Roberts, inspired by a photograph by Kalli Piht

FOREWORD

The original Estonian story, Forest Brothers was published in 2012, but took three years to write. What I was hoping to capture in the book was Estonia's struggle in both wars, and to recognise the Royal Navy's role in helping Estonia in its war of independence. From the moment I discovered the latter, I wanted to do something that paid tribute to this forgotten piece of history.

On completion, I was left with a desire to further explore the back story and so the story of Finnish Boys came to life.

I would like to thank Deborah Lea for proofreading my work and Kalli Piht for the original image. Rita Roberts for her painting and Aile Roberts for always putting up with me and my persistent desire to visit some of the lesser known places in her land. For that forbearance, I dedicate this work to her.

BACKGROUND

It is June 1941, twelve months after Russia has forced a military presence on Estonia. Now a part of the Soviet Union, its people live under constant fear. In one night, ten thousand people are rounded up for deportation to Siberia, in what is now known as the Red Terror.

The Molotov-von Ribbentrop pact has carved up the Baltic lands between Russia and Germany. Now the alliance is tenuous. Hitler's Army have moved up from Poland and are waiting to pounce. The Red Army will be pushed out of Estonia until 1944, when the Germans find themselves in final retreat.

Germany has few allies, but one is Finland. A country formed from the aftermath of the Russian revolution. One that has only recently survived a winter war with the Soviets in 1939.

Estonians who manage to escape North have been formed into a unit in the Finnish Army.

The UK has its back to the wall in the battle of Britain and the USA is trying not to get embroiled in the war, so both are conspicuous by their absence.

The story begins on the night of the Red Terror, in Rapla; a small town in Central Estonia.

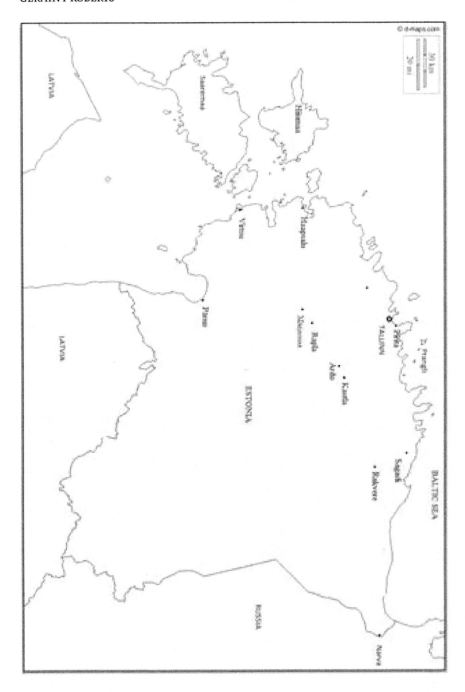

CHAPTER ONE

The Baker (June 1941)

M ärt loved the smell of fresh bread. Ever since childhood, the aroma of baking had made him relax. At least for a short part of the day he could feel good about himself; for there always seemed to be something that would set him off into a spiral of regret. Märt smiled at the thoughts.

Why so cynical today? You have a good business here. People like you - when you let them get close enough.

Kari was preparing to unlock the front door and open the shutters to let in the grey morning. Always arriving early to work, she radiated a warmth that brought people through the door. Even in the dark times that they lived in, she still tried to keep positive.

'I wish I could learn from you,' Märt muttered.

Kari looked up and smiled, even though Märt knew she had not heard. Always bright, always happy. Still a looker, Märt thought. Had there not been ten years difference, Märt would have considered his chances.

Ten years and a husband, of course. Märt felt like laughing at the thought of romance. At forty years of age, it was a bit late to go chasing girls - especially older ones.

'It's going to be a fine June day,' Kari said. 'Hot.'

'I will probably sleep,' Märt replied. Then realising how melancholic he sounded, he added.

'Maybe I should go fishing later on, Kari.'

'Yes, you could sleep by the river.'

'Well, let's sell some bread first,' Märt said with a flicker of a smile. 'I will get some peppermint tea, it always relaxes me.'

Märt normally spent most of the working day preparing the dough, baking or the final cleaning of the back area. Today he felt he deserved the luxury of making an appearance at the counter and bask in the morning sunshine.

He made two mugs of hot water and added some herbs. The aroma was calming, and he managed a smile as he walked into the shop and saw the line of people waiting to buy bread.

They like my bread.

Märt always felt satisfaction at the thought. He placed the mugs on the table.

The front door burst open, as a man swaggered into the bread shop. It was a deliberate act, to maximise the melodrama. He slammed a paper on the counter and produced a small nail and hammer. He fixed the nail through the paper into the counter, then turned to face his audience.

'By order of the Rapla Workers Committee, this bakery is hereby nationalised. It will now be worked by the people, for the people. The shop is closed for today.'

The man stormed out without another word. He hadn't even looked at Märt.

The whole room was stunned by the audacity of his action, but the red armband that he wore on his coat had paralysed them.

Slowly and sadly, the customers turned and shuffled back out of the shop, leaving Märt and Kari staring at the empty room. Märt grabbed the paper, ripping it from the smooth counter he had crafted himself.

'I don't think you are supposed to move it,' Kari whispered.

'Screw them!' Märt replied

It wasn't right. It wasn't fair. But as Märt read the words on the paper, he knew there was nothing he could do about it. He wanted to screw it into a ball, but he could not put it down.

'He is one of the morons working for the People's committee,' Kari said with a sigh. 'An outsider from the villages. Liisbet says he is a lazy man, no interest in honest work.'

'Ideal job credentials,' Märt snapped.

He had prepared a fresh batch of dough that morning, ready for it to rise and sour as the days went by. Now he all his good work would be taken away from him.

'I'm going, Märt, I'm leaving Rapla,' Kari said. 'I can't work for them. All the Reds seem to walk around like him; as if they have the right to do anything they want.'

'Your Liisbet is one of them,' Märt said. He knew his disappointment at the young woman's actions made him spit the words out. He always found Liisbet a friendly, happy child.

As she had grown however, the young people's zeal to change the world had begun to grow within her. Unfortunately, her path involved joining up with the Red bullies.

'I can't stop my niece from making her choices,' Kari replied. 'Although one day she will regret them, I fear. Märt, my husband was talking about escaping to the forest. I did not believe it was that bad. Now...'

'I understand,' Märt watched the door move slowly in the breeze. He went to shut it. The conversation was private, and you never knew who would listen in – or who they would tell.

'You would go to join the forest brothers?'

'Märt, I see no future in staying in the town. There are some rumours. They frighten me.'

Märt nodded slowly. 'Take whatever bread you want - you will need it.'

'You could come too.'

'Honestly, Kari, I don't know what to do. This place, it's my life. Without the bakery, it ends.'

She came up and squeezed his hand.

'Don't wait too long.'

Märt sat in the bakery shop for hours, until the sun's set-ting rays began to filter through the shutters. At one point, he slept with his head on the counter and had been rewarded with a stiff neck for his trouble.

He still did not know what to do; should he give up his life and all he had built up or drown in the shame of submitting to the new order?

Märt cursed as the door of the tiny shop opened. He was sure he had locked it. To his surprise, it was Liisbet. Märt had little patience for her. It reminded him too much of the drama of the morning, as he gazed at her red armband.

'Kari said you would be here still', she said

'Well, Kari was right,'

Märt looked down at the proclamation again. He did not need to see the words; nothing was going to change. Märt looked around his small shop, noting that flour dust still lay on the empty shelves from loaves now sold. He had spent so many years building up his business, from the time he had left the Kaitseliit, the civil defence. He had been learning every day in his bakery. Learning to make good bread. Learning to run a shop. Learning to like himself once more.

'She said you had a visit today.' Liisbet said.

'Cowards!' Märt muttered, as he thought of the scene once more. *Hope your people's bread poisons you. Hope you choke on it.*

'You know this already or you are not a good party mem-ber, Liisbet.'

'What is going to happen?' Liisbet asked.

Märt paused to look at the counter and for once appreciate the smoothness of the wood.

'I will not bake any more bread, ever.'

He was angry at his own words, spoken out loud. They hurt him; the truth hurt him. He felt helpless, but he would not change his mind.

Traditionally, people baked their own bread in Estonia, sharing a communal oven. In many parts, the population was spread over a distance in small farms and logging camps. As Rapla grew, people became more urban in thought. Märt had put a simple idea to a small group. *I bake your bread and you have time to earn more coin.*

Märt looked at the word '*Leib*' painted on the window. It was nothing fancy, although people at first were suspicious of him. Then slowly they came. He smiled to himself.

'They liked my bread.'

'They still like your bread.'

'They will never get to taste it again.'

Liisbet looked at him for a long time. She had taken to wearing a beret and a dark jacket to try and appear to be part of the militia. With her youthful appearance and small frame, she looked more like a sea cadet.

'I have a friend who is in trouble, would you hear him out?'

Märt was surprised by the words and forced a noncommittal shrug. Liisbet opened the door fractionally, making a faint hand signal.

In seconds and without much noise, the Englishman swept in, shutting the door behind him. Märt did not know the man's name, he was just known as the Englishman in this town.

The man was always trying to make conversation, mainly about things that Märt found irrelevant. He was of medium build and probably in his forties.

Märt felt he himself probably looked the same these days. His once sandy hair was now almost completely bleached. He certainly felt old before his time, even if he was probably younger than this man.

'Good evening,' the Englishman said politely, nodding to Märt.

Märt nodded back without a word, there was no need for more mindless chat. The man stayed at the doorway, but his eyes looked at the paper still held in Märt's hand.

'Or perhaps not so good. I heard about that.'

'What will you do?' Liisbet asked.

Märt shrugged. 'Dig ditches, I don't know. I'm not staying here for sure.'

'Where would you go?' The man asked and Märt tensed.

'What do you care? Why is it your business?'

'You bake good bread. I think there are many who are jealous of this and your success,' Liisbet replied.

'It means nothing here,' Märt snapped. 'Success is rewarded by a knock on the door in the night. A long journey east to Siberia on some charge invented for the purpose.'

He stopped. Why talk to this girl? He used to think fondly of her, but she had matured to be quite a single-minded woman. She had her own ideas and was not afraid to let others know of it.

Now she had joined the militia, she could have him imprisoned for what he had just said. Yet something was odd about the whole visit.

'How the hell did you get here anyway? There's a curfew in town.'

Liisbet made a face, 'It doesn't stop those who are careful, or those with friends. Why do you run, Märt? Why not just keep your head down and wait for it all to settle down?'

'When will that happen?'

'The British will influence Stalin. They will make sure that Estonia gets a fair deal,' the Englishman said. 'It's been a few months, that's all. Give it time.'

Märt's frustrations exploded in his reply. 'Do you know

what you say? You are a fool. Russia thinks they own us. Germany thinks they own us. Whoever wins this war will not leave.'

'So, live with it, learn to adapt.'

Märt felt as if he was being pushed to anger.

'Who the hell are you to tell us how to think? You do not know what you are talking about. If someone started shooting down your passenger aeroplanes, then forced their soldiers onto your lands. If they then said you were part of their country, how would you feel? You hypocrite!

Germany is beating London to a pulp and your Churchill stands defiant showing two fingers to Hitler. Yet you still tell us to roll-over and submit?'

'Keep your voice down,' Liisbet said. 'There are patrols in this town at night.'

Märt thumped the wall in his anger. 'Stalin is your ally, Englishman; you're probably a spy anyway.'

'The Reds want me dead,' the man said calmly. 'I have seen too much. I just wanted to see if you had also.'

'So, run.'

There was a brief pause, and then Liisbet spoke quietly.

'He needs a guide.'

'To where?' Märt said.

'To the coast.'

'So, take him. What use is this journey anyway? The Russians destroyed all of our boats to stop people escaping.'

'Even so.'

'And why should I?' Märt demanded.

Liisbet produced a crumpled piece of paper which she gave to Märt.

'You are on the list. They will come for you tonight.'

'When?'

'Two, maybe three o'clock. When everyone is asleep,' the Englishman said

Märt stepped forward in anger. 'And how do you know this?'

'I am on the list also.'

Märt snatched the paper from Liisbet's hand and scanned it, then looked up slowly.

'Why?' he whispered.

'They want people out of the way who are dangerous.' Liisbet said. 'Those who may object to changes or report back to others. People who may organise resistance to their plans.'

'So, this man is a spy?' Märt said.

The man shrugged nonchalantly back.

'I do nothing special. I see what goes on and I tell people what is happening.'

'That's what a spy does.'

'In my day it was called a journalist.'

Märt snorted in contempt and turned to the girl. 'Why should I bother, Liisbet? The English are allies of Stalin, surely I should want to run to the Germans?'

Liisbet raised her gaze to the roof in frustration.

'And look what the Germans did here in response. Calling their people back to the motherland, to leave Estonia and resettle. They ran away, is that the sign of a friend? Or have you turned towards those who joined the League of Veterans and become a dedicated fascist?'

'What do you mean turned? What makes you think I wasn't a black shirt before?'

She smiled slowly. 'Now you are testing me. I know you, Märt. What you say, who you sell to? You haven't ever shown yourself to be one of them. Yes, you have been involved in government work in the past, but you are certainly no Nazi.'

'How the hell do you know what I have done?'

'From your file, Märt.'

'What file?'

'The one they have on you. The reason that you are on the list? You are dangerous to them.'

Märt stared at the small shop. He had taken years to build it up and was proud of his achievement, but now to have these people walk in out of the blue and tell him to throw it all the way? Impossible! And yet, it was precisely what he was thinking. These were very difficult times.

'Where do they take the people? Is there a camp in Estonia?'

The man shook his head and Liisbet said.

'They take you to the station in Rapla, then you are herded into cattle trucks and the journey begins. It ends in Siberia and the gulags.'

'Some have a short time there,' the Englishman added. 'Five years, perhaps. Some will die there. Those who are allowed to leave the camps can never return to Estonia.'

'And where are you going?' Märt asked.

'Finland.'

'Why not Sweden?'

'It's closer.'

'What is your name?'

'Harold, but don't worry. The world calls me Harry.'

Märt went for his trusty bottle of vodka and poured himself a shot. He didn't bother offering one to the others. In truth, he hated the taste, but vodka had many uses. Mixed with black pepper, it settled stomachs. On the skin, it reduces the swelling of bites. Tonight, it dulled the pain of all that was and that had been.

There was a long silence, Märt then grabbed a bucket of dough and spread flour on the counter. He took hold of a handful of the dough and slapped it down, beginning to knead it into small rolls.

'What are you doing?' Liisbet asked.

'We will need food, for it is a long journey ahead. The fire is still warm enough to bake.'

'You will take him with you?'

Märt snorted in derision. 'For sure, I just said so, didn't I? How you expect me to get from here to anywhere or anything, this is beyond me. I have no vehicle and it is a long walk to the coast. Where will you find a boat?'

'You get me to the coast - and I will find a boat, don't worry. Are you sure that you want this?' Harry asked.

'I don't want this, but I have no life here. That paper tells me it is so, I have no choice. You had better accept what I say before I change my mind.'

'Do you have a message for anyone here?' Liisbet said.

Märt shook his head. 'You know this is a dangerous thought. Who would be safe with that information?'

Harry looked towards Liisbet. 'Are you sure you will not come also?'

She shook her head. 'I will be alright here. There are still people to care for.'

He went to her and held her head in his hands.

'Listen my dear girl, the people who are coming are killers. They do not value life and those they send out to do their bidding, they are so scared for their own skins, they will not think twice of committing a crime. If you find a chance to leave, take it. This is a dangerous land.'

She hugged him tightly. Her eyes blurred with tears and then looked across to Märt. It was the closest to affection that he would get, he knew. Then she slipped through the shop door and was gone into the night.

Märt moved towards the new batch of dough that he had souring for the next week's bread He had a feeling it would be a good batch, one of his better ones. Even the old folk would lick their lips in appreciation. It was so unfair, but then nothing had been fair for a long time.

'You know when I thought it would change,' Märt said. 'When we won our independence and we felt free and Estonian. Then the freedom became less and less. Then there was the corruption. I didn't feel concerned, I thought we would prevail. Even when the Reds tried to rise up in '24, I didn't feel worried.

Then Konstantin Päts ruled as a dictator for twelve years. Now this. My world feels empty. I have no hope, no land, no life and no future.'

Märt looked across to Harry and said. 'And now I have no choice left. For sure I am coming with you! I have nowhere else to go.'

He picked up the new batch of dough that was maturing and looked on it sadly.

'At least a day's work left on this stuff and I am going to throw it out into the back-alley for the rats to feed on. At least they know they are rats. I will deprive those who do not.'

The alley behind the shop was used by many people for sleeping off a rough night's drinking. Some had tried to break in to get shelter and Märt had fitted an iron bar across the door to stop them trying. There was a skylight on the small sloping roof above and Märt put a ladder up to reach it. It was not difficult to crawl through and he held the hatch open to allow Harry to follow. The Englishman was less graceful and then turned to close the latch.

'Why do you do this?' Märt said.

'So that it takes longer for others to discover you have gone, should they wish to follow.'

Märt stepped forward and lobbed his keys through, then

15

leant in to dislodge the ladder with a crash, before closing the latch as cleanly as he could.

'Now they will have to break down the door to get in.'

They both slid down and then let themselves down slowly to the ground. Harry stopped Märt as he began to move.

'Stop, first and close your eyes. Let them adjust to what light there is.'

Tiny specks of illumination glimmered from the houses whose owners dared to be awake, but it was not enough to navigate by. In the sky, the moon fought a running battle with thick white clouds, the patchy open sky being pock-marked with millions of distant stars.

After a while, Märt recognised the nearby silhouette of the twin spires of St Maria Magdalena church. He felt like praying, the thought was quickly lost in a wave of cynicism. He'd never been listened to before, what was the point of trying now? It was a shame, he decided. The church suddenly felt beautiful to him, he would miss it. How it would survive in this new god-less order, he could not even begin to imagine.

'Where are you going?' Harry asked.

'To find the railway line. It is straight and level to walk by and away from the road patrols,'

'Where then?'

'Towards Virtsu.'

'Why Virtsu?' Harry asked and Märt cursed.

'If you ask so many questions, we will never leave this alley.'

They kept close to the buildings, Märt prayed there was no object on the ground that they would stumble into with such a sound as to draw the attention of patrols. There would surely be many around this night, as there had been for the last few weeks. Even now, he could see a light bobbing to and fro at a street junction ahead.

'Someone is coming,' he whispered.

'Where can we hide?' Harry asked.

'Back to the alley, quick.'

They swiftly retraced their steps and stopped to listen. In the distance, a man shouted a question. Märt caught his breath, trying to let the air from his lungs in slow busts. He felt the blood thumping in his chest but focused on slowing his breath and intake.

'Is there another way?' Harry's voice sounded faint amongst the thumping, even though they stood next to each other.

'Come,' Märt said and moved swiftly down the alley. He could hear footsteps approach and it added to the urgency. They ran to the end and rounded a corner, stopping as their lungs had tightened with the pain of lack of air. The flicker of lamplight glimmered down the alley and hovered for what seemed like an eternity. Then it faded away and Märt gathered another huge breath.

'Now we go quickly. The forest begins soon after we leave town. We can talk there, not before.'

He tapped Harry's arm and moved down the street, cautiously checking they were not being followed.

'Are we on the right railway line?' Harry asked.

Märt cursed, as Harry had not waited beyond the first tree of the forest. *Don't spies ever shut up?*

'Listen,'

Märt held up his hand and the man stopped. He could hear a faint rustling sound in the field behind them. Perhaps it was just an animal like a boar rooting for potatoes. Some of the stalks started swaying. Closer and closer the sound came, as they waited.

'Soldiers would not be so secretive,' Harry murmured. There was another rustle and a figure stood up nearby them.

'Soldiers would not be so stupid as to talk,' came a hissed whisper of a woman's voice.

'Liisbet? What are you doing?' Harry asked.

'I got thinking you were right. People know you were with me,' Liisbet replied.

'Why would they talk?' Märt asked.

'Everyone would talk to save themselves tonight. You do not know what I have heard. All the government, the generals, even Laidoner has now been taken.

The people are next. I will be marked for the train because people know we have a relationship. Besides, Harry, I thought you liked me.'

The sound of a kiss made Märt's teeth grate and his voice was stiff as he said.

'No time for lovers, we must move now.'

'Where do you go?' Liisbet asked.

'Virtsu.' Märt replied.

'Why Virtsu? The North coast is nearer to Finland.'

'Because that is where we are going.'

The whispered conversation had become harder as they had gathered pace.

'Please, Märt,' Harry said patiently. 'Why do you pick the port for Saaremaa?'

Märt sighed and stopped. 'There is talk of resistance in the islands. Forest Brothers operate there. Perhaps we will get help.'

'No,' Harry replied. 'There is more to this. What takes you that way? It takes you through Märjamaa, where you lived and... ah. Is that where she lives?'

'Maarja worked in Tallinn for the government. A civil servant,' Märt said. 'She may have contacts. She certainly needs warning in case they try to come for her.'

'Who is this?' Liisbet asked.

'My wife,'

'Why does she not live with you?'

Märt sighed. 'Because she is no longer my wife.'

There was a pause and Märt took a deep breath.

'She deserves a chance, that's all. The farm is on the way to Virtsu, we can follow the train tracks, then head north if you wish. Or go off on your own, Harry. Now you have Liisbet, you have someone who knows the way.'

'I will go with you, Märt,' Harry said.

'Then we must hurry. There is no time, and it is a long walk.'

Liisbet sighed. 'No, you don't understand. This is not happening just in Rapla. This is happening everywhere at once. If you want to warn her, we must go back and steal bicycles to get to her in time.'

'I think we will be too exposed on the road,' Märt snapped and Liisbet grunted in irritation.

'I know this land and I know where the Reds will be. If you want to save your woman, you had better start listening to me. Are we going to be taking her family also?'

'Be glad I let you come,' Märt muttered.

'Be glad I warned you in the first place,' Liisbet said her voice sounding sharper.

'Hold there now!' Harry's voice rang out, calmly but firmly. 'We have a long road ahead and many enemies. We have to work together - or we are lost. Liisbet and I will steal the bicycles and you keep watch, Märt.'

'From where?'

'The police station,' Liisbet said.

'They will not be watching, then?'

No, you fool, they are too busy rounding up people in

trucks.'

Märt let that last remark ride, although it caused a taste in his mouth. For the second time, they returned to Rapla and Märt began to wonder if he would ever leave as he stood in shadows watching the road.

There was the sound of activity, but thankfully nobody came close as Harry came out running between two bicycles and Liisbet followed on another.

'Now, let's get going to Märjamaa!' Harry said and Märt needed no second invitation.

The journey was anything but smooth. The merest threat of the light of a possible approaching vehicle, any sound that might have spelt activity from militia, had them diving for cover.

'I can hear a train,' Harry said, as they sped down the road. They stopped and listened at the hiss of steam far off into the night.

'We can cut over fields to the railway,' Liisbet said.

'Come on,' Märt replied. 'Leave the bikes in the ditch. It will be faster if we can steal a ride west, but only if it is a goods train.'

He led them to an embankment, and they crouched low to wait. The rails had begun to vibrate in anticipation.

'It is coming the wrong way,' Harry said.

'No, you are wrong, Märt replied. 'Get ready.'

The rumbling increased and then they spied a large shadow moving towards them, faintly lit by a yellow glow at the front. Liisbet crouched ready to jump but was pushed down by Märt. The train passed by its wheels squealing in complaint, and soon its presence was only marked by a red taillight bobbing away in the night.

'Why did you stop me?' Liisbet said.

'Because they had guards on the outside,' Märt replied, adding with more than a hint of dryness in his voice. 'Otherwise it was perfect. It appears they are in a hurry to move everyone tonight and so should we be.'

He started back for the bikes and the other two followed. The cycle trip was without incident, by-passing the village centre of Märjamaa without any problems. Märt gathered pace as they neared the farm and he flew down the track from the main road, ignoring any potential dangers. It felt that fate would be kind to them that night. Märt quickly buried the thought; fortune had never been kind to him so far and he would be better to ignore any anticipation on that level.

His feeling of anxiety made the air thick to breathe. He was also panting with the exertion of the long ride. Märt steered them away from the road and down a path into the nearby forest.

'This forest path is less obvious - in case there are people already there.'

He carried on slowly towards the farm. For a moment, he remembered the past.

He would cycle out as a young man, to steal a midnight kiss from his love. Those were happier times, when life revolved around the farm, the harvest and Maarja.

Märt sighed as the forest ended abruptly. He stopped to park the bike against a tree and crouch in the long grass. In the faint light of the starry sky and the cloud covered moon, he could see the outline of buildings.

He remembered the small farmhouse, the lean-to shed and the barn across the courtyard. All appeared without life, as if deserted.

'If soldiers were here, they would not bother being quiet,' Liisbet murmured.

Märt shuddered at memories of long ago. 'This is not always the case.'

'Wait!' Harry said and they began to hear the complaining engine note of a lorry whining nearby, the tyres crunching the path as it came.

'We go further into forest,' Märt said. 'Bring your bikes.'

They ran for cover and settled down to watch the as a lorry drove to the farm. Once it stopped, men jumped out from the back.

From the light of the headlights, Märt could see rifles in their hands. One ran to the door of the farmhouse and hammered on it. A few others made their way around the back.

There was no reply, so the soldier hammered again and shouted to be let in. In the end, he broke the door with a few chosen blows of his rifle butt and went inside. A torch light angrily flashed within as the man moved around, complemented by the sound of crashing. Märt began to wonder if they should not begin to withdraw further into the forest. Then he felt a prod on his back and a woman's voice whispered.

'Don't move.'

'What do you want me to do, Maarja?' Märt said evenly.

'We wait and watch,' she whispered. He felt her crouch by his side.

Märt was desperate to look at her face. Part of him wanted to keep looking ahead, for fear of what emotions he would see. That part won the battle in his mind. There would be time again to look upon the face of the woman who long ago had brought him much joy, only for him to bring her great sorrow.

'I will wait for your orders,' Märt said.

'You have changed, Märt,' came the stiff reply.

'You listen.'

CHAPTER TWO

The Forest

T he soldier had reappeared from the farmhouse and started ordering the others to search the other buildings.

'Perhaps they will come here?' Liisbet asked.

'Then they will be fools,' Maarja replied. 'Four men against the forest will be four dead men soon enough. What are you doing here, Märt?'

'I came to warn you.'

'A bit late perhaps, they have been here twice already. I must be so dangerous.'

'I came as fast as I could,' Märt said. There was no reply.

'What now?' Harry asked.

'We wait until they leave,' Maarja said. 'Who is this?'

'An Englishman called Harry,' Märt replied. 'I need to take him to Virtsu.'

There was a pause in the conversation as the soldiers re-appeared, without much urgency in their actions. They took delight in cursing as they loaded up into the lorry and set off.

Maarja cursed them back in reply then said. 'Now you all come with me.'

The group moved into the darkness of the forest. Märt half-closed his eyes, to help him imagine where Maarja was on the trail, pinpointing the gentle sound of her footfall.

He felt someone grab the back of his shirt for guidance. He hoped the ground was flat and root-free, so they would not fall. The breathing of his colleagues became more and more prominent in his mind. The journey seemed to take hours.

Märt knew it would have been less, but each tentative step appeared laboured and slow.

'We've arrived.'

Maarja's words were quiet but firm.

'Where are the others from the farm?' Märt asked.

'This is as far as you go.' Maarja said. 'My family do not need to see you and perhaps it is better you do not know their whereabouts, so you cannot tell others. Where, how many, and so on...What is going on? Why does the world behave like this?'

'They are rounding up those who would resist absolute power,' Harry said. 'It's how the Red army works. Get rid of those who would fight, send in the destroyer battalions to roam the land, killing and maiming at will. Then everyone left is so terrified they are nothing but sheep.'

'Estonians are not sheep,' Liisbet hissed in outrage.

'Those who are not, need to pretend to be. Run or hide, it's all that is left. Even then it takes just a wrong word or someone to talk badly of you to the wrong people.'

'How would you know?' Märt asked.

'I have seen it happen before, it's their classic advance. They put pressure on the government to 'invite' them in to set up military bases. Then the machine goes into full gear. All the potential enemies of the state are rounded up and shipped out. Then the nation suddenly declares it has an overwhelming desire to be a daughter of the Soviet Socialist republic.'

'It won't happen here,' Märt said.

'It is happening here,' Maarja replied. 'This man is right. It is what we feared in 1919 and has come to pass now. Where do you go to?'

'The quickest way to the coast for Finland,' Märt replied.

'You have a boat? I heard the Reds have taken all they can to make sure no-one escapes the glorious revolution. Will you swim to Finland?'

'The Englishman will conjure up a boat.' Märt said dryly.

'Of that I have no doubt,' Maarja said. 'Don't you feel strange helping one of Stalin's allies, Märt?'

'I trust the man and the Soviets want him on the train, as well as you – and me, so I don't think he's an ally of Stalin.'

'Come with us,' Liisbet said. 'You seem to know what is going on more than we do.'

Maarja shook her head. 'There are people who need me here. I need to keep them safe in the forest. With no transport and little food – and one rifle for protection, it will be hard enough.'

'What will you do?' Liisbet asked.

'I heard them talk. These soldiers are only really after numbers, quotas. If they do not catch us, there will be some other unlucky people on another farm who will go instead. We will wait for a while and then go back when it is safe.'

'Do not return to the farm,' Märt said firmly.

'Would you wish me to live my days in the forest, Märt? 'Would you have me freeze in December when it is minus twenty?'

There was a raw edge to her voice.

'Märt is right,' Harry said. 'If they have been back three times, there is more here than just numbers and quotas. You are ex civil-service, and they will look for you. Move away or out, do not expect things to return to normal.'

A youthful voice broke through the dark shadows.

'*Ema*, where have you been?'

'I told you to stay with Uncle,' Maarja said. 'We went to look at the farm. Soldiers came back, but it is alright.'

The sudden warmth in Maarja's voice was like warm sunlight breaking through the clouds on a frosty day.

'I know this path, even if blindfolded.' The voice replied,

then with a curious edge. 'You have been gone a long time. Where have you been?'

There was a long pause, before Maarja snapped. 'The least you could say is Hello to Juhan, Märt.'

Märt felt paralysed and with a grunt of pure scorn, in the faint light, he saw the silhouette of Maarja turned to walk away.

'I moved away, Juhan. Your mother and I began to stop...' Märt paused remembering the scene. *I was no longer wanted*, he thought. 'I had to move away. You have grown up.'

'Yes, I will be seventeen next autumn. The farm keeps me busy and I grow strong with it. What do you do now?'

'I bake bread in Rapla.'

'Well perhaps I may visit some day. I hope you brought some, we are hungry at the moment.'

There was a sense of wrong in Märt, as he passed over a couple of rolls. He could not keep the conversation going. There was a deep wound within him and part of it was not seeing Juhan grow up at his side. He had visions of summer days, with Juhan fishing at the river and hunting in the forest. They were good times, but they now filled him with pain.

'Juhan, I am sorry...' Märt began.

'It is alright,' Juhan said softly. 'I know what happened.'

'You do?' A fear gripped Märt in his chest.

'Yes. You fell in love with another. It happens.'

'Yes, yes.' The lie tripped easily off Märt's tongue in relief. 'But I still feel so bad to leave you like that.'

Juhan gave a chuckle. 'No matter, we are still friends.'

'Yes,' Märt replied faintly. 'Yes, we are.'

'I will tell you all about what we've done with the farm later. You will be impressed. Perhaps if it is safe...'

'Juhan, it is not safe. I don't understand fully what is going on and why, but our Russian guests are turning slowly into monsters. Whatever happens, promise me that you will keep your mother safe.'

'For sure,' Juhan said cheerfully. 'That is easy.'

Eventually they reached a clearing. Maarja gently called, but there was no reply.

'Who does she call?' Liisbet asked.

'Her uncle and aunt, they live in the farm,' Märt replied.

'They were supposed to follow,' Juhan said. 'He was talking of going back to the farm, but *Ema* stopped him.'

'There is no-one here to meet us,' Maarja said. 'Or I have got lost. Perhaps we should wait until morning. Rest here, it is at least dry.'

CHAPTER THREE

Captured

T he double click of a rifle being loaded stirred him from his slumber. He awoke to focus on the grey uniform of a soldier pointing a gun at him.

Märt stopped moving as soon as he saw what was happening. His eyes scanned the area, taking in the sight of Maarja, Juhan, Harry and Liisbet standing, hands high in surrender. The soldier had company. Märt recognised locals with red armbands. They looked uncomfortable and Märt could smell their fear.

The soldier shouted a command that needed no translation. Märt stood up slowly and joined the rest. They were marched through the forest and back to the farm, where the covered lorry was waiting. Another sullen soldier started shouting instructions. The captives climbed into the back and were forced to sit apart. Two men guarded the tail, the rest went to the front and the lorry began to move out.

Märt closed his eyes to imagine the journey. It appeared they were going back to Rapla. His heart sank, with the thought that all that effort was for nothing.

He looked at the group huddled in various corners of the covered lorry. Maarja looked sad. Liisbet had a haunted look on her face. Even Juhan frowned. Harry was strangely distant.

The truck rocked from side to side on the rough road and then ground to a halt. There was a lot of shouting from outside and soon it turned into curses. The young militia man guarding the group began to get agitated. His eyes began to dart back and forth from the group to the flap. Then frustration got the better of him, as the fight developed. He slipped out of the back to join in.

'They argue over simple things,' Liisbet said. 'The Rapla men want possession of us, but the Märjamaa men refuse to hand over the lorry.'

'Do the Rapla team know of your defection, do you think?' Harry asked.

Liisbet shook her head. 'Probably not, I doubt if they have had time to think about it.'

'Well there's never a better chance than now,' Harry replied. 'Whatever we do, we act as Liisbet's prisoners. Let's go.'

'There's no-one at the back of the truck,' Juhan said, already looking out. Märt thought of reproaching him for his reckless action. He saved it for another time.

'Let me get out then,' Liisbet said. As she slowly climbed over the tailgate of the lorry, someone called to her.

'Liisbet, what are you doing?'

'Those fools would drive off with our prisoners, our quota,' Liisbet shouted back. 'What will the soldiers do then to us? I'm going to take them out of the truck and guard them until you've chased off this Märjamaa scum.'

'Do you need a hand?' The voice called back and Märt could hear her laugh in derision.

'With this lot? Just give me your rifle. I'll shoot the first one that gives trouble. Go on, quickly. You will need your fists more on those Märjamaa idiots.'

The flap opened up again and Liisbet's head poked through.

'Now or never, come!'

'Good girl,' Harry muttered.

They quickly moved out one by one, Märt chanced a look around the truck to check for trouble.

'I wish I could stay and watch the fight,' Juhan whispered.

'Go to the forest with the others, idiot!' Märt snapped.

The look on Juhan's face made him regret his hasty words. The panic of the moment had made him curt. He started to apologise.

'You'd better come with me then,' Juhan replied and was gone.

Märt needed no second invitation. Keeping low, he ran quickly across to the forest land where Maarja stood waiting for him.

'I thought you weren't coming,' she said.

For once the words made him smile. She turned and ran into the forest, leaving him to follow. He quickly caught up with her. She had stopped and was whispering to a man stood in shadow, who turned out to be Juhan.

'The others are ahead waiting for us,' he said. 'Where are we going?'

'To the coast. Harry wants to go to Finland,' Märt replied.

'Great,' Juhan said with a laugh.

'We are not going.' Maarja's whisper rang through the silence. 'We have to go home.'

'You have no home,' Märt said. 'You are marked at the farm. It will only be a short time before they come again.'

'Then we will stay in the forest like the others who have escaped being caught.'

'So, you will come back with us then?' Juhan asked Märt.

'No,' Maarja replied. 'Märt must take the Englishman to Finland.'

The bitterness rose in Märt's throat, almost choking him.

'Then I will go with him. He must have help,' Juhan said.

'No,' Märt said, although he felt detached from the words.

'You must stay and see your mother safe. She needs you

here. Besides, we must keep it a small group. There is a better chance of getting through when there are less numbers around.' His eyes blinked and watered like they had been stung.

'Are you sure?' Juhan said.

'Yes,' The emotion dripped from so thickly the emotion dripped from his own voice so much, that Märt didn't even recognise the sound.

'Then you will come back after?'

'Yes,' Märt said and Juhan chuckled.

'Then that is good.'

Märt reached out to clasp his hand, which quickly turned into an embrace.

'Be strong young man. Be lucky.'

He turned to where Maarja stood.

'Be careful and be safe. Take care.'

It wasn't long before he realised that she had gone.

I never meant to hurt you, please believe this.

The words were a whisper, lost to the empty forest. Märt followed the path until he found Liisbet and Harry.

'I hope you knew it was me coming,' he said, the pain in his chest now unbearable.

'Yes, we did,' Liisbet said simply.

'Where now?' Harry asked.

'I am guessing we are now close to Rapla once more,' Märt said. 'We should move North around the town, find the railway line and follow it for a while. Then keep pushing that way to the coast.'

'And the others?'

'They will not be coming.'

There was a brief pause before Harry said.

'Did you bring the rifle?'

'They need it more than us.'

'That remains to be seen,' Harry said.

'Let's go,' Märt said, walking past the other two heading in parallel to the forest edge.

'We'll keep in line with the edge until I find landmarks, then I will know where to head next.'

Märt moved without effort along the forest path. It seemed to provide steady footing, though he would not have cared either way. He just wanted to walk and keep walking until he could go no further. In the darkness, his emotions could be masked. He had no need to hide the tears that streamed down his face.

CHAPTER FOUR

Flight

Maarja stumbled for the umpteenth time as she walked along the forest perimeter, just enough to be out of site to any who chanced to look towards them. She cursed herself under her breath at her clumsiness.

'It is too dark for you, *Ema*,' Juhan said calmly. 'Perhaps we should stop until the morning.'

'It is fine, Juhan,' she replied. 'I am just thinking too much. A lot has happened in so short a time.'

She would not tell him of the tears that blurred her vision as she stumbled along in the open starry night.

They carried on in silence. Maarja reckoned it would take a day to get back home, assuming they could avoid any patrols by the soldiers or the local Reds.

'What is happening with all these trucks?' Juhan said. They stopped at the sound of yet another vehicle on the road. From their recent experience, all Maarja could feel was fear.

'We have to get away from them, Juhan. It's why I want to keep walking. We can stop and rest later on if you like.'

She had no desire to feel the muzzle of a gun once again in her back on waking - like the night before.

'Do you think they are looking for us?' Juhan asked. Maarja gave no reply, for fear of exposing her own anxiety. She stumbled again and this time, Juhan held her to stop her falling.

'We must stop, *Ema*. The stars are bright, but the light does not break through in the forest. If you turn your ankle, we will have worse problems.'

Maarja sighed in defeat. 'Yes, I suppose we must. The trucks are not looking for us, at least I don't think so. They are taking away people the Reds don't like. If you take away those people, nobody is left to stop them.'

'So, we must keep hiding,' Juhan said. 'They won't come into the forest. They don't know it well enough.'

Juhan would always sound cheerful, even in the middle of a crisis.

'Perhaps you are right. I am scared, Juhan. I am scared to sleep for fear of being found. I am scared for being overrun by these people in their trucks. I don't know this country anymore. I am simply scared.'

'Don't be, *Ema*. I am here with you.

She felt his arm curl around her back. It was a comfort and she warmed to it.

'Promise me this. If it comes to it and I am taken and you are not, you just run. Get away. Leave this place. You cannot fight these people. There are too many.'

'Let's sleep,' Juhan said quietly.

'I cannot,' Maarja said softly in reply.

'I think we are clear of the town, far enough away from any patrols. I don't think anyone will be searching for us here,' Märt said.

'You think so?' Harry replied. 'I would think they would be keener to find a foreigner on the loose.'

Liisbet broke her silence with a cry of frustration.

'Somebody tell me what is happening! We were happy to embrace the new ideas, that we would all be free and equal. Then they tell us to round up our own people and take them away. My teacher was one. He was a lovely man and when he saw me, he wept,' overcome with emotion, she began to sob.

'It is when I started to question what I was doing.'

'The world has gone mad,' Harry said softly, moving to embrace her.

Märt was lost in his own misery. He had tried to save his own, but they chose not to come.

'Well, at least we found the railway line,' Harry said.

Ahead was a short clearing, between two patches of forest, running straight across their path. Harry gave a small smile,

'It will not solve anything, but it is a start. Rest here a while, I will keep watch for now.'

The early morning dew made the grass sparkle in the morning sun. Maarja loved this part of the day. The land was fairy-like in its beauty. An overture to another long hot sunny day.

She started to plan the work that would be needed on the farm, as she had done daily for twenty years. Then she stopped to watch a ball of midges swarming in the cool morning air. The realisation hit her - she was not at the farm.

'Good morning, *Ema*,' Juhan said moving to her side. 'You slept long.'

She looked at the forest around her. Beautiful as always, but today it felt like a prison. The past life on the farm was like the early tentacles of warmth in the air. The present was the cold breeze sweeping up to douse her in an ice-cold shower of reality. She reached out to clutch the air. Juhan reached out and she fell into his arms, as a wave of pain and misery engulfed her.

She cried for the past, she cried for the present and the bleak future that appeared all around her. All the while, Juhan held her like a child until she could move away and gather herself.

'I'm so sorry, it's just everything. Losing the farm, Märt...'

'I know, *Ema*,' Juhan replied.

'I was so alone once - and he helped me. He was there and then I...'

'He broke your heart,' Juhan said.

'It was already broken, 'she whispered, her lips trembling. Then the door shut within her once more and her strength flooded back on an emotional tide.

'We need to go back to try to find out what happened to everybody.'

'And then?'

'If it is bad, I suggest we go south, towards Pärnu. I have cousins there. They will hide us.'

Deep inside, she wondered whether it would be that simple.

The first glimmer of dawn shone through the forest, waking Märt from his slumber. He stood up and looked for his companions. Liisbet lay on the ground asleep, whilst Harry sat with his back to a tree, facing out of the forest. There was a rumbling sound from the direction of the railway line below. Märt went over to Harry, who stirred and awoke at the approach.

'So sorry, I thought I was strong enough to keep watch all night,' the Englishman muttered.

'That was a foolish thought' Märt replied. 'A train approaches. Liisbet, wake up! This may be our train.'

They moved to the forest perimeter, the rumbling slowly increasing in urgency in their ears. In times past, Märt enjoyed hearing the vibration of the rails with an approaching train.

The thrashing of the driving rods of the engine fascinated him, as they pulled the wheels around and drove the engine forward, amid eruptions of steam.

The smell of burnt coal and dirty steam was not unpleasant to him. The engine was a living, breathing, restless animal and he was especially fond of watching them at speed.

Today, as he looked slightly down on the track, the spectacle had certainly not changed. As the engine passed, the driver stared straight ahead with his hand on the regulator, whilst the fireman was busy digging into the mountain of coal in the tender. This time however, the pair were joined by two soldiers who stood on the footplate at either side. Behind the engine was a long line of large cattle wagons. A soldier sat on the top of each, gun at the ready, watching the world cautiously as it passed them by, making Märt instinctively duck behind the bushes.

Every wagon door was shut and at first, Märt thought they were empty. Then he spied flashes pink, around the vents at the top of each truck. It was when he saw an arm that he knew they were the faces of people. The arm stuck out of a gap in the vent at the top of the wagon, flailing as if trying to clutch at freedom, clawing to keep some element of balance.

Then he saw others. Many held out in plea, most drooped to the side. There were faces in the shadows. He could sense the despair.

Märt thought he could hear the moans of sorrow and fear, even with the noise of the moving train in the background. A sudden panic rose within him as he thought of Maarja and Juhan.

'This is my fault,' Liisbet's voice broke through the anguish in his mind.

'No, it's not, Liisbet,' Harry said gently. 'You found the right path in time. Märt, do not think this either. Your family is safe, I am sure.'

'So, what can we do for them?' Märt asked. For the first

time in his life, he felt truly helpless.

'Nothing, except watch and remember. Make sure the story is told to others.'

Märt turned to Harry and saw the Englishman's tear-streaked face.

'I will never forget this,' he whispered.

'Where do we go now?' Liisbet asked.

'We follow where the train went,' Märt replied. 'It is going north towards Tallinn and across to Narva and St Petersburg, at a guess. We can go part of the way, until it gets more urban.'

'What about your family?' Liisbet asked Märt, who sighed.

'I have no idea what will have happened. I can only hope that they escaped and stayed in the forest.'

'You could have stayed...' Liisbet stopped when she saw the look in Märt's eyes. He moved past her to pick up his knap-sack.

'It's time to leave. We should make the most of the cool morning, take rest in the early afternoon and then carry on in the evening. It looks as if it will be hot again today.'

'Very hot inside those cattle trucks,' Liisbet muttered, not meeting Märt's eyes.

'It is July. It is hot everywhere,' Märt snapped. He took a deep breath. 'I know a farming family a few days north. We should start there.'

The day began to warm. By mid-afternoon, the heat had become oppressive. It made Märt think about discarding his jacket. The thought of a shivering night in the forest stopped him. He hoped today would not end in a severe rainstorm. He would welcome the cooling water in the heat of the day, but his clothes would become clammy overnight and would smell thereafter.

The sight of the train of cattle trucks had filled him with dark thoughts and fears. The poor wretches inside those mobile prisons would not appreciate the beauty of the day, as they were taken to oblivion in their far-off prison. Many were probably unable to see what may turn out to be their last day in Estonia.

CHAPTER FIVE

Into the Forest

Her farmhouse was still deserted, the door was hanging open. Maarja went in and looked around the inside, thankful for the shade. Against the heat of the midday sun, it was a blessing.

'The cellar is still stocked,' Juhan said looking up from the open hatch.

'There is a good supply of jams and pickles at least.'

'Nobody has been here recently,' Maarja replied, her heart sinking. 'I was hoping for a sign that uncle and aunt were around. The vodka has gone - the soldiers took it.'

'We could sleep here,' Juhan said. 'It was a long walk from Rapla.'

'Perhaps we would be too much in danger if someone came?'

Juhan shrugged. 'If I put a metal sheet on the road before the track, no vehicle will come close without us knowing. I don't see the Reds being so keen to walk from Märjamaa to here.'

'Then we will sleep and have the back door ready for a quick exit. Hopefully, they are not still looking for us.'

She felt so weary with the talk of rest, her mind was half-way into bed.

Maarja snuggled into the blanket, with the thought of another ten minutes of warmth and the feeling of being wrapped in cotton wool. She was hungry, but food could wait, as sleepiness reached out to embrace her. She began to go through the daily tasks in her head. *What did I do last?*

She sat bolt upright and looked around her. The farm felt less secure, as the memory of the past few days flooded back.

'Juhan?' She called softly, then louder as panic rose within her breast and she could faintly hear a noise that sounded like a vehicle.

'Juhan?'

'I'm here,' came the inevitable bright reply.

Maarja sighed with relief and delved into the wardrobe and drawers to find a change of clothes. Perhaps she could wash at the river first? The noise of a vehicle was still in the air, as she dressed and moved downstairs. Juhan had found a loaf of bread. Though the random cuts made on it gave the impression he had taken away the mould.

'Here, I picked some gooseberries from the garden. I have some dried fish and sausage, with tea from peppermint.'

'What about the vehicle I can hear?' Maarja asked. Juhan just shrugged.

'It is on the road to Virtsu. I put the metal plate on our road last night and it has yet to sing to me of anyone's approach.'

She sat down in relief and began to nibble at the food. The bread was sour and made her think of Märt, both for the craft and the bitterness.

Her stomach craved for her to carry on eating, overriding her sad memories.

'Where are aunt and uncle, I wonder?' Juhan said.

'We should go to the forest and look for them,' Maarja replied. 'Perhaps they are just too scared or confused to come home. The Reds could come back here if we got too comfortable.'

The engine noise was fading outside easing Maarja's anxiety. She went to the river to wash, even though she had concerns of meeting someone. What if they were hostile?

To Maarja's relief the riverside was empty but held an eerie silence. She began to wash her face and hands, expecting a soldier to jump out of the bushes at any time. Then with another deep breath, she stripped and jumped in.

The shock of the cold felt good to her. She felt cleansed, almost reborn. A dragonfly was busy investigating the reeds. Maarja could not stop smiling at the insect's dance.

On return, she found that Juhan had already filled some packs for them.

'What journey are you expecting?' she asked.

Juhan smiled and gave a shrug. 'I don't know, but if the men come, we have the basics here ready to escape with.'

'And food?'

'I store it in a handy bag.'

'You are so practical, Juhan. Did you pick all the ripe fruit and vegetables from the garden?'

She meant it as a joke, a tease to her son, but Juhan looked serious.

'Yes, *Ema*. Cucumbers and potatoes, berries and currants. We will eat well for a few days.'

'We cannot stay here and tend the garden. We would never know if the Reds or their allies will return when the mood took them.'

Juhan's smile was sad. 'It was as well that I grew up with a liking for forest berries and mushrooms. I have packed fish-hooks and string and taken uncle's hunting rifle.'

'Go and wash, Juhan, then we will go and search for him.'

They left the railway at the first sign of a military presence. In a clearing ahead lay a small crossing and checkpoint. Liisbet spied it almost immediately and they quickly sought shelter in shadows to observe the building.

'They do not appear to have seen us,' she said. 'We could move around them.'

'It may take a bit of time,' Harry replied. 'The land is flat and there is little cover.'

'We have to move away from the railway, anyway,' Märt said. 'We may as well do it now. It is a day and a half to the farm at our walking pace.'

'Why do you want to turn now? Shouldn't we keep to the railway and aim closer to Tallinn?' Harry's question buzzed around Märt's head like a wasp, making him feel challenged. He managed to keep calm in reply.

'This guard post is away from any town, but the closer we get to larger places, the more military we will have to avoid. Next time, they may see us first. Trains would be good to jump, but I think they will be guarded. The farm is still on our way north, but away from Tallinn. We are starving, so I am taking you to a place that will welcome us.'

'How do you know the way?' Liisbet asked.

'There are landmarks, like villages, towns, lakes. I know something of this area.'

Märt knew he sounded brusque, but the pain inside him was too great.

After a few hours of stumbling through the wooded land, they reached a road familiar to Märt.

'This will lead across the marsh to the farm,' Märt said. 'We walk faster on this road. We must still keep our senses alert though to any sight or sound, so no talking unless to warn of danger. Any human activity is a danger to us, do not think twice of this.'

'No problem with that,' Harry replied. 'We've hardly been talking up to now.'

Märt sighed in irritation. The farm he was taking them to was good at maturing its own alcohol. He could do with a drink right now.

'We should rest where there are berries. We need to eat what we can find. Mushrooms we can take for later.'

'What berries?' Harry said.

'Blueberries, strawberries, raspberries, Lingonberries possibly. Cloudberries if you are unlucky to be in a swamp. You don't know this?'

'Yes, Märt, I know nothing of this land. I know a lot of the people, but nothing of this land.'

'Look out for snakes also. They like to sleep in the warmth and will attack if provoked. They are long and grey.'

'I know what a snake is.'

'And also, you have to...'

'Märt, you can fight with me all day if you like, but at the end of it we will still be stuck here, running from the Reds.' Harry's words were calm, but firm. A latent anger was brewing in both men.

Märt did not think of a reply for a while, but it was hard to suppress an incendiary comment. He was irritated, hurt and angry.

The image of the train and seeing Maarja again had sent his senses into freefall. Sleeping rough had done nothing for his temper either.

'Perhaps we should rest here and make use of the berries.'

Perhaps I will stop lashing out and become human again.

His mind fell back to a scene from the past, one that had played over and over again in his mind for years.

'Is this true? Did you really do this?'

Maarja's hair was unkempt, her eyes red raw with weeping, but she had tensed like a wounded vixen waiting to defend her lair. Märt reeled from the slap delivered to his face, as he nodded in reply.

'Why would you do this? Why would you do this?'

She yelled at him and launched a flurry of punches. He fended her off but did not retaliate. She flung herself at him and he had to hold her wrists up until she fell back exhausted.

'I love you,' he said.

'No, you don't. Nobody who loves would do this.'

'I never wished to hurt you.'

'Well, you did,' she whispered. 'I feel ashamed. 'I feel defiled. Dirty.'

Her words stung him. It felt as if a dark void had opened in his mind and he tumbled into it.

'I will leave if you wish.'

He hoped to God she would not agree. Her eyes winced with pain and she went to the window to stare out at the farm.

'I think you should. I can never trust you again. I cannot look at you for loathing. It is over, you must go.'

Märt gasped with the sudden pain.

'Juhan...'

'...Is my responsibility. You didn't think of him before. Why worry now?'

He began to protest, but she raised her hand to stop him. She still could not turn and face him.

'Go. Leave me. Never come back. There is no place for you here.'

Märt moved past her to the door. He knew she was stifling her sorrow. He had had enough of fuelling it.

Why do I hurt the ones I genuinely love?

There was no answer, no flash of inspiration or enlightenment. He wondered how Juhan had grown up so happy and positive. He was glad it had happened but wished he had been there to see it. His eyes narrowed, as he winced at the thoughts of what might have been. The nightmares had come to him too regularly these past few days.

Normally he could easily suppress them, but meeting Maarja again had made it impossible to ignore this time. Now Märt felt he was dying inside.

The early morning sun's rays channelled through the wavy lines of trees, highlighting the undergrowth and grass that grew patchily in the clearings.

Liisbet gave a gasp of approval as she discovered a patch of golden mushrooms. She started to fill her pockets.

'You were right, Märt. We can cook these when we are able.'

Märt went to help, he felt he owed the other two some civility, so he finally began to recant his tale.

'When I was in the Kaitseliit, I had some cause to be in the area north of here. We were a small group, but one day a nearby farm caught fire. We were there and we helped. I hope they still remember.'

He could not forget the smoke choking him as he struggled up the stairs. His eyes were streaming as they tried to rapidly blink the pain away.

Märt charged the door of the bedroom to find a small boy huddled in the corner and sobbing. As he picked up the child and turned, a rushing sound came from within the house and flames shot through the door.

There was no time for delay, Märt rushed to the open window, the child held in one arm. He sat on the sill and let himself down slowly with one hand as low as he could, before he had to jump. He landed and collapsed backwards, levering the child to land on him. His back felt on fire and his buttocks were bruised, but he knew he had not broken any bones. He knew they were safe.

It felt like a miracle that they managed to save the farmhouse. Märt's unit was granted leave to rebuild the farm. Märt helped where he could as he recovered. He felt proud, but scared about the rescue.

He had realised as he rushed through the burning building, that he did not care whether he would live or die...

'My family, well Maarja is a strong woman and very resourceful. I did her a great wrong many years ago. That is all.'

'That is not all, but enough for us to know.' Harry replied. 'Though I think that she realises she still has feelings for you.'

'But not enough to want to be near me. I will speak of this no more.'

He strode on thinking of old farmhouses, slanted wooden fences and warm smiles of gratitude. For a few hours, they made steady progress and then Harry stopped and glanced at the sky.

'Perhaps we should look for somewhere to rest for the hotter hours,'

'Let's move on a bit farther, away from the road first,' Märt replied.

He led them through the forest, whilst keeping his eye on the angle and intensity of the sun and the time. He could only do this when he could see daylight break through the canopy, so a lot of the time he moved forward by instinct. They aligned themselves to a forest track and their way became brighter once more. The trees formed wavy lines, highlighted by the sun.

The ground below was green with vegetation, a soft respite to their aching feet. They soon found berry bushes on either side of the track and Märt called a halt.

'We are far enough from anywhere. Let us eat the berries.'

'With a fire I can cook these mushrooms,' Liisbet said, although her voice belied her weariness. 'Build the right fire and we can roast them above the flames.'

'I can make the fire,' Harry replied, producing a petrol lighter.

They were all silent as they collected the berries, eating as they went. No matter how many they consumed, the hunger remained.

'The last of the bread,' Märt said, producing three hand-sized rolls from a pocket. 'They never searched me. It is only something to line the stomach, small as it is. Next stream, we should stop to drink.'

He knew it was obvious, but his thirst made him say it out loud.

Liisbet sat away from them in a clump of berry bushes. Slowly and deliberately, she picked one berry and placed it in her mouth. Slowly, she reached for another.

'What's the problem, Liisbet?' Harry asked. She didn't reply, so Harry moved over to her and she raised her head to look at him through teary eyes.

'I cannot stop seeing them in my mind. Those people on the train, I saw some of their faces, those children. I did this.'

'No, you did not,' Harry said firmly.

'In my belief that things would change for the better, I helped welcome in those who did this. This is the result.'

'Well you were right about things changing,' Märt said quietly. Quickly he added. 'Though not how you expected them.'

Harry held her to let her cry on his shoulder.

'I see them in my dreams, those faces, so helpless. What have we done?'

'It is not what we have done,' Harry replied. 'It is what we can do. Never give up, little one.'

Märt continued to forage for berries. The look Harry had given him was more than hostile. He focused on his own gloom, remembering the waving arms from the train. He would not begrudge Liisbet her grief.

A movement made him look up. Liisbet stood over him, holding out a handful of berries. Silently, he took them and nodded his thanks.

'I hope your woman is safe.'

'She is not my woman.'

Liisbet reached out to touch his arm, then she moved away to find more berries. Märt shook the fog from his head and moved forward, Liisbet's voice filled the air.

'Let's make a fire and we can toast the mushrooms on a stick. If we get to find a place where we can stop for a longer time, perhaps we can fix a snare and catch rabbits.'

'I doubt if we will be somewhere long enough,' Harry replied. 'So, we buy, beg, borrow or steal what we can find. I need to sleep. Can we organise watch – two hours each?'

Märt's dreams were troubled. He saw the waving arms on the train once again, as it steamed past him. They were waving him to come with them.

He ran and ran as fast as he could, but the train was always just out of reach. Then the back fell open and Maarja stood there looking at him.

He looked in her eyes and the pupils were black. They grew larger until they filled his vision and he felt sucked into them like a vortex. He woke with a start. The sweat that covered him now began to cool rapidly in the cold night air and made him shiver. Märt saw Harry was sitting up awake and moved to join him. Harry noticed his approach and nodded a greeting, before remarking.

'I had a thought that we should chance a visit to a village. See if we can buy supplies, barter, whatever we can do. I don't think we can survive forever on berries and mushrooms.'

'Perhaps not,' Märt replied. 'I could set animal traps or fish if we stayed in the same place for a while. But exposing ourselves from the forest? It is risky.'

'We do it at the start of day and check out the movements around the place beforehand, or we find a farm? Where is this one you want to visit, by the way? We have been walking for a while now.'

'Another day, maybe two.'

There was a pause and Liisbet began to raise herself up. Märt asked the burning question in his mind.

'Harry, why are you here?'

'I was sent to keep an eye on things in 1924, when groups of communists tried to stage a coup in this land.

I liked the place and... well, they wanted to keep an eye on things. Especially as Europe began to fall in love with fascism and the League of Veterans had rose up here. When the black shirts began to look dangerous, and President Päts suspended democracy, I was suddenly in demand again by Her Majesty's government.'

'I thought England didn't care.'

'The United Kingdom of England, Scotland, Wales and Northern Ireland is always interested in the world, especially in what Germany and Russia are doing.'

He moved away to relieve himself and Liisbet came to stand by Märt.

'You can trust him, Märt,' she said. 'He is a good man and he will not sell us out to Germans or Russians.'

'How do you know?'

'I know,' Liisbet replied, suddenly tensing. 'If not, I would have had him arrested long ago. And don't worry, it is risky going to a village, but I will be doing the talking.'

CHAPTER SIX

Encounters

T he forest edge was ankle-deep in blueberry bushes. Maarja wondered where the rest of their food would come from whilst they stayed on the run. The carpet of blueberries went far in, as the tall trees with their high branches offered limited shade. The occasional clumps of grass broke up the bushes. The trees stood like sentinels, offering an embrace of sanctuary away from the madness that the land had become.

Maarja felt safer, although memories of their capture came flooding back. They retraced their steps to where they had been caught. The knapsacks and bicycles still lay on the ground. Juhan found Maarja's rifle in a bush.

'It was quite simple,' she said. 'They had orders to take us but if they couldn't, the bastards just made up the numbers with someone else.'

They split up to search whilst keeping in sight of each other, moving at different sides of the path to try and search for clues. Maarja was clinging to the hope that within the madness of the world, some semblance of sanity remained.

She was sure that Juhan was bending down to pick the blueberries as he went. A wave of irritation ran through her, but before she could scold him for his lack of concentration, he gave a cry and stopped.

'What is it, Juhan?'

Juhan's voice was flat. 'Please don't come here, *Ema*.'

She ran across with fear clutching her throat. 'What is it? What...?'

Maarja gave a moan of anguish at the body swinging in the breeze. In her shock she gazed around, although the light that seemed to have exploded in her mind made her stagger. She stood on something hard and without thinking began to pick it up. It was a shovel. At the edge of her now blurred vision, she saw a roughly made wooden cross, behind a turned piece of earth.

'Oh God, Oh Jesus Christ,' she muttered. 'Could we have saved you?'

'I don't think so,' Juhan replied softly. 'He looks as if he has been there for a few days.'

'We cut him down,' Maarja said firmly, her voice breaking at the tail of her words. 'We cut him down and then we bury him with his wife. They should lie together in peace, away from this madness.'

'What then?' Juhan asked.

'How the hell do I know?' Maarja shouted. 'My world has fallen apart. How the hell am I supposed to know what to do next?'

She could not stop quivering with the anguish and when Juhan went up to her to envelope her in a hug, she could only cling to him and sob as if the world had ended. Finally, she stepped back and wiped her tears.

'I am so sorry, Hani, I was not prepared for this. It was bad for me to shout at you so.'

'It's okay,' Juhan said with a sad smile. 'You were shocked, that's all.'

'You are always too forgiving,' she sniffed.

They buried the old farmer with his wife at the tree. It was a heart-breaking act to uncover the body of the woman that Maarja and Juhan had lived with for many years.

'How did she die?' Juhan asked.

Maarja marvelled at how the young man took it all in his stride.

'I don't know. There's no sign of bruising or blood.'

She forced herself to clean the face a bit and noticed the burst blood vessels around the cheeks. It was not how Maarja had remembered the woman from her days at the farm. She began to doubt if she could clearly remember anything that had ever happened.

It was difficult to sift between what was or had been reality and what was imagination. The reality always seemed so good even though the present seemed so scary.

'I think she had a heart attack,' Maarja said.

'I think so too,' Juhan agreed. He had completed the grave and now sat cross-legged, beginning to carve a name on the cross. 'When this is over, we should get a nice black iron cross, made of thin pieces, like the Swedes do.'

'Yes, you are right,' Maarja replied, though she felt distant, like being encased in cotton wool.

'Juhan, I think we should go down towards Pärnu, where my cousins live.'

There was a pause and she leapt in to break the silence. 'I just cannot do this without more family around. We are on our own here; soldiers just arrive out of nowhere and do what they want. I don't feel safe and I don't want to go back to the house. There's too much pain around here.'

'I understand,' Juhan replied. 'We need supplies, maybe spare shoes for all this walking. Maybe just some spare soles and nails and a hammer. I will go back to the farm and prepare them.'

Okay, but perhaps we can use the bicycles, as long as we don't run into any Reds. I will come with you and have one last goodbye to my memories, good and bad.'

'Perhaps we can go to Latvia. It may be better there.'

Maarja shook her head. 'It's not going to be better.'

'Well, if not Latvia, maybe Lithuania or Poland. Maybe the Germans there are kinder than the Reds.'

'Unless we get a boat to Sweden, I don't think we will be safe, Juhan. I don't see the Germans being too much better. They had history in this land of being the squires, the landowners. Yet they stood by and watched us be taken apart by the Russians. I can't see them rushing back.'

Märt was lost. He knew it, as Harry tried to be diplomatic.

'Trees grow, Märt, the land changes. Perhaps we should forget this farm and just head north?'

'Perhaps we should stop here and hunt?' Märt replied. 'I did this many times with my father.'

'How do you do this without weaponry?'

'We look for signs on the ground, tracks in the dust, shit, that sort of thing. Then we set snares where the signs are greatest.'

'Or we look at this village,' Liisbet said, pointing through the undergrowth at a flash of red. A roof that appeared to be in the distance, a first sign of life.

'It may be just a farm,' Märt replied. 'Yes, it's certainly not Tallinn, but perhaps we can get food. We need to be careful in our approach,'

He scanned the area.

'It's too quiet and we should remember what happened at Märjamaa.'

How can I forget?

They watched the building for an hour before they decided there was nobody there. Märt moved to the house wall and then he crept around to the door.

It was locked. He moved around to the back. There was no movement, bar the darting actions of clouds of insects in the sunlight.

'The back door is open, let's go inside,' Harry said returning to the others. Liisbet made a face.

'We can apologise later,' Harry said.

The house was deserted, the place was neat, but had no indication of any abnormal activity having taken place.

'They must be hiding,' Liisbet said.

Or dead.

Nobody said what they all thought. Märt started to tap the floorboards with his foot.

'What are you doing?' Harry said.

'Looking for a cellar,' Märt said. 'If they want to store food, it would be where it is cooler.'

He tapped his foot again and lifted a threadbare rug, before pulling up a hatch.

'Do you have a light?'

Harry passed a cigarette lighter and Märt struck a flame to look around.

'There is little here.'

'What are you doing?'

Märt heard a strange voice call. He looked over a parapet top see a tall, bearded man at the doorway, holding a rifle. The man had a thin face and was clearly on edge. Harry had his hands raised.

'Don't shoot, we are not enemy,' Märt said as calmly as he

could.

'Lower your weapons, we are here on orders,' Liisbet shouted as she crept into view. She had put on her red armband and cap and tried her best to look like a worker brigadier.

'We have special orders for this village.'

'Like those who came through the other houses?' The newcomer snapped.

'What do you mean?' Liisbet asked.

'Go see for yourself. But don't take anything here.'

Time appeared to stop for a while before Harry said.

'We are not Reds, stranger. Liisbet uses the armband when we need to hide what we are to some people. We are refugees, fleeing north. We escaped the deportations.'

'What deportations?' The voice was level and without emotion and the gun had not wavered in the farmers' grip.

'Perhaps it did not happen here,' Harry said with a sad smile. 'The Reds rounded up people in Rapla and Märjamaa and shipped them off to Siberia. Hundreds were on the list and we were part of it. It was Liisbet who saved us.'

The man gave a curt nod in acknowledgement. 'So, what are you doing on my farm?'

'We are hungry, and we thought this place had been abandoned,' Harry said. 'We hoped to find food.'

The man relaxed his grip on his rifle, although Märt noticed he replaced the catch.

'You can take what you want from my neighbour. The Reds came to us also. It is why I was in the forest. I go to check on visitors from afar before I meet them with my gun.

Follow the road; there is a farm, Siim's place. They were taken in the lorry and are on that train. Don't take the wrong path or I will know you are Red. If you are captured, *when* you are captured, I will not have you leading them to my family again.'

'You do not have much food,' Märt said. 'So why not go to

your neighbour's place. They have no use of the food.'

'I will not visit their farms. We may not have been friends, but I will not make gain from their misfortune. Get rid of that armband. It's not convincing and if Forest Brothers catch you, you *will* be dead. Now you must leave.'

Slowly they moved out of the house and past the farmer. He waved at the road for them to take and his manner made Märt know that the conversation had ended. It was not until they were out of sight of the farmer that Märt spoke.

'He is right, Liisbet. Take the armband off. It is a life long gone now and you will get more trouble in wearing it.'

'I don't think...' Liisbet began.

'Märt is right,' Harry said gently. 'Throw away the armband. It is not part of you.'

'It is the true way,' Liisbet protested. 'Equal shares for all, so that everyone gets a fair reward for their work.'

'Man is not ready for such sharing,' Harry replied. 'In this world, I have seen too much thirst for greed and desire for power.'

'Then we are lost,' Liisbet said, her shoulders slumping as she stared at her boots.

'Not while we live,' Märt said and made for the road. 'Now I am hungry, let's go.'

The road had been long and hard. The temptation to rest at villages on the way was there, but Maarja was wary of who they could trust.

'Some of those who rounded us up, were people I knew. They said hello in the street. They bought the food we grew. They could not look me in the eye. But I would have trusted them before the Russian army came across. Now...'

'So, we just assume everyone is out to hurt us?' Juhan asked. 'It feels like we are closing out the world.'

'For now, what else can we do?'

'Perhaps we should move the bicycles out to the road?' Juhan said. 'We would go faster. We are walking more than cycling at the moment.'

'No, I want to stay in the forest,' Maarja replied. 'But we do need to rest, I am very tired.'

'What about over there?' Juhan said. 'There is a stream, where we can fill our bottles.'

They sat for a while, weary from the many hours of walking and cycling. Maarja's hips ached and she wondered if she could get up again. Then Juhan stood up and peered in the distance.

'It looks as if we are not the only ones making this journey. I see a group on the horizon. Perhaps we should join up with them?'

'I don't think this is wise, Juhan. A large group attracts attention. Perhaps we should try and find somewhere to sleep and then carry on after they have gone.'

They used the time to eat and drink. Keeping out of sight, they observed the group as it passed them on the road. They looked weary, even shell-shocked to Maarja. She hoped that good clothing was inside the bags on their backs, what they wore was threadbare. The leading man looked fearfully all about, the woman kept a furtive eye on her children who stumbled looking straight ahead.

There appeared to be no direction or plan in their travel. They just appeared to want to move anywhere, as long as it was away from where they had come from. It was a pitiful scene. Maarja wondered if that was how she and Juhan might appear to strangers. The group made no indication that they knew they were being observed.

Maarja heard a vehicle approach, the engine note was aggressive in tone and it cut to coast as the lorry pulled up in front of the group. A man jumped out, wearing the customary red armband that Maarja has come to loathe.

'What are you doing here?' He shouted at the group.

'We are travelling to the south, towards Viljandi,' the man gave a quiet reply. He did not look up.

'Who gave you permission? Who said you can do this? Where are your papers?' the reply was angry at the impertinence.

'We just want to leave, sir,' the man sounded world-weary and on the verge of crying. 'Please...'

'Get in the lorry, Now!' The Red started waving a pistol around.

Maarja watched as the group began to trudge towards the vehicle, the air of hopelessness was absolute. The soldier pushed the man in the back, causing him to stumble. A kick in the back was his reward. They loaded the children and then reached for their bags, only for the Red to snap impatiently.

'Leave your bags, there's no time. Get on, now.'

The shoulders of the hapless parents were now slumped in resignation as they got in. The vehicle was soon turning around and returning from whence it had come. Juhan sighed.

'We spend less time on the road.'

Maarja nodded slowly. 'And avoid villages.'

'Shall we see if we can use anything left?'

Maarja shook her head and bit her lip. 'I know you are not callous, Juhan. I know that those poor wretched people will not return, but I cannot face it. Even if there is something there that would make our life easier. If they are lucky, they will be on the next train east.'

'If not?'

'They are dead.'

Juhan nodded slowly. 'Which is lucky?'

They walked on, lost in their thoughts.

'Why did you send him away?'

'Why do you ask this, Juhan?' Märt's face appeared in Maarja's thoughts.

Juhan said nothing for a while and they carried on walking in the forest. Finally, he said.

'He would have been useful to have around.'

'Perhaps,'

It was a struggle to even say the single word in reply. Maarja did not want the interrogation that she knew would follow, so she grudgingly added.

'He would have caused too much pain. He hurt me.'

Juhan looked across and said nothing. The green surroundings now felt close and oppressive to Maarja, she even shied away from the touch of a leaf. Then she had to stop.

'Not physically, he did not hurt me like that. Just there.' She pointed to her heart.

Juhan sighed again. 'Do you forgive him for running away with someone else?'

'He didn't.' She wasn't going to say the words. She didn't want to keep talking about Märt. It was all too much.

'I never said he ran off with another. He did something that hurt me. But whilst I think he has fine qualities and I remember happy times, what he did causes me great pain every time I see him. I thought it had gone, but I now know otherwise. Please don't ask, I rather would not talk any more about it – or him.'

'Okay,' Juhan said softly. 'I will let you tell me when you want to.'

Maarja knew that Märt would not be a finished story for Juhan, nor for her.

'The light is fading, and horse flies will feast upon us if we don't leave the river, Märt,' she said, giggling at the thought.

'I would stay if you wish it, just don't send me away,' the baker said in his quiet way.

'What is wrong Märt? Afraid of the dark?' she teased.

'No, I am afraid of life without you, Maarja,' Märt said. 'Over these years, I have grown to love you.'

Maarja was in shock as a deep thrill migrated up her back.

'You never spoke of this before.'

'I felt you were mourning, and you had no need of other worries.'

She sighed. 'Those days are past, Märt. I would say I look forward to the future now, thanks to you.'

'I love you, Maarja,' he said shyly.

'I love you too,' she said, although in her heart she did not know if it was politeness. Or was she living a lie? Märt offered her security and stability, something she had craved for a long time. Was she just in love with that?

'You're the only man that hasn't walked out of my life,' Maarja said, giving her son a quick kiss on the cheek. 'You're the only one who hasn't abandoned me.'

CHAPTER SEVEN

Reds

W*hat do I do now?*
Märt felt a great weight on his shoulders. The pit of his stomach appeared to have dropped and his frame tightened. It made his chest feel constricted. The edges of his eyes felt moist. He could cry - perhaps it would even make it better. He knew he would not. All he was left with was a dull ache that would never go. Especially not now he had seen Maarja again after so many years.

He knew what happened, as it had before. He would feel distant and distracted. He would not feel the sunshine and his mind would drift back to what was and what could have been. The answers would never be there to heal him.

Not this time, Märt promised himself. I have people to look after. I have a purpose and belief. I cannot afford to grieve. Yet he still wished it had been different. He wondered how Maarja was faring. He hoped she was well and for the first time in many years, thought about the men she may meet in his wake.

'What is the matter?' Liisbet asked. 'You have a look on you that would slay demons.'

'Just realising you cannot change the past,' Märt replied. 'I wish I had remembered that all my life.'

Liisbet appeared not to have heard the reply and Märt was relieved by the silence and concentrated on the future. However, his ego kept part of him focusing inwards on the dreams and desires of the past.

They continued down the path, Märt preferring to feel the gravel under his boots than to walk on the grass at the verge.

The road continued around a wooded area hidden by bushes and as they rounded this, they saw the road split into two paths. Märt stood and took note of the land to try and work out which was the right one.

'He didn't mention two farms,' Harry said.

'No, and the right hand one looks like it is not as well used. It either leads to a barn or the forest, I am thinking. We should carry on left.'

They carried on down the road again, the land to the right of them becoming swamp. Trees grew out of the waterlogged ground. The low drooping branches looked wretched in their watery home. The forest opened to a group of buildings.

The house itself had a small lean-to barn. Behind this, another closed barn stood, covered in patches of rusting metal. A small smoke sauna lodge was nearby and a well stood in the courtyard.

The farm appeared deserted, although this time, the door was half open. Märt felt little need for stealth, driven by his desire to purge his hunger. He made straight for the doorway and went inside but stopped on the threshold and turned to his companions.

'I am a fool. Liisbet, keep watch. We do not want uninvited attention again. Harry, I need some help.'

The two men went inside and were immediately hit by the stench of death. Harry put his hand to his mouth to stop gagging and then groaned. A man was slumped on the ground. There were dark stab wound on his arms and legs and back. He had been dead for a while. A line of blood led from him like the trail of a slug. The main wound on his back was wide and popular with flies. His hands curled up showing his past pain.

'They made sport of him,' Märt said simply. Harry spied a bottle of vodka on it side and moved towards it.

'There is another body here behind the table. A woman.'

'A body?' Harry said vaguely.

GERAINT ROBERTS

'Yes, her throat is cut. She is dead.' Märt replied.

He made for the staircase and quickly moved up it. One room was occupied by the body of a small child. It had been bayoneted to the floor.

Märt stopped and closed his eyes. He listened to the gentle call of birds and the sound of the rustling sway of the branches of trees coming from an open window. The occasional buzz of insects could be heard in the air. He wondered where the nightmare had begun.

As he turned to walk back downstairs, he spied a long metal rod in another bedroom. Further investigation found a large hunting rifle, which he shouldered.

Märt quickly went through the drawers nearby and located a few boxes of ammunition, which he stuffed nto his pocket. He checked his actions, as he felt a surge of greedy empowerment and took a deep breath.

Then an image came in his mind of someone doing the same at Maarja's farm, as she lay downstairs having been given no mercy. With a curse, he slammed the drawer shut and moved down the stairs. Harry stood by the door, which he had pulled shut bar a crack, from which he furtively looked outside.

'There are people coming,' he said quietly.

'Where is Liisbet?' Märt said. 'Why did she not warn us?'

'She is across the road hiding in the bushes.'

'Why did she go there?'

Harry shrugged, but his gaze did not break from the doorway.

'To relieve herself or to be sick, I don't know.'

'We can get out of the back,' Märt said.

Harry gave a quick look at him, which was ice cold and full

of contempt, before looking back on the road.

'I'm not leaving without her.'

'I was not suggesting we did. I will go and circle around the back behind them. I have found a hunting rifle and some ammunition.'

Harry nodded and his eyes narrowed. 'I can hear them now. They are not talking Estonian or Russian.'

Märt listened for a moment. 'Latvian Reds.'

Harry nodded. 'That's how you get people to do your dirty work, you bring in strangers.'

'Not all Latvians are like this,' Märt said.

Harry cocked his head. 'One for discussing later. I am worried they will find her.'

Märt moved through the house, loading the rifle as he went. It had been kept in particularly good condition. The mechanisms moved smoothly, having been well oiled in the past. He reached the door and turned the handle slowly. Putting his leg against the lower half, to cushion any shuddering, he gave the door a hard pull. It wasn't smooth, but his leg stopped the door from vibrating with noise. *It was a start*, he thought, as he kept the rifle raised high and started to move around the house.

There was a small wooden fence, just below hip-height and Märt looked for a gate. Finding none, he sat on the top and rolled his hips over dropping softly to the other side.

Remember your training. They taught you for a reason. They taught you well.

He reached the corner of the house and looked around it.

There were three men, dressed in ordinary clothes. One had a leather hunting jacket on. It was far too warm to wear on such a sunny summer's day, but Märt guessed he wore it for some semblance of rank. He looked at the Latvians critically, to size up the threat, noting immediately they all were armed.

One held a semi-automatic rifle, and he was standing a bit

to the side, looking at the scene away from the farmhouse. Liisbet was on her knees in front of the leader, who ranted at her and took a swig from a bottle of vodka. The third man stood nervously nearest to the house, gun at ready. Märt could only assume Harry was still inside but had not been discovered.

'You'd better do it woman,' the leader spat. 'Earn your life.'

He took out a hunting knife and grabbed Liisbet by the hair, pulling the back of her head closer to him. Liisbet whimpered with the pain.

'Open your mouth, bitch.'

Märt noticed she still wore her red armband, as did the men.

The farmer was right. That rag was no bloody use.

Even now, part of him felt like walking away. It was not his battle. Once again, he thought of Maarja. The leader brought his knife under Liisbet's chin.

The man nearest the house began to speak. Märt tensed, it looked as if Harry had been seen. He aimed at the man, who was walking to the house, and the world suddenly went mad.

The cracking sound of a rifle shot came out of the forest and the leader screamed. He fell to his knees holding his shoulder and dropped his knife to the floor.

Märt identified the semi-automatic as the greater danger. He quickly changed his aim. As his shot rang out, he noted a red trail spurting out of the man's chest as he fell to the ground.

Märt quickly reloaded and found Harry standing over the last Red. A cord wrapped around both his hands had strangled the man. For the first time, Märt realised this Red was no older than a boy.

He tried to put the thought of Juhan from his mind and quickly ran to check Liisbet. She stood over the leader, having rammed his hunting knife deep into his groin. Her face was a mask as she twisted the blade.

'Bleed, you bastard! Bleed!' she screamed between sobs. Harry stepped over and quickly embraced her.

'It's enough. He is a dead man.' He gently took the knife from her hands. 'It is finished, girl. It is done.'

'It's not enough,' she whispered, her lips trembling. 'It's not enough.'

She tore her armband off and flung it at the face of the corpse.

Märt went to check the others The young man lay still, his eyes wide and his tongue still hanging out with his last choking breath. Märt had a muted feeling of satisfaction as he looked at the chest wound that his shot had made on the other.

You've not lost your skill, he thought.

He was still wary, for the first shot had not come from him. He pulled his rifle to a ready position as a figure stepped out from the forest growth. It was the farmer. He walked towards them, his gun remaining in a casual, but ready position.

'Are they dead?' His voice breathed raw emotion, whilst the scowl on his face highlighted a long scar down the right-hand side. It made his expression look demonic as he looked at the scene.

'Yes, they are,' Märt replied. 'Thank you for your help.'

The farmer grunted. 'Those destroyer scum should have been killed at birth.'

'Not all Latvians are this way, 'Märt replied.

'I know. I fought in the war of independence. We would have liberated Riga, but for the British stopping us. But every land has its share of scum.' He looked warily at Märt. 'These are animals, but what are you? You handle your gun like a soldier.'

'I was *Kaitseliit*,' Märt said. 'And I hunt like a good country boy.'

'*Kaitseliit*? Why are you still not in the Defence League?'

Yes, why not? Märt thought. *Away from this mess and fighting those who would do us ill.*

A whirl of images spun through his mind.

There was an office in Kristiine barracks in Tallinn to which Märt dreaded going. The old Colonel sat behind his desk and sunlight streamed through the windows, lighting up the dust dancing in the air.

'*You have a rare talent, young man,*' *the Colonel said.* '*My senior officers say you have the ability to gather men and lead them. People feel confident with you there, sizing up the situation, thinking of plans on your feet. It's what a good officer does.*'

'*Thank you, sir,*' *Märt replied.*

'*Yet you still want to leave?*'

'*I must return to Märjamaa. There is something that I must do.*'

'*You have a strong, quiet manner. Nobody knows much about your past. They think you have a great secret.*'

'*It is a secret, Colonel, and it will remain as such. I am afraid I will not speak of it.*'

'*And you are easy with foreigners. Not normal for an Estonian. They say you were in the French Foreign Legion.*'

'*Let them say what they will.*'

The Colonel could only sigh at Märt's stubborn resistance. '*I wish I could help you.*'

'*Believe me, sir. You can by letting me go.*'

'*Well, we'll miss you. Just don't stay out of practice. Dark clouds are gathering in. The old masters look to return and take what they think is theirs, you mark my words.*'

'*I won't get much practice baking bread.*'

'*You never know, soldier. You never know.*'

'I had to return, that's all.' Märt felt in no mood to oblige the farmer with the full story. 'I'm a baker, not a soldier.'

'Not much of a tale, perhaps you should say more.' A hint of annoyance was creeping into the farmer's voice. The situation was causing enough stress and Märt's apparent dismissive response began to irritate him.

'That is all you will get,' Märt said.

'I have a gun ready,' the farmer's casual tone belied the tension of his trigger finger in the gun.

'So, use it.'

Märt glared at the man and as they locked gazes, it was plain to both that neither felt like weakening.

'I may tell you one day,' Märt finally conceded. 'But not when I know nothing about you, farmer.'

The farmer shouldered his rifle in a sudden movement and held his hand out in greeting.

'My name is Peeter.'

Märt grasped the hand in response. 'Märt.'

'Your friend the foreigner, he is an assassin, no?' Peeter asked.

'Something like that,' Märt replied. 'An English spy, I think.'

'The girl?'

'She was a red until five minutes ago.'

'Do you trust her?'

Märt shrugged. 'While the English spy is here, yes. She saved our lives.'

'Okay, if you say so,' Peeter said with a nod. 'You took the rifle from the house?'

'I had no choice. I was looking for food. We have not eaten for two days.' Märt knew they had spoken of this before. Yet he had a feeling somehow that they had stepped into forbidden ground by coming to this farm. Especially as he watched Peeter's expression.

'You meant for us to go to another farm?' There was no reply to Märt's question.

'Where are you headed?'

'The marshes near Jägala river, close by Ardu. Then we carry on north.'

'We must dispose of these bodies,' Harry said, walking over to the two, Liisbet reluctantly followed, holding his hand. 'Others may come, we must try and hide our trail'

'Why is an English spy not fighting with the reds?' Peeter asked.

'Because the English spy does not like what he sees,' Harry said with a gleam in his eye.

Peeter nodded slowly once more. 'Well, it's good to see you have more sense than your Winston Churchill. There are other more deserving people who deserve a decent burial.'

Liisbet suddenly broke out of her dream like state and spoke 'My God, this is your farm. It's the way you look at it. These are your family.'

Peeter nodded. 'My father, my wife, my son. All murdered by those bastards.'

'Then we must bury them,' Märt said.

'It is why you are at the other place,' Liisbet continued 'You cannot face being here. It's why the food is nearly gone over there and full here.'

Peeter shrugged, although his shoulders also appeared to have slumped. 'Do you blame me? My neighbours were taken by lorry a few nights ago. They won't be coming back.'

'Not at all, it must be hell,' Harry replied and then placed his hand on Peeter's wrist. 'Peeter, we must eat, we have to ask that you please allow us food from your farm. Firstly though, we will help bury your family and then dispose of these destroyers.'

Peeter looked away. 'Take what you will, it no longer means anything to me.'

Märt stared at the sturdy farmhouse. It looked so secure and firm and yet had been so vulnerable to the hell spawn that had visited.

'Peeter, come with us. We have a long way to go and I think we could use your rifle skill. I am afraid there is nothing here left for you but pain.' Märt said.

'What will my leaving give to me?' Peeter replied.

'A chance,' Liisbet said. 'Perhaps a future.'

The farmer looked long and hard at his farm. He tried to smile, but he almost broke down. There was a single line of moisture running down the side of his face; his scar formed a barrier that made it move at an angle.

At first, Märt thought it was sweat, then he realised there was nothing else on Peeter's forehead and the man wiped the tear away.

'I will come with you. We will bury my family near the house. Then we will throw these drunken bastards into the marsh. Then we eat in the memory of my loved ones and we can pack and leave. I have rucksacks. We can go to whatever future holds for us. Yes, it is a good plan. I will follow you, Märt the baker.'

Märt's face clouded as he heard the words. The words echoed through his mind again and again.

I will come with you

It reminded him of gazing into Maarja's eyes. He was sure they wanted to soften that day, but her words had cut him deeply.

'You say you left the Kaitseliit to come back here? But you have no home here, Märt. Time has passed, but the pain will never heal in me for what you did. I cannot look at you for hurting. There is nothing left.'

Märt felt his chest would collapse with his own pain and re-

morse. To his own ears, his voice sounded distant and broken.

'Many times before you said things to me, did you not mean them? Tell me you do not love me, if they were never, ever true.'

Maarja's eyes seemed to grow with the tears, but her voice was firm.

'I do not love you, Märt. There is nothing left here for you. You have no future here.'

CHAPTER EIGHT

Family

'Where are we?' Juhan asked.

'Pärnu County, I think,' Maarja replied. She hoped she was right. Her boots felt rough and she feared her feet they would blister, with all the walking they had done.

'Pärnumaa?' Juhan said. 'Well that's good news. The forest begins to look the same after a while. Beautiful, but quite mysterious and uninviting.'

'As long as the Reds think that, we shall remain safe in there.' Maarja replied.

'I would like to see Pärnu's beaches,' Juhan said. 'They are supposed to be long and sandy. When do we actually get to Pärnu?'

'We are not going all the way to the summer capital, Hani. My cousin's village lies just outside. Hold!'

She hissed and ducked into the foliage, beckoning Juhan to follow. They stayed still waiting, not daring to speak. Then Maarja tensed.

There were now clearly voices ahead, steadily growing in volume as they got closer. The new arrivals wore ordinary clothes, but there were no armbands. They had no military bearing but were armed with rifles.

The men made their way slowly through the lines of trees. Maarja's hopes began to fall as she saw the leader indicate to the rest to spread out to search.

'We know you are there,' he called. 'Come out so we can see

you. We don't want to hurt you, just to talk.'

Maarja held her breath as the men showed no signs of moving on. The leader shouted again.

'Come on, we need to talk,' he shouted.

'Why should we trust you?' Juhan shouted back. 'The last people we saw in the forest were put into a lorry and taken away.'

Maarja gave him a withering look and received a grin back.

'That's not what we are,' the man shouted. 'We are patriots. *Metsavennad*. You have nothing to fear; unless you are Reds.'

'If we were Reds, why would we be walking in the forest?' Juhan shouted.

The man cocked his head and started slowly moving towards them. Maarja suddenly realised the fallen bicycles would soon make their position obvious.

'Well, YOU don't have a lorry and neither do we, so perhaps we should both accept ourselves as true Estonians.'

This time, Juhan did not answer and the man looked at his companions and gave a short flick of his head to indicate where he thought they should search.

Maarja shuddered. Juhan had moved further around. She wished she had followed him.

'Okay, here I am,' Juhan surprised everyone by standing up.

'*Tere, tovarich*,' the man said. Although his gun was not pointing at Juhan, it was held at the ready.

'I am not a comrade,' Juhan replied.

The man chuckled and shouldered his weapon. 'No? Well, neither am I.'

'*Tere homikust*,' Juhan said with the hint of a wry smile.

Maarja hesitated with the fear of the unknown. There had been so much abnormality going on in the land that she no longer knew who to trust. She trusted Juhan to the grave and he had shown faith in these men – or was he trying to be a decoy to let her escape? Finally, her concern for Juhan overcame her fears and she stood up. The leader smiled and bowed.

'Aha! There you are! welcome lady. Come back with us to camp, it is safer than sticking around here. There are a few in this area who would do you harm.'

'You are not one?' she asked. He shrugged in response.

'If you are what you show yourselves to be, then you are welcome.'

'Do you know my cousin then? Konstantin?'

It was an impetuous move, for she had no idea if her cousin would have fled to the forest, stayed in the town or become a Red. Maarja just needed something, some tangible link from the past that she could cling onto.

'Konstantin Päts? Yes, I remember him. He used to be the president of Estonia. Got fed up with the people trying to destroy democracy, so he suspended government and ruled the country for the last ten or twelve years. A hypocritical bastard, though at least he was our bastard.'

Maarja was not impressed with the swagger in his voice.

'Fine, but I meant Konstantin Tamm and I can see damn well that you knew that.'

'You're a live one, aren't you?' the man said with an approving look that made her uncomfortable. 'Yes, I know him. If he can vouch for you, it would save a lot of talk.'

Maarja was getting annoyed at the way the man where the man was looking at her. From a feral point of view, he would be a starving wolf. She clicked her fingers.

'Hey! I'm up here.'

The man flushed at the dig, especially as his colleagues roared with laughter. Maarja took a deep breath and tried to relax. It was better probably to not antagonise anyone until she knew the lie of the land.

It was good news that her cousin was *Metsavennad*, at least if this man could be believed.

There was no escape, she had to trust them and hope the people were as honest as it would seem. She looked to Juhan and was relieved to see his smile of reassurance was back. For once, she had worried herself over the way he looked at her. Was that a frown of doubt also on his face?

Märt and Peeter went to start digging graves for the farmer's family. At first, Peeter dug in silence. Märt respected this, knowing he had nothing to say back of merit. When they had finished, Peeter put down his shovel and sighed.

'I heard them come to take that family away. It was three in the morning that a big green lorry turned up. Lots of banging and shouting and then they were all gone within an hour.'

Märt was sure that Peeter had not had anyone to talk to since the shootings and so he let him continue, even if he wanted to lose himself in his own thoughts about Maarja and Märjamaa.

'Then a few nights later, those three animals turned up at my farm in the same lorry. I was coming home after fishing in the lake and they drove past while I was still close by the forest. They did not see me, for I hid as soon as the lorry was in view. The one in the hunting jacket was laughing, he was waving his hands outside my house and they were red with blood.

At first I thought they had returned to the other farm, but then I realised no-one was left there. I dropped my fishing and ran and then...'

The tears ran down Peeter's face as he looked at the graves that they were close to completing.

'I have not been in the house since. I could not.'

The aroma of cooking meat hung in the air. Peeter had mentioned he had sausages in storage and Harry and Liisbet were in the house preparing a meal. Märt now felt weak through the digging, the light foraging and the stress of their flight. It had all got too much. He felt old.

'I said why are you travelling with them?' Peeter asked.

'I have nowhere to go,' Märt replied. 'My woman is dead to me.'

Peeter dug out another spade full of soil and stopped to look over.

'At least she is alive.'

He carried on digging without a further word.

'You cook well,' were Peeter's first words after they had eaten within the farmhouse. He had spent the meal, staring around him, as if this was his first visit. Märt was surprised the farmer had even managed to cross the threshold, he would have struggled had the situation been reversed.

'You assume that as I am a woman, it was I who cooked?' Liisbet said.

The tense atmosphere in the house appeared to be getting to everyone and Liisbet took a deep breath before muttering an apology.

'I merely helped. Harry is the cook.'

The Englishman was sitting quietly in the background, observing the interaction. A clever man, Märt mused, and dangerous also. He would add his thoughts, but only when needed to steer the talk in the direction he wished.

'We head towards a village called Ardu, do you know it?' Märt asked Peeter, feeling the need to get away from small talk.

'If you came from Rapla, you have certainly come a strange way to visit Ardu,' Peeter replied between chewing a mouthful of food. He took a drink and then continued.

'Yes, I can show you the way towards Ardu. A day's walk should get us there. Do you know where you go then?'

'Get me there and I will know,' Märt replied. 'We have food now that we can take with us, guns also. Liisbet, can you shoot?'

'Märt, patronise me and you will find out.'

'He does not,' Harry replied. 'Be calm, we are all friends here.'

'You want a fight, girl? That is fine.' Märt snapped, glaring back at the blonde girl, the tension finally getting to him.

The events of the past few days had taken their toll on them all and although Märt understood where the anger came from, it still irritated him.

He wanted Liisbet strong, alive and independent. He realised Liisbet's petulance showed that the drama of the journey had taken their toll on her also. He was angry that she too was human, though he would not choose to admit it.

'We have a new pathfinder,' Liisbet said evenly. 'You do not have to come.'

'I am not travelling without my friend Märt,' Peeter said, staring straight at Liisbet. 'This man, I trust. You, I am not so sure.'

He omitted Harry by name, but the inference was there also.

'We have to trust each other,' Harry said firmly, He slammed his hand down on the table and it killed the argument, as everyone reflected with the shock of the sound. Harry continued in his calm manner, but there was a new edge to his voice.

'We must not fight. All of us have been hurt by events, but that should bring us together, not tear us apart. We do not need to fight when there is so much around us. There are plenty out there who would gladly hurt us just as easily as clapping our hands.'

Peeter got up and moved to open a cupboard, returning with a bottle and four small glasses. He removed the stopper with his teeth, poured a measure into each glass and placed them on the table in front of each person. He picked up one of them.

'I do not know any of you, but perhaps I have heard and seen enough in the past few days to recognise who is friend and who is not. An enemy of my enemy is my friend. This is to my family.'

He downed the drink.

Märt looked at the vodka.

'Liisbet, your aunt was a good woman and worked well with me. She trusted you and I trust you and your friends and the people who save our lives. This is to my family.' He downed his drink, enjoying the burning sensation in his throat.

'Märt. My aunt thought well of you also. Now I know you as *Kaitesliit*, I also know you are a true patriot. So much has happened. I am hurt, but I realise that I am not alone. I am learning to trust people by their actions, not by their badge. This is to my family.' Liisbet downed her vodka. She flushed as the vodka hit her stomach.

Harry sat watching them, eyes gleaming. He raised his glass.

'You are my family.'

He downed his drink.

'And now the circle is complete.'

CHAPTER NINE

Forest Brothers

K onstantin Tamm was a heavyset white-haired man with a walrus moustache. With his rifle slung on one shoulder he looked ready to shoot wild boar. He scanned the group approaching warily.

'Who are these that you have brought to us?' He shouted.

'Relatives,' the leader said.

'Whose?' Konstantin shouted.

'You tell me.'

Konstantin squinted and looked carefully, then muttered to himself.

'No, I don't think so, don't know them at all.'

Maarja muttered a curse. 'Do I have to kick your arse, like I did when we were children playing in the garden?'

'Maarja? Maarja Tamm? You went off to some fancy house in Tallinn when your *Isa* went to work for the government. Too good for Pärnumaa folk, I remember.'

'Well, Pärnumaa is an attractive place these days, Konsti.'

'Can you cook?'

'I can do more than cook. I can hunt also.'

'Still the tomboy, Maarja Tamm.'

'Still the big soft bear, Konstantin.'

He gave a roar of laughter and stood with his arms open to grab his cousin in a hug. The pure joy seemed to become infectious. Maarja smiled and for once the years seemed to fall from her, making her beauty glow from within.

'Who is this?' Konsti asked, acknowledging him for the

first time.'

'My son, Juhan.'

'Well, I was hoping he wasn't your man. Where is *he* then?'

'Away.' The sun drew in from Maarja's expression and Konstantin's smile dropped.

'Okay, a fine Estonian boy though, I assume.'

'Juhan is my fine Estonian man now,' Maarja said.

'Well, there will be plenty of time to catch up You can help me catch some fish as we talk.'

Maarja was wakened in the middle of the night by a feeling of being touched. She was quick to realise it was not a dream and her arms quickly moved to block the hand cupping one of her breasts from behind. She tried to get up but was forced down. A hand was clamped over her mouth.

'Come on woman, you know you want this. All this playing hard to get, you can't keep your eyes off me. I've seen how you are looking through your eyelashes.'

Maarja began to panic as the man's weight forced her from rising. As her arms began to thresh, she received a blow on the head. It made the world spin away and then come back. Voices buzzed around her, though she had no idea what words were being said. Then someone was fully on top of her. She frantically struggled, but the body did not move. Maarja squeezed and pushed with a great effort until she was free.

In the limited light from the myriad stars in the sky, she could see a large shadow of a man had picked up the body that had fallen on her and slowly dragged it away. She knew it was Konsti and the attacker was Riki, the man who had found them in the forest. Her breath came in fearful gasps, but she hoped Konsti would not kill him. With a scrabbling sound, Juhan was by her side.

'What happened? Are you alright?'

Maarja nodded and then spoke, realising Juhan would not see her head movement.

'Our friend that we met in the forest, he thought he could get frisky. I think my cousin has taken him away.'

She felt as if she had been on a long run, as her heart still thumped around her temples. She resolved to carry a knife at all times.

'I am sleeping by your side from now on, *Ema*. I was a fool not to see it before. They will have to get past me first.'

Maarja's lips trembled with thanks. 'You're good to me, Hani. You rest, I will be alright now.'

They settled down, but Maarja could not sleep now for troubled thoughts about what might have happened. What may happen if Konsti was not there in the future?

'You have a face like a beetroot, Riki' Konstantin said with a laugh at the man who now had a visible lump on the side of his head.

'I went for a walk in the night,' Riki replied in embarrassment, moving past. 'I must have hit my head on a branch.'

'Too much of a weak bladder or too much vodka?' Konstantin said to the man's back and the nearest men laughed and shouted after him.

Riki said nothing, although his face looked red-raw. As he moved past Maarja, he dropped something in her lap, making her start in fear. Riki could not meet her eyes and Maarja looked across to her cousin, who gave a nod in reply.

She looked down and picked up the knife sheathed in leather. It looked good for hunting. A part of her relaxed.

There was still a bad taste in her mouth and an uncomfortable feeling in her stomach, but she felt she would have to live with it. Konsti had delivered his punishmen.

To banish Riki, would leave the possibility of being betrayed to the Reds. To kill him could shatter the harmony in the camp. Konsti had chosen to teach Riki a hard lesson in the hope that he was a fast learner. Maarja still knew she would need her wits about her, as well as her family, to be fully safe.

It had been an uncomfortable night, even though they had moved out of Peeter's farmhouse and back to the neighbours. Märt could not stop thinking of Maarja and Juhan. Would they survive this madness? What the hell was going on with the world?

The past few days had left him with no thoughts but to escape to Finland and restart his life. Many youngsters had run there at the start of the war, the Finnish Army had created a unit for Estonians, they called themselves the Finnish Boys. Their name was legendary by hearsay. It was said that the reasons the Russians had broken every boat in Estonia was to stop more people crossing the Gulf to join them. Now, it felt there was nothing else left.

For a moment, doubt grabbed him. He had stopped being the leader. He was no longer making the decisions. Then he dismissed the thought. Who told them when to stop, when to rest, when to listen for strange noises?

Märt heard the sound of a lorry approaching, the laboured engine in low gear moaning as it negotiated the potholes in the gravel track.

The slow pace almost taunted him and he reached for the rifle by his bed and ran to the other rooms. Peeter met him in the corridor. Harry and Liisbet arose from the same room.

'We need to get out of here, Peeter, where can we hide?'

'If they have not come into view yet, then we run across the lane. There is good cover there.'

'Alright, let's go now, everyone!' Märt shouted.

There was no thought to hide their stay, for the lorry sounded very close. Märt hazarded a quick look round the corner of the barn down the lane. To his relief, he saw no vehicle, but he could see the early sign of its headlights, so he sprinted across to the forest. Peeter indicated to move further away and Märt followed waving for Harry and Liisbet to follow. As they made their hiding place, the sound of the lorry was raw and Märt knew it would soon be in view. He could only hope that they had not been seen.

They all lay on the ground, waiting for the moment of discovery. A battered old olive-green lorry wobbled and lurched down the track -. Three men sat in the cab, whilst another three looked out lethargically at the back, rifles by their sides. They gave no impression that they had seen the group as the lorry limped on down the lane.

'Our luck holds,' Märt whispered. 'They are going for your house, Peeter. Can we get closer?'

'Yes, why?'

'Because I want to sort out these people once and for all.'

'And bring more destroyers over here?' Liisbet said. 'They are probably looking for those other three bastards.'

'Well, now they'll be looking for nine,'

'It won't stop them coming,' Harry said. 'And the more you dispose of, the greater the number of the next batch to arrive.'

'What would you do?' Märt asked. Harry did not take his eyes off the house as he spoke.

'Get to a safe position far enough away to be hidden but able to fire if needed and have a good escape route. Don't shoot unless you have to, I have a feeling we will need bullets before we get to Finland.'

'I'm happy with that,' Peeter replied. Märt indicated him to lead and the farmer took them closer towards his farm.

'This is where I shot the others from.'

'Alright,' Märt said. 'Spread out and wait for my signal.'

The men were standing around the lorry looking bored. One took out a cigarette pack and a few others joined suit. There was a loud curse as one demanded a cigarette and light. He began calling out names, the language was foreign to Märt, but the tones were obvious. He threw his cigarette away and started shouting again. He started to enter the house, and then called out. Another followed with a can of fuel.

'They are going to burn the house,' Liisbet said. Peeter's face was a mask.

The door burst open and another man stepped out. He wore dark clothing and his face was blackened by mud. He raised a rifle to fire at the leader.

The shot passed through the Destroyer, spattering the man behind with blood. A window broke and a rifle appeared at the sill. A shot was fired hitting the fuel tank. It exploded and the man carrying it was engulfed in flames. He fell to the floor screaming.

Peeter raised his rifle and fired at the remaining group of destroyers. One man fell, the three remaining overcame their shock and ran for the lorry. One rushed to the cab and had the engine revving at a higher rate than he should in his panic. He released the brake and the lorry lurched forward down the track.

The sudden forward motion threw the other two on the tail. One fell off, whilst the other disappeared, only to stand again on the lorry. Another shot rang out and he collapsed.

The man left on the ground started to run for the lorry, but soon realised that he would not meet it. He slid to a stop and tried to start running back down the track. Märt chose the right moment to stand out from the forest and called for him to stop. The man kept running in his panic. Märt called again in Russian and stood in front of him. The man stopped and with a whimper fell to his knees, beginning to gibber at Märt uncontrollably.

'You haven't killed him?' Peeter asked.

'He has a lot to tell me,' Märt replied. 'Do you know these men at the house, Peeter?'

'They look like locals. I could swear one is my neighbour, who I took for being deported. They must have escaped.'

'Go tell them we are friends. They look a bit keen.'

'They got the ones in the lorry too,' Harry said.

Märt did not reply, but turned to his captive, noticing the man's eyes were wide with fear.

'Do you speak Estonian?'

'Some,' the man replied followed by a cascade of half broken pleas.

'Shut up and listen. These men will kill you if I hand you over to them. This man owns the farm you tried to burn. His family was murdered. You had better tell me what I want to know.'

'I am not part of this. I was not there,. I swear. We were looking for lost comrades.'

'What are your orders?'

'I follow the big man and you shot him at the doorstep. He gets orders from the Russians. I just need to follow them. We are told to eliminate all resistance. I...'

Realising what he had said, the man cringed even further. 'I swear I have not killed anyone, comrade. Please, I have children.'

'Give me that man!'

The shout came from the group of ambushers and a man walked swiftly towards Märt with Peeter following. He held a large hunting knife with the blade drawn.

His body language warned of violence and the captive cried in fear.

'Talk to him, I will keep this Red here,' Harry said.

Märt stepped forward to meet Peeter and his colleague.

'Give me that man, so I can kill him.' The newcomer threatened.

'No, wait. He can talk; tell us numbers, bases, plans. We saw local Reds mop up who was supposed to be their enemies in Rapla, how widespread is it?'

'I don't care. These bastards have been going around this area taking what they want, destroying what they want and raping and killing for no reason. This is not civilised. They are animals and they deserve nothing less than an animal's death.'

Märt stood across the man's path.

'Wait!'

The man's knife came up.

'Keep out of the way.'

'Easy now, Siim,' Peeter said reaching out to try and stay the knife arm.

The captive looked on in terror and gave out a howl of fear. He stood up and started to run pushing past Harry and made for the lane. Märt began to run after him and a shot ran out. The man arched his back and fell, arms flailing. Then he lay still. Märt looked around and saw Harry get up from a hunter's crouch.

'He's no use dead, but he's a greater danger at large.'

'He could have told me a lot,' Märt said with regret

'He told me a lot,' Harry replied. 'Well, only a few words, but I can guess what is happening from them. That and what Liisbet has said and what I know of the Soviet machine. They are doing the same as they did at Rapla and more besides.'

'Then you come back with us,' Siim said approaching them.

'I am happy that Peeter says you are with him, but I need to know what brings you here and other things. Why do you want to keep this man alive - but your friend is quite happy to kill him?'

'You trust me, Siim?' Peeter said.

'Come along, Peeter you come and tell us what happened. I am glad to see you, but what has happened with the family?'

Peeter had no words to reply. Märt took the man by his arm and led him away.

'We will talk of that later.'

They were taken to a camp in the forest, where a primitive shelter blended in with the woodland. The group sat around a fire, keeping close for warmth. Märt had taken to honing the point of a stick with his knife, whilst Harry was speaking at length to the men.

'We know the Reds organised deportations and now they are trying to break down society. Destroy your national identity and keep you on the back foot, so you are always on the defensive and running scared.'

Liisbet stood up to speak. She looked exhausted and Märt was convinced he heard her slurring her words a bit as she said.

'In Rapla, we were told to find all figures of authority; judges, politicians, *Kaitseliit*, army, people involved in government. Even organisers of sports clubs and people who had made fun of the Stalin or the Soviet Union.

Then we were told that we had to add other people. No reasons, as long as we had the numbers, we could take who the hell we wanted. That's when I ran.'

Liisbet sat down, the effort had drained her. Harry continued.

'They also use their secret police, to round up those who were missed. Then they bring in the Destroyer battalions. These men go around creating mayhem. They have no rules, so they can do what they want. It means those remaining in the towns and villages are always in fear of them.'

'What's the point?' Siim asked.

'To kill off all opposition before you begin. To make sure

that nobody gets in the way of the Soviet Union, changing what it wants when it wants. To make sure you do what you are told.'

'And what about us living in the forests?' Siim asked. 'We won't do as we are told.'

'They cut you off, so you starve. Then they hunt you down,' Harry said bluntly.

'Or you keep going,' Märt said, still whittling down his stick. 'And you are there when the West comes across to free us.'

Harry nodded in agreement.

'So, you will bring your English over to rescue us,' Siim said, the tone of disbelief ringing in his words. 'Perhaps I should put my faith more in Hitler's army of shorties.'

Harry smiled thinly. 'I don't mind if you do. Just keep alive for whoever comes to drive the Soviet machine away.'

He turned to look at Liisbet and leant over. She had slumped forward, and her breathing was shallow. Märt went over to check and Harry looked up at him.

'She has a fever and is shaking. We need to get her warmth and rest.'

'Hey, you don't bring anyone here with a bug. If we all catch it, we will die.' One of the men said, but Siim waved him back.

'I am concerned,' he said and reached forward to pull back the collar of her top. A tick could be seen, encased in a blue-red blood sack. 'If this one has infected her, she is as good as dead. We cannot treat a swelling of the brain. I hope it is swamp fever. You can put her in the shelter, and we will try to keep her warm.'

After they moved Liisbet into the shelter, Märt signalled to Harry to speak outside by the fire. The orange embers of glowing wood seemed to mesmerise him.

'I am not leaving without her,' Harry said.

'I did not ask you to,' Märt replied.

'What is there for you to do, anyway? You have no mission.'

Harry shrugged. 'There are things I can observe and send back about Comrade Stalin's men. Assuming they aren't driven out of here.'

'Will Germany do that?' Märt asked.

'Did you know Comrade Molotov and Herr von Ribbentrop met up a year back? They carved up the Baltic. Estonia went to Stalin.'

'So, the Germans will not come?'

'Personally, I would not trust the ambition of Stalin or Hitler. That is why I send information to London.'

'So, you do not wish to leave now?'

Harry shook his head. 'No. I must go to Finland, but not without Liisbet.'

Märt spotted Peeter and went over to him. 'Did you hear?'

Peeter nodded. 'Nothing surprises me about our English friend.'

'What do you think?' Märt asked.

'I think he loves that girl. Will you go?'

Märt nodded. 'Probably. I would like to have done at least one good thing in my life.'

'There you go again with those words. You have too much to hide. It weighs upon you.'

Märt decided that Peeter was never going to stop until he knew Märt's hidden past.

'Alright my friend, but there is a time and a mood. Now may be the time but I will never be in the mood'

CHAPTER TEN

The Village

M aarja was surprised to be still alive. Had she been writing the book of her life; she wouldn't have seen that twist to the plot. Branches and leaves for shelter and bedding?

At least it was July, with its hot days and warm nights. She wondered what would happen in December, when the cold started to seep into her bones, the snow was all around, and even the islands were linked to the mainland by ice.

She looked at the cabin built of stout logs. They had used trees that had moss on them. The moss would insulate and camouflage. They appeared to expect to be there for a long time. The fight was in them - from the way they carried themselves to the weapons they branded.

'Riki is acting like you don't exist,' Juhan said, bringing a bowl of soup across from the fire.

'Yes, it is quite a relief,' Maarja said.

'He's too scared of getting his balls cut off by Konstantin,' Juhan said before slurping a spoonful of broth. Maarja choked on her soup at his words, so soberly put.

'Do you think we live here?' Juhan asked.

'Perhaps,' Maarja replied. 'They train you.'

Juhan nodded and stared at the others sitting around. Not much conversation was happening, most sat lost in their thoughts.

'They teach me how to fight and kill. Do you approve?'

'Whatever keeps us alive, *kallis*. Promise me you won't kill unless you have no choice.'

'There is always a choice, *Ema*. I won't kill.'

She paused and ate more soup. 'Just remember my words.'

It was possible he would never listen, but she had to speak. The silence was unbearable.

'Thank goodness for the farmers giving us food,' she said.

'Yes, *Ema*. Their grain helps us survive. I wonder what we will do in winter though.'

'Berries, preserved as jam, mushrooms. Maybe find some fish or game. The problem is you need fresh food - or you fall sick.'

Juhan handed her some bread. 'Perhaps they have other plans.'

They continued their food in silence. Maarja hated the thought of eating black bread. It reminded her of Märt.

The baker was all sour and dark, just like this bread. Had she made him - or did he do it himself? She was too hungry to leave the crust and wolfed it down.

Her cousin came over to them as they were finishing. He went straight to Juhan.

'You are needed.'

'What's happening, Konsti?' Maarja asked.

'There's a small settlement a half day from here. The local Reds are planning their own clearance, though without trains or lorries.'

'I'm coming too,' Maarja said.

'I'm not taking a woman with me, sorry.'

'Konsti. I'm not discussing it. You just give me a bloody rifle and I am coming with you.'

Konsti glared at her before sighing.

'What the hell, you scare me as it is. The Reds will shit their pants. Riki! A rifle for Maarja. Don't argue.'

'I wasn't,' the chastened forest brother said, going to the shelter and returning with a rifle.

'And I assume if I tell you how to shoot it, you will castrate me with my own knife,' he said.

'Something like that,' Maarja replied, her voice oozing honey.

'No time to argue,' Riki muttered.

'Follow!' Konsti shouted from the edge of the camp. 'Any stragglers will feel my boot. Come on, people will die without us.'

The journey became a fast march and there was little time of inclination for conversation. Maarja thanked herself for wearing leggings.

'Why the sudden rush,' she shouted to Riki. In spite of her ordeal, she found the courage to even acknowledge the man who had tried to assault her. She never would trust him. Even now on the march, her hand itched for a knife.

'There are true Estonian patriots who are in danger of being butchered,' he said. 'And Konsti has a sweetheart in the village, I think.' He sped up to keep out of earshot.

'He definitely doesn't want his bollocks chopped off, I think,' Juhan said and Maarja tried to stop a loud guffaw of laughter.

She felt a quick thrill of fear about what they may find and quickly put it to the side. She would do whatever was needed without flinching. Anger was within her, waiting to be unleashed and she wanted to focus it on those who were party to Estonia's fall. She wanted to hurt someone.

They travelled by road, the group no longer caring about stealth. Maarja had spotted some spare soles at camp. Perhaps someone knew how to nail them on to the soles of her shoes. She could now feel each step, it was obvious the leather was thin.

The village ahead was situated on level ground. The sprawl of houses hugged the road which drove through the middle. The spire of a whitewashed church was prominent in what must be the village centre.

The fields surrounding it were manicured following the harvest and now made the village look like an island on a sea of brown soil.

Konsti did not slow as the group moved straight towards the houses. Juhan nudged his mother and pointed at a line of trenches in a field.

'Are they preparing for battle?'

Maarja did not reply. She could not help feeling the forest brothers were bringing it to the village. They were quickly met by a man running from his house. He had a quick, urgent conversation with Konsti.

'There is someone hiding in the shadows of that house,' Juhan said. 'Look you can see his arm and the red band on it even.'

'Arsehole!' Riki said and ran over, reappearing with a man holding his hands high in surrender. 'Take the weapon and move him along.'

At the urging of his contact, Konstantin started to call the locals out. Most came willingly and acknowledged the villager as they arrived. Then the man pointed to another house and his tone grew more urgent. After a quick command, Riki took a few forest brothers and ran to the back of the house. There was a sound of a door being forced, then a lot of shouting. Suddenly, a man burst through the front door and ran onto the street. He stopped in shock and was quickly captured.

'Urmas says many are meeting in the town hall,' Konsti said. 'We should get there quickly before they realise what is happening. Juhan and Maarja. Keep these prisoners here. Shoot them if they resist.'

He did not wait for a reply and Maarja watched them rush off, she felt vulnerable. One of the captives started talking.

'Who are you?'

'*Metsavennad*,' Juhan said. 'Why are you digging trenches?'

The man looked away, and then asked. 'What is your purpose?'

'To stop you from harming those who do not like your ways,' Maarja said. She raised her rifle and cocked it. 'Don't make any sudden moves, we are farming folk and used to shooting vermin.'

She could hear sounds of gunfire from further down the road, coupled with large amounts of shouting, a crash of glass and more firing.

'Juhan, stay focused,' Maarja said. 'These people will attack at any point if they can.'

'They won't have any success,' Juhan laughed and quickly brought his rifle to bear on one of the prisoners as he had taken a step forward. In the background there was more gunfire and shouting, followed by a cry of pain. Then there was silence.

'*Ema,* you should go and see. I will keep an eye on these men.'

Maarja shook her head. 'No, we stay here and wait.'

'Your men have been killed,' one of the pair of prisoners said. 'There is no way they could survive the will of the people.'

'You talk like a fool,' Maarja said. The man smiled. At another time, Maarja would have said he was good looking with his blue eyes and carefree smile. Not today. He sighed.

'Go and check or if you can believe me, it would be safer to hand over your weapons now.'

Doubts began to nag in Maarja's mind. She had not heard any of the forest brothers call for a while. She glanced aside and tightened her grip on the rifle as she saw the man had stood up. He smiled and opened his arms in a submissive gesture.

'Come on woman, you know I am right. I'll make sure you

won't be harmed.'

The emotion of the past few weeks swamped her. Visions of Märt spun into view and of the man who she had loved before. The one who had broken her heart. Märt had mended it, only to shred it raw once again. He had left and she had needed to rebuild her life only for him to return. The chaos that normally followed in his wake was inevitable.

'It's alright,' she could hear the voice of the prisoner soothe as she sobbed. 'You have nothing to fear.'

'Everything has gone wrong,' she said to herself. 'All I trusted to stand with me are gone. What is there left?'

'I'll just take this.'

Reality whipped her back from her dreams. She could smell the man's breath and lashed out with the rifle.

He fell back in surprise, as it let off a shot that went close to his cheek. The sound echoed back from the forest. The rifle fell to the ground and she calmly bent to retrieve it.

'I said sit down,' she shouted. The man seeing his chance slip away tried to charge her. Instinct took over and she brought up the rifle butt and pushed it down to collide with his groin. He fell to the ground and she stood back gathering herself with deep breaths.

'I told you, no more chances.'

'It's alright,' the other prisoner shouted, looking directly at Juhan's rifle, now brought to bear. 'Don't shoot, we'll behave.'

'Hey!' A voice shouted from behind them. 'Konsti sent me back to help. What is going on? Have you had problems?'

Maarja sobbed in relief, catching the sound in her hand.

'Come here and take over. Shoot anyone that moves.'

'No problem.' Maarja turned and closed her eyes. It had been too close. She started to stumble up the road without thinking, only vaguely aware that Juhan was by her side.

'*Ema?*'

'I nearly lost control there and it might have cost me my life. Why has it come to this?' Her mind started asking the question over and over again.

'Hey, Cousin. What's up?' Konsti deep voice broke through her panic.

She looked up to see him at the head of his band. A group were marching ahead of them, hands clasped on their heads. She stumbled to reply.

'Nothing Konsti, I was worried when I heard the shots, that's all.'

They were already past her and Konsti shouted over his shoulder. 'No problems for us in the end, just sorting things out now.'

Maarja looked around her. The small, neat wooden houses, so Estonian in their character, looked hollow and empty. She thought she knew her country. Perhaps she did, once.

Back in 1919, when the War of independence had started, she had fallen in love with a foreign sailor. It had all felt so easy; so warm and complete. Problems had been so easy to overcome. There had always been simple solutions.

Then he had gone and Märt was there for her, providing comfort, helping her find a path through her pain. Juhan had arrived, a great joy in her life. He still was, but now her world had fallen apart again around her. It felt like nothing had gone to plan for the last twenty years and now everything was black.

'Ema, we need to find some food,' Juhan was saying

'Yes, food would be good,' she said faintly. 'Food and rest.'

They were taken in by a grateful villager, who fed them and then gave her a blanket and a bed. Nothing was said and Maarja was grateful for the privacy.

It was delicious to have warm sheets once more and her brain was fuzzy with the benign dozy feeling of their comfort.

It was hard to leave it, when she was finally awoken by a gentle shake of the shoulder.

'*Ema*, we are leaving,' Juhan's voice cut into her dreams.

'Huh? Yes, I suppose we must,' she said with genuine regret.

Slowly she gathered herself and arose. The villager had donated to her a sweater to replace the dirty top she had. It felt warm and she would feel the better for it in the approaching colder months.

'Which way?' she asked.

'Back the way we came,' Juhan replied. 'I will show you.'

They quickly made for the main street, where she could see the forest brothers gathered at the end of the village.

'Come on sleepy,' Konsti said with a grin. 'It's time we moved out. Word will get around eventually and the Russians will want to come here and investigate. The villagers will follow us into the forest for a while, just in case.'

She followed them out down the main road. The group morale was buoyant, people openly swapping jokes and stories. There was a lot of bragging and Maarja began to ignore it as they passed the trenches.

She noticed the locals were now digging and then she realised they were filling them in. Maarja was puzzled, for the trenches would make a defence difficult for any army to breach. It forced them to use the road and was easier to defend. Why fill them in? Then she saw something sticking out and it all became clear.

'The Reds, where are they, Konsti?'

The smile had gone but there was no trace of remorse either. 'The villagers killed them.'

'They killed their own. Just like that?' Maarja was stunned by the news.

Her voice dropped to a whisper. 'That's murder. They can't

do that.'

Konsti stopped and place a kindly hand on her shoulder.

'Those trenches, what were they for? The Reds had dug them to shoot those who remained true to Estonia. For days they had goaded them saying those ditches were going to be graves. Is this not self-defence? They only got what they deserved. What they wished on others, they got themselves. I call that justice.'

He walked on, leaving Maarja standing on the road, tears in her eyes. The forest brothers followed and soon, only Juhan remained.

'*Ema*, are you alright?'

'There must have been another way,' Maarja said, smearing a tear to a dirty smudge on her cheek. 'We couldn't be so ruthless.'

'They would have done the same,' Juhan replied.

'That doesn't make it right!' Maarja jammed her hand in her mouth to stop the sobs. 'We helped this - when we kept the prisoners under guard. I feel tainted. I feel used.'

Maarja looked distantly to watch the forest brothers as they continued their walk. Nobody looked back and soon they were out of sight.

'We have to leave, Juhan, as soon as we can. I cannot be part of this. It is not right. Nothing is right. You cannot send a man to his death knowing there has been no trial.'

She was young and very pretty and she knew it. She loved the fact and basked in the glow of admiring glances. She loved the attention - it gave her power. Today she needed it. Maarja gathered her courage and strode through the office. The door at the end of a dimly lit corridor looked massive as she approached. Like a barrier that could never be breached. She was surprised how easy it gave out a hollow sound as she knocked.

'Come.'

Or at least that is what she thought the muffled sound was as she turned the handle and entered the room bowing her head.

'Minister.'

'What is it, Maarja,' the minister said. He looked tired and on edge. Maarja thought she had already started badly.

'The prisoners on Naissaar. The sailors from the Bolshevik ships. We are executing them.'

He did not reply, she fumbled for more words.

'We have hung a few of them already, I heard about twenty.'

The minister looked over his small round glasses to stare at her coolly.

'How is this your business?'

Maarja stopped to choose her next words. This was going to be difficult.

'I received a deputation from the English Admiral. They demanded that we ceased immediately.'

The minister was looking at papers and did not even bother looking up.

'A young sub-lieutenant, no?' He asked almost absent-mindedly.

She flushed and swallowed heavily. 'It was, yes. He was sent by the admiral.'

The minister sighed, with a feeble attempt at melodrama, though it made Maarja feel under attack.

'It is one thing to take a foreign lover at times like this, but you should not be talking state business at the pillow.'

Maarja felt numbed with a shock that cascaded from her head downwards. She could not decide if it was embarrassment or rage. The minister looked up from his sheath of papers.

'Was there anything else?'

Anger coursed through Maarja like she had never felt it before. The issue was important, yet it was being dismissed through her humiliation.

She moved closer to the table and gently pushed the papers down. She was ready to ram them down his throat.

'These are our allies - and they are just supposed to stand by as we do this? They will not sit back if you just ignore them. The English do not like being ignored.'

The minister sighed and snapped the papers away. He stood and leaned closer to her.

'This is none of their business.'

'It is their business; <u>they</u> gave us the prisoners from the ships they captured, but not to kill them.'

'Whose side are you on here?' the minister demanded, his voice raised and his brow white with anger.

'Is it your country or that of your lover?'

Maarja shook her head as if slapped. The words still echoed around the room like a bell. Any worries about her job and her career had gone. She no longer gave a damn.

'I will tell you what is going on here,' she said, her words almost frosting on her lips. 'The Bolsheviks are invading this land. They want to regain Estonia as part of their revolution. Laidoner and his army fights to keep us free and pushes them back. The Bolsheviks tried to send in their navy to pound Tallinn to ruins. If they had the freedom of the seas, they could land an army behind our lines. They could destroy all our coastal towns; they could surround us. The English are stopping them. They captured some Red ships and gave them to us.'

'To our Navy,' the minister said.

'My God! We didn't have a navy before that,' Maarja snapped. 'If we don't treat these allies with respect, they will go and we will lose many, many people to Lenin's forces. We may lose Estonia to him or to the Germans in the south.'

She slammed her hand down on the desk and watched with satisfaction the ripples in the ink well. He knew this already, but he was just a stubborn Estonian man. She had not finished with him yet though.

'And my personal life has nothing to do with you and is certainly not something you can use to slap down the office girl when she is saying something of worth.'

Expecting an eruption, Maarja was surprised to see the man turn and reach for a decanter of port, which he poured two glasses. He offered one. Perhaps her dismissal from the job she loved would be numbed by the alcohol.

'You have spirit girl, be careful how you use it. There are reasons why this was done. Naissaar is a strange land. Perhaps this is what makes people so on edge. It probably makes us look no better than our enemy. I see this and I will send a message to the Admiral.

You are right, we are winning this war whilst the English watch our backs as we carve our nation's path. They brought us coal and weapons. We need them to keep feeling they are part of this fight.'

He still held the glass out and she finally took it and sipped the liquid. He nodded in satisfaction as it washed the anger from her.

'You cannot send people to their deaths without trial.' she said her voice barely a whisper.

'No, my dear and you cannot dictate policy to a minister, but it still happens. Tread carefully, bide your time and wait for the moment. Then strike swift and sure, make the strike deadly, you may only get one chance. That is how you get the greatest success.'

CHAPTER ELEVEN

Fire (July 1941)

P eeter gave a wry smile. 'Well, now I see why she isn't coming. Will helping Harry heal your soul?'

Märt snorted his derision. 'Probably not. Yet I will try anyway.'

'Well, whatever you do, count me in. I have no desire to
stay here anymore and I think someone needs to watch your
back.'

Liisbet's fever had not broken in three days. They had
tried to help it with Camomile and herbs. She was conscious
enough to acknowledge the efforts that people were making
but showed no signs of recovering. Harry was by her side,
whilst Märt and Peeter foraged. They had spent a successful
morning fishing and their catch was now lying dead waiting to
be cooked.

'I use better hooks than these,' Peeter complained.

Märt gave a rare smile. 'I once took a boat to the centre of
Lake Peipsi to fish, when I was on location with the *Kaitseliit*.

When I got back, my superior officer said something about
disobeying orders and abandoning my post. I had to give him
the best fish to shut him up.'

Peeter chuckled. 'So, was it worth it?'

'Märt nodded. 'I caught up a lot of sleep that day on the
boat.'

Peeter sighed. 'If we get back into the house, I could get
some decent fishing stuff, then we'd be catching more than we
can eat.'

'Do you know how to get there?'

'Sure, it takes us away from camp, but we can get there and back before someone notices.'

'You take me there, woodsman.'

They carried on walking in silence for about ten minutes before Peeter stopped and smelt the air, muttering, 'there is a fire somewhere close.'

'The Reds are firing the forest?' Märt asked.

'That would be ambitious,' Peeter replied. 'Especially as the wood is wet, so there would be more smoke. It's not coming from camp, wrong direction.'

He cried in realisation and he sprinted away, leaving Märt struggling to keep up. Peeter stumbled but regained his balance in his headlong momentum. He continued his crazy run until he reached the edge of the forest.

He stopped and his shoulders slumped. Across the field and down the perfect line of wooden fences marking out the boundary, lay his burning house. There had been a lot of fire damage already, the roof had collapsed and most of the barns were gone.

Even the small smoke sauna lodge was burning. Orange flames licked the underside of the roof of Siim's farm in the distance and the silhouettes of men could be seen about like ants.

From the rush of flames, they were throwing more petrol onto the fire.

'I expect that means we are stuck with these fish-hooks,' Märt said, feeling that only cynicism could help the moment.

Peeter gave a shrug and made a face. 'To be honest, they are doing me a favour. I would never go back to live there and I certainly don't want anyone else taking it over. The land can go to nature for what I care. Hell, I would give them a hand if I had known that was their revenge.'

He turned and walked back into the forest.

'I hope Siim takes it so well,' Märt muttered and followed.

Märt looked over the camp on his return, observing the small groups of people scattered around in makeshift shelters of brushwood. He disliked the way a scared young child was watching his every move with wide eyes.

What has the world become? He asked himself. *Where ordinary people are driven to this? Where nobody feels safe?*

He didn't try to smile at the child, it would probably look demonic. Harry met him at one of the shelters.

'How is she?' Märt asked.

Harry gave a half-smile. 'She is in this world at least and she eats. Yet she gets no better.'

Peeter's angry voice sounded from behind Märt, as he caught up.

'What is she, young enough to be your daughter? You have a mission, you say. Yet you stop to save her at the cost of what?'

'The mission, as you call it, is not worth endangering her safety,' Harry replied quietly his words ice cold.

'But if it is a mission of national interest, surely you are endangering others by delaying it?' Peeter asked.

Harry smiled, although the chill was still there. 'My mission is not totally without a sense of timing. And perhaps now is not the time anyway. And yes, when you talk of endangering others, it is why I head for Finland, not Russia. I need medicine, Peeter. Is there a Doctor in this area? Someone we can trust?'

Peeter stared at Harry for a while and then nodded. 'There is one such person we could trust, in the village. But to get him out here? There is a curfew and a few people I do not trust would sing to their new masters if they found out.'

'Then we go at night to him and ask him for medicine,' Märt said. 'And if he is as true as you say, there should not be a problem.'

Harry nodded and moved away.

Peeter placed his hand on Märt's shoulder.

'You have put great faith in this man, but do you really know him? Do you trust him?'

'I cannot explain, Peeter. This man is using us to achieve what he wishes, but I feel it is for our own good somehow. I can't say why, it's just right.'

'Now you sound like Liisbet,' Peeter replied and walked off.

'We're lost,' Juhan said finally, finding a large thick branch to sit on. What shall we do?'

'It's my fault,' Maarja admitted. 'I just felt so detached from Konsti's camp. I could not force myself to focus.'

'I know, *Ema*. The executions were a shock to me also. But if we are not with them, where should we go now?'

Maarja gave a sad smile. 'I don't know, Hani.'

'How about we find the village again and take it from there.'

'Good idea, Hani, but can we rest first?'

'Sleep for as long as you need, *Ema*,'

Maarja stretched and closed her eyes. 'Is this our life now? Walking and sleeping rough?'

'I hope not,' she heard Juhan's voice in the distance, as sleep took over. 'I need a decent meal at some time in the future.'

She awoke quickly in a panic, then listened carefully and fell back with a sigh. The lack of noise reassured her that they were not being chased.

Then she arose again, realising the one thing missing in the forest. Her fear grew, she did not know where Juhan was, nor what to do next.

Should I look for him? If so, down which path? Should I shout out his name? Wouldn't that attract attention to anyone else in the forest? Should I just stay where I am? What if he was in trouble?

She was uncomfortable and frightened and felt powerless for the first time in her life. For many years she had secretly thought she was blessed with luck. Today it felt it had all run out. She just didn't know what to do next.

'Come on Maarja, get control of yourself,' she whispered, closing her eyes, whilst slowing her breathing. The feeling of panic slowly faded, like ice thawing on a lake and she opened her eyes once more.

Look for traces of humanity . It was difficult for the ground was fairly hard and had no muddy imprints. Late summer was a difficult time for trackers. Even so, Maarja started to check for signs like broken branches and flattened grass. Anything that would help her locate Juhan.

She moved slowly, checking each pathway a short way for signs of passage. Finally, she made out the faintest scuffing in the mossy grasses. Further along, the moss was a thicker, luscious green carpet that was beginning to choke the trees. Maarja spotted a more definite footmark on a clump of moss, the heel pointed towards her. She had found her trail. Her feelings of hunger had disappeared, as she strode on.

The trail led back along the path to the village. It made it more difficult to find clues, as occasionally she could see other footprints.

The air was warm, and a wave of fatigue washed over Maarja. She didn't want to stop for fear of losing the trail. Where was he? She stood up and rubbed her stiff back.

The light in the forest grew. She couldn't remember any clearing, so surely it was the forest edge. Her pace quickened and then she stopped when she saw a face staring impassively at her through the branches ahead. Fear tensed her chest and choked her breathing, as she gathered her rifle with difficulty and pointed it, shouting.

'Come out!'

There was a rustle of branches, before an old man walked onto the path with nervous steps and hands raised.

'Don't shoot! I am from the village. I saw you when you came in with the *Metsavennad*.'

Maarja's hands tightened on the gun.

'If you were hiding from the village, you must be a Red escaped from your neighbours' revenge.'

He shook his head sadly. 'No, I am hiding because the Reds have come, listen.'

Maarja paused and began to hear the sound of moving vehicles and the clank of metal. She was surprised she had not heard it up until that point.

'What's going on?' she asked.

'Stalin's tanks,' the man replied. 'Come on, I will show you.'

He began to walk and then stopped. 'I will walk in front, you still do not trust me, child.'

'A lot has happened, old father,' Maarja said without apology, as she lifted her rifle.

'You are right,' the man replied heading off. 'I had a neighbour. He would help me gather fruit in my orchard. He helped me fix the house. I shared a bottle of spirit with him many a time. He now lies in the ground and but for your men, I would have been there instead.'

'Do you know this for certain?' Maarja said.

The man chuckled without turning around.

'I know that many of the village were calling to us, telling us how they had dug our graves ready. Many times they did this - and for many days.'

'You do not mourn their passing?' Maarja asked, moving to the man's side as they reached the edge of the forest and gazed across the field towards the village. There was no reply.

A few tanks were rumbling up the road towards the outer houses. A red star was painted on their turrets. From where they stood, the men next to the vehicles were like pins, albeit with waving hands and loud voices.

As they watched one tank turned towards the nearest house. Smoke poured from the cannon as it fired, the building collapsing with the impact.

A loud boom followed, echoing around the land. The tank moved forward, collapsing the front wall as it progressed, and then it withdrew. A fire had begun to start in the ruin and the flames began to be visible.

'You ask if I mourn their passing,' the man said quietly. 'I do not. I mourn the passing of human kindness.'

The tank turret had now rotated around to point at a house across the street. Another blast of flame and smoke was followed by a rumbling echo, as the building almost nonchalantly collapsed like a pack of cards.

'My house,' the man said simply.

The cameo being played out by the tanks was mesmerising as Maarja watched the houses burn.

The lead tank lurched forward and then stopped. A figure rose up from the top of the turret. There was animated conversation with one of the nearby soldiers before the figure disappeared back into the tank.

It reversed into the wall of one of the ruins and headed off back down the road. Its partner followed obediently. The other figures mounted a motorcycle sidecar and moved off.

As Maarja watched them depart, she wished she would never see another tank again. She sighed, it was a futile thought, given what was happening in Estonia.

'Where will you live now?'

The man shrugged. 'I will sleep in my dead neighbour's house. It would be the least he can do for me after the last two weeks he has put me through.'

There was a clink of metal behind her and Maarja spun round in fear. She sobbed as Juhan came into view carrying a sack.

'What are you carrying, Juhan?' She gasped.

'Field rations from those Russian boys, they were carrying too much.'

'A shame you have nothing to open them with,' the man said.

Juhan smiled and produced a can opener from his pocket.

'Don't ask how,' Maarja said to the clearly surprised villager. 'Just appreciate that he does it.'

The man gave a curt nod. 'I will. Come and rest at the house for a while. You can wash and have hot food.'

Maarja looked at Juhan as the man walked across the field and the young man nodded back. 'With luck he has comfortable beds.'

'Why is he doing this?' Maarja asked.

'He's probably hungry,' Juhan replied.

CHAPTER TWELVE

Encounters

P eeter led Harry and Märt as they crept towards the village.

'We go slowly past this building, for they would sing our presence all the way to Moscow.'

One by one they crouched down and moved swiftly, using a hedge as cover.

'That was easy - but be careful of any activity. Nobody should be out, so do not trust anyone you might see.' Peeter warned.

They jogged down the road looking at the houses. Märt held his rifle close to muffle the noise. Then Peeter ran around the back of a house and tapped softly on the door. The door opened a crack and then wider to let the men rush in.

'Peeter!' A woman's voice whispered. 'I heard you were dead!'

'No, no, but I need the help of your husband. Where is he?'

'Taken away,' the woman's voice echoed as if hitting an empty void. 'Two nights ago. I don't know if they want to use him or...'

Peeter gave the woman a quick hug. Märt wondered if the lines on her face had only appeared since the world had gone mad.

'You have someone sick?' She gathered herself and was immediately focused.

'Yes,' Harry said. 'A young woman. She has fever after a tick bite on the neck.

She has shakes and her dreams are violent and sweating. She will eat sparingly, sleeps most times and shows little sign of recovery after three days.'

'Harry, this lady is not the doctor,' Peeter said softly.

'I have some knowledge. Where is she?'

'In the forest,' Harry said sadly.

'Well, I am afraid I am too old and slow to go there this night,' the woman replied. 'Also, the medicine cabinet is locked - and they have taken the key.'

'So, you have no idea where your husband is?' Peeter asked

'None.'

They stood in silence and then the woman seemed to grow taller as she said. 'Follow me.'

They went into the front room and she moved towards a glass cabinet.

'You go and watch the window and look for anyone approaching,' she said to Märt.

He moved to obey. 'Nobody as yet.'

There was a crash of glass and a slight rustle behind him, then the movement of boxes, before the woman let out a groan and sounded breathless as she got up, waving away offers of help.

'You give her this and perhaps these tablets. One every day, no, two. I hope this helps you. Now, Peeter, you must hit me.'

'What?'

'Thieves broke into the house. I could not stop them, they stole from the medicine cabinet that I cannot open by order of Comrade Stalin and his monsters,' she said firmly. 'I'll forget that last bit. I was unable to stop them and they hit me. I cannot see their faces. Oh...'

There was the sound of a punch and Märt turned to find the

woman slumped in Peeter's arms.

'You are a brave woman,' Peeter muttered and kissed her brow. I'll leave you on the chair.'

'On the floor,' the woman sobbed gently. 'Go...'

'We have company,' Märt said. 'A few men heading this way. Time to leave.'

'Take the back door and head straight into the forest,' Peeter replied. 'Follow me.'

Harry paused and gently touched the woman's cheek before joining the mad dash for the safety of the forest. Behind them, the sounds of men shouting broke the silence of the night. House lights started appearing all around the village. Märt caught up with the other two and as they hit the forest perimeter. Peeter paused and turned.

'They will not follow. They do not know the forest well enough, especially not at night.'

'The woman?' Harry asked.

'I think they may believe her tale that she was hurt after finding robbers in the house,' Märt replied.

'If she was deemed a nationalist, perhaps she would not be in the house, but on a train to Siberia. Peeter, can you take us back to camp in the dark?'

'Märt, I played in the forests as a child. There is nowhere I do not know blind-folded.'

'Well, take us back. But remember the darkness makes us blind-folded.'

They heard a click of a rifle as they approached. Peeter made an owl hoot and a brush of branches sounded before Siim's voice came from the dark.

'You would wake the dead. Did you bring anyone with you?'

'No, they are too scared to get within a metre of the forest,' Peeter replied.

'I thought you would sleep rough and make your way in

light?' Siim asked.

'We had to get back. We have medicine to dispense,' Peeter said. 'Take us to Liisbet.'

'Should it not wait until morning?' Siim asked.

'No,' Harry said. 'Please.'

There was something in the tone of Harry's firm reply that made Siim stand. 'Alright,' he said. 'Just be careful where you tread.'

They scrambled their way to the camp and Harry made straight for one of the shelters. Gently rousing Liisbet, he made her drink the remedy and take some tablets with water. Then he returned to find Märt and Peeter by the embers of a campfire.

'Märt, Peeter. Thank you for this night's work. It was more than I could ask.'

'We'll see what happens overnight,' Märt said. 'Get some sleep, Harry.'

There was no reply, but Märt heard him move away. Although there was silence, he knew Peeter had not moved.

'He is right, it was well done, Peeter.'

'I hit a defenceless old lady tonight, Märt. It does not feel good.'

'I think you saved the life of a brave woman this night, and that it took courage to do. Get some sleep also.'

Liisbet began to improve as the week progressed. Whatever the medicine had been given, it worked quicker than even Harry had hoped. The fever broke and Liisbet began to take an interest in the world again. Then her hunger returned and soon she began to forage for food with the rest. Harry gathered Märt and Peeter one evening, to discuss the next steps.

'Liisbet is strong enough. We will be going soon to head for Finland.'

'Are you sure you are strong, young lady?' Peeter asked.

'Yes, thanks to you all,' She said. 'Harry told me what you did.'

'Don't thank me, thank the Doctor's wife,' Peeter said, but would not look at her.

'I will leave with Harry tomorrow,' Liisbet said

Märt wondered what the world would hold for them all, then Peeter interrupted his thoughts.

'Well I'm still going with you. I can't stay here. Too many memories coming back and biting me when I least expect it, just like horse-flies.'

One by one, the three looked across to Märt. For once he held a small stick, without sharpening it. He stared back showing no emotion. Then he flicked the stick away.

'I am family; where else would I be going?'

'What is this?' Siim asked approaching.

'Siim, we need to continue our journey,' Märt said. 'What you have done for us we can never repay, but we must carry on.'

Siim nodded with a grunt of acknowledgment. 'Whilst I understand your reason, I regret that we lose some practical people. Even so, I suppose it would be easier for a smaller group to survive. The forest will only yield us so much food.'

'Ask the local farmers, Siim. They will help with what they can. It is our way.'

'Perhaps, friend Peeter, stay lucky and stay safe.'

Tanks played a big part in Maarja's dreams now. The guttural sound of the engines as they bulldozed through the houses was all around her. The rattle of the links on the metal tracks, the whirring

as the turret moved and the shouting of men – always a shouting of men.

She couldn't bear it and went to stand at the doorway of the house. The tank was directly outside. Slowly and deliberately, the turret moved around to point directly at her.

She saw the puff of smoke from the barrel. The shell began to come out of the gun, corkscrewing towards her...

She awoke to find the sound of engines still hung in the air. She rose quickly and dressed. Juhan waited for her in the corridor.

'Tanks?' she asked in fear and he nodded.

'Yes, Ema. With a white cross. They are German tanks.'

'What? Germans?'

Juhan smiled. 'Yes, Estonia is safe, now the shorties have arrived.'

Maarja stumbled to the doorway and watched as a procession of heavy armour passed her, all the white markings so welcome from the terror of the red.

The journey was tiresome to Märt. Each day was the same; in the forest, foraging for food, whilst keeping eyes and ears open for approaching dangers.

They moved forward, but he still felt he had not delivered his promise and he needed to show determination, to keep their morale high.

'We have made good progress in my mind at least,' he said to Peeter. 'We are close to reaching the area that I am seeking in Kõrvemaa, although it has taken much longer than I had thought.'

'Well, we were over three weeks waiting for Liisbet to get strong. I am surprised that our foreign friend could afford the time,' the farmer replied.

'He says there is plenty of opportunity for whatever he wants to do. It looks as if he wants to find the right person at the right time.'

'Or maybe he is making it up as he goes along.'

'Probably right there, Peeter,' Märt replied.

Harry had sped up and caught up with Liisbet, who had gone on ahead. Now they both returned and Liisbet clutching a poster.

'I found this on a telegraph pole,' she said.

'What the hell are you doing out of the forest?' Märt demanded 'Didn't you think you might have been discovered.'

'It's nice of you to care,' she replied sweetly.

Harry's lips twitched in a hidden smile, as he said. 'Listen to her. Or if you cannot, at least read the poster.'

Märt picked up the poster and opened it. Peeter came over to check it with him. It was a printed message, full of exclamation marks and large text.

COMRADES OF THE ESTONIAN SOVIET SOCIALIST REPUBLIC!

Rise up and fight to defeat the Finnish white snakes!

Loyal comrades must act and resist the cursed invaders and preserve our motherland!

'Well they can go to hell,' Peeter muttered. 'Since when have we been Soviet?'

'Since the bear took residence in the land,' Harry said.

'What about the Finnish? What does this mean? Has Finland invaded?' Liisbet said - her voice eager with excitement.

'Finland allies with Germany,' Märt replied. 'So, it may be true. They may also have sent their Estonian units back here to fight - The Finnish Boys. Whatever it is, it will make the Reds more jumpy - and there are now more strangers to keep an eye out for.'

'Maybe you should not be going to Finland,' Peeter said to

Harry. 'Not if Finland is coming to you.'

'Let's just keep our eyes open and not assume anything,' Harry replied.

Märt did not know if Harry was talking about the Reds, the Finns, or his own band of stragglers, but he grabbed his rifle and started moving forward. 'Let's move on. Next time Liisbet, don't stray so far. You could get caught by the people who are putting these papers up.'

Maarja sat in the hallway of the local school. The building was peppered with men dressed in the field grey uniform of the Wehrmacht.

It felt as if someone had taken the village and moved it hundreds of kilometres west into Germany. Many smiled as they passed her. The contrast in the friendly treatment she now received, as opposed to the sullen reception of the past few months, was not lost on her.

She was shown into the head teacher's study, where an officer sat behind a desk waiting. It was a surprise to her how normal the man looked. The stiff blond-haired, blue-eyed man with a duelling scar was the German stereotype. This man was short and striking, but not particularly attractive. His dark eyebrows rose above his reading glasses as he looked up and the ghost of a smile played on his face. Maarja was immediately on the defence from the intensity of the stare.

'Come in,' he said, standing to receive her with a formal nod. She swore he had clicked his heels and for a second, she tensed at the display. Then he relaxed and moved around the desk to bring a chair for her.

'I have had a fire made, so we can be warm. This evening looks cold, *nicht wahr*? Besides, you look tired, from what I hear it has been terrible here.'

'Yes,' Maarja said. 'Perhaps the warmth makes me feel

sleepy. That and my first real wash in ages.'

'It is difficult, living in the forest.'

She hesitated and he smiled.

'The villagers, they tell me this. Don't worry; I'm not here to interrogate you. I do need to find out some things though, to make sure my men are safe and that we get the Ivans out of this land quickly. You are not from here.'

Maarja shrank before his piercing eyes. She felt a paradox of feeling in danger, yet strangely being compelled by the man to respond to the conversation.

'Your accent,' he continued. 'It is not the same as these people.'

'No, I am from further North.' There was no harm in saying this, Maarja decided, looking at the flames dancing in the fire. Almost all of Estonia was further north. She did feel sleepy though.

'What is Tallinn like? I have heard a lot, but never really had the chance to visit.' The question was harmless, but Maarja was wary.

'It is very beautiful. The old Hansa town on the hill, the cobbled streets and church spires. Then there are the long walks in the summer on the beach.'

'It sounds an attractive place,' the man replied. 'Perhaps you could show it to me one day. How long had you lived there?'

Maarja flushed at the flirting. 'I did not say I had.'

The man shrugged. 'No, you did not. But you are quite eloquent. Too much for a peasant woman. That makes you either Tallinn or Tartu. Pärnu is to the south.'

'My father was once a lawyer. He paid for my education.'

'Only for it to be wasted by war. It is a sad time.'

The officer sighed and looked aside. His face looked sad, then he tried to smile.

'I am sorry, I have not said. My name is Günter Schulz. I can sympathise with you, for I was an academic, I studied philosophy. War changed that and now I have to put my mind to finding people. Those who would do us harm.'

'You missed your chance here,' Maarja snapped back. 'The villagers shot them all.'

The man laughed. 'Yes, so cynically put. But what I am to do is to find much bigger fish. I am to find those who would damage us, spy on us also. Even English, though how the hell would an Englishman get here, I ask myself.'

Maarja's heart skipped a beat, as she was reminded of the parting in Rapla forest in that dark night a few weeks ago, following the escape from the truck. There was the one man that she had tried to forget about, Märt; but she had driven him northwards.

'I met one,' she said slowly.

Why not? Weren't the Germans their liberators? And Harry had taken Märt from her. Anger flushed through her, suppressing the thought that she had herself sent her ex-husband away.

'He is from England and called Harry.'

'Ah, so. Harry,' the man replied. 'Show me where you saw him please.'

He pushed forward a map that was open on the desk and she placed her finger on Rapla.

'Here, about three weeks ago. We escaped from the roundup of people to Siberia.'

She shied away from his look of intensity and her words evaporated to nothing. She looked away until the tension felt to recede in her as she heard him sit down.

'It is most ignorant of me. You were rounded up for deportation? That is terrible.'

Schulz looked concerned and Maarja's cynical laugh was curtailed to a snort.

'Yes, it was not good. They came to take us to the cattle trucks, but we escaped them.'

'Cattle trucks? That is barbaric. Why did they choose you?'

She shrugged. 'Perhaps they just wanted numbers or perhaps because I once worked for the Estonian government. I don't think it's that though, it was so long ago. It was the War of Independence. I dealt with the eastern front.'

She stopped for fear of rambling. Every sentence seemed to dig her deeper into a mess. Why did she bring up the subject anyway? He was very persuasive in his approach to the queries. It was almost hypnotic.

Perhaps it was because she resented all that had taken away her loved ones. The Reds for her uncle and aunt. Märt for ruining her life and Harry for seeming to take away Märt.

Schulz smiled slowly. It was warm, but somehow his eyes felt like she was watching gravestones falling. It was stress, she told herself. This man was listening to her, at least.

'My husband - my former husband,' she corrected herself, 'came to me with a man and his girlfriend. They were trying to escape the Reds.'

'Thank you, Frau Tamm,' the officer said softly. 'One moment.'

He briefly went to the door and spoke to the guard before returning.

'I have asked for some food and perhaps wine. We have a lot to talk of and it is a hungry time for us both, I think.'

She felt more at ease once she started eating. She felt no danger in discussing anything with her rescuers. After all, they were returning Estonia back to its nationhood. She spoke of Märt and her farm, the escape from Rapla and the time in government.

She only stopped when she thought of her British Navy officer. It felt dangerous to mention such a liaison, however long ago it was. Her pain was still was so raw, that she could not see the wound ever healing. In her tale, she made him out to be local, it was safer that way.

The food was delicious, and so welcome. They had liberated some Georgian wine from somewhere. Maarja did not care where, the warm feeling it left in her was overwhelming.

Schulz listened patiently and asked questions. She was pleased with the attention and the interest. It had been a long time.

'Maarja, you have told me many things,' he said. 'Fortune shone on me when you walked through the door. One man I have to find is this Harry. He is one of many. I hope to catch him before he goes to Finland.'

'Why is this?'

'He is a dangerous agent. An assassin, once dormant here but now activated by Ivan. His job is to get across to our Finnish friends and cause trouble through misinformation, destruction and killing. He is specially trained for this and I have to stop him.'

'How can we do this?' Maarja asked. Schulz smiled, acknowledging the 'we'

'By beating the Russian forces. It is unlikely that he would find a boat at the moment. If he has been hiding, then he has no desire to be captured by Soviet forces, so he will be on the run. I have a feeling he will be obvious to find, especially with your former husband and the girl. I just have to keep listening for news and send agents out to search for him.'

'Send me.'

The eyebrows raised a fraction.

'To do what, precisely?'

'To locate him, to steer him towards you. To kill him if that is what is required.'

'How would you find him?'

'I would look for Märt.'

He pursed his lips and stared thoughtfully at the map. Maarja's reasoning gathered momentum.

'I am Estonian. It will be easier for me to blend in than to send a German, who will stand out as a spy. They will be found out very quickly. To many of my people, you are still the old squires, coming back to grind our noses into the dirt.'

He still would not reply. She decided that now was the time to be direct. In that moment, she felt she had never needed to do something so much as this task.

'Look at it this way; I am a gift to you. You have no chance of finding him without me and my contacts and my Estonian ways. I worked in the government a long time ago, but I travelled - and I made friends. I know the land and I know our people. If he is still in this country, I will find him.'

'Behind lines is hard. You have no support, you are on your own,' Schulz said.

Maarja shrugged. 'I will take my son.'

'Perhaps he should remain here. It is easier to move alone and if you are captured, they would use one as a lever to get information out of the other.'

'You do not understand, he is a lucky man. He has a great talent for finding ways out...' she stopped and glared at him. 'He comes or I do not go. He is not your hostage, Günter Schulz.'

He opened his hands in a disarming gesture. 'We are allies, do you not think?'

'Yes, we are allies,' she replied. 'And I have trusted to that idea by telling you everything I know. I need to have Juhan with me; I would not do anything but worry without him.'

He had begun to tap his fingers on the desk. It was not out of irritation, more thoughtfulness.

Maarja began to liken the dull percussive taps to the ticks of a clock. As it was, time seemed to stand still around them.

'It is decided then, Maarja. You go with your son. You will first receive instruction and I will get you to the front line. You can stay here for today, but we must move quickly. Our forces are advancing. Harry may be running ahead of us.'

'Where do you want me to go towards?' Maarja said. A sudden mixed emotion filled her of being sent back towards Märjamaa.'

'I will first send you to a Finnish reconnaissance unit that has set up behind lines. They may have an idea of where to start. You can link with them and report back to me.' He stopped and looked at her in open admiration. 'You know, you really are a gift.'

She looked at his open smile and his appreciative glances. His smile was returned, but polite and tinged with frost.

'For operations, yes. In that sense we are allies.'

CHAPTER THIRTEEN

Kõrvemaa

P eeter led them down a series of roads that skirted the perimeter of the forest. They eagerly made the most of the daylight offered, that was all denied to the gloomy woodland behind it.

The edge of the road became flanked by thick bushes. Every time they heard a vehicle approaching, it was easy to step into the shadows.

After a while, Märt called to stop, and they moved to a group of tall, thin silver birches growing in close proximity to each other.

'If someone is travelling by road, the flicker of shadows made by the trees makes us difficult to see us,' he explained. 'As well that is so, there seems to be a steady flow of traffic and it all seems to be moving east.'

'Yes, something is planned,' Harry said. 'And we appear to be walking into it.'

'We could head further north?' Peeter said.

'No, this is all wrong,' Märt said. 'There are army and ir-regulars coming through. Too many civilians with rifles, in the middle of a land that is supposed to be conquered.'

'So, should we avoid it?' Liisbet asked and Märt shook his head.

'There is a fight brewing somewhere and I think we should warn those who are about to meet it. I for one do not want to see anyone else suffer from the invaders.

If this is a battle against Estonians, I too want to be part of the fight. I have had enough of running away in my own land.'

'I will follow you also,' Harry said. 'I want to see everything.'

'Then it is settled,' Liisbet said. 'I will also embrace the blue, black and white.'

She sighed at their blank expressions.

'The Estonian flag, you idiots. I too am tired of running.'

'Welcome home,' Märt muttered dryly. 'The farm of my friends is close by in the forests near Ardu. I want to first check that all is fine there and that they are safe and well. Maybe get some news. There is a lot going on here and maybe something is happening in the world that has yet to reach the forests that we have walked through.'

Märt remembered that the roadway formed a pleasant approach to the farm. The road swung away from the forest on one side to a fallow field, bounded by a fence of wooden staves set in the ground diagonally, in the Estonian way, all joined by twine.

Märt admired the regularity of the fence. He remembered the summer days when he had helped build it for them.

His eyes began to follow the run of staves until it curved around towards a charred remnant of stones and blackened beams, still smoking in the aftermath of the fire - and whatever misfortune had caused it to pass.

Märt had no doubt over the cause. With dread in his heart, he loaded his rifle and held it ready as he slowly approached from the field.

Peeter grabbed his arm.

'Go easy. Remember to tell friend from foe.'

Märt nodded and continued.

He saw six men standing around the ruin, five had rifles at their shoulder. The other was opening a bottle and took a long swig. A feeling of doubt crept over Märt as he watched their actions. They were picking through the debris as if looking for something. Survivors? Was the drink vodka? Was it to douse the pain?

Then the man with the bottle said something and a few of the men laughed. One shouted a jovial reply. Märt's blood began to boil with raw anger. He ran forward and crouched, bringing his rifle to bear.

A coldness fell over him and he signalled the others to spread out. Harry went to the forest, Peeter took a position at the fencing and Liisbet came to Märt.

'Stay close,' was all that Märt could whisper amid his white anger. His fears looked as if they were being realised. The dream was becoming a living nightmare

The bottle flew in the air, as the man dropped to the floor. The expected trickle of spirit did not reach his lips and started a low flame on a particularly hot charred beam. The man gagged, having been shot through the throat.

More shots rang out and the men looked to take cover in the ruin. There was a great confusion amongst the group of men as to the direction of the attack. One hid behind a ruined wall looking at the forest. It made an easy target for Peeter, who shot twice and hit him.

Märt resisted the urge to charge directly at the men. He wanted so much to beat them for what they had done. He moved closer in, hearing a scream nearby. Peeter had charged forward, an answering cry came from Liisbet behind Märt. One of the men raised his weapon to repel the attack and Märt shot him. The crossfire proved too much for the marauders and one turned to flee. Peeter knelt down and trained his rifle on the back of the departing man. A single shot echoed through the clearing and the man fell like a hunted rabbit.

Märt ran to the ruins and looked at the carnage. He called for the others to stop as he sized up the situation, always checking for new dangers. Liisbet started pushing around the ruin looking for survivors.

Peeter was checking the dead men to be certain they were not feigning. Harry was nowhere to be seen.

'Peeter, take care. I saw only four fall. Peeter!'

Even at a distance, Märt could see the farmer glare at him, before retreating.

'I have shot rats before, I know what I am doing,' Peeter shouted.

'Fine,' Märt said. 'So where are the other two, hey?'

'One is at the edge of the forest,' Peeter said. 'He died trying to run.'

'The other?'

There was a sound of collapsing stones and Liisbet cried out in alarm as a figure leapt out and barged past her. Märt screamed for the man to halt and fired a warning shot. The man stopped and lifted his hands high, so as to leave no doubt he was surrendering. Even so, his eyes looked back and forward for a means of escape. Märt was reminded of the Latvian Destroyer that was shot at Peeter's farm.

'Peeter. Stand down. Peeter!'

The farmer retracted his rifle back to his shoulder and glared across at Märt.

'We need him to talk, Peeter.'

Märt turned to the captive and noticed that a wet patch appeared to be growing around the crotch of the man's trousers.

'You have life. If you want to keep it, you had better tell us what is going on. Who are you? Come! My friend is keen to avenge his family. These farmers were my friends.'

The man was trying to look submissive, but Märt was aware that he was furtively looking around and trying not to be seen to look for methods of escape.

'Not my fault. We were ordered here.'

'Ordered what? Who?'

'It is the resistance in *Kõrvemaa, the army is coming to deal with it. We were told to come here and soften up those who support the fascists.*'

'*Where is the family?*' *Märt said.*

The man shuddered and looked away and Märt yelled.

'WHERE ARE MY FRIENDS?'

'Orders,' the man said very quietly and with a quavering voice. 'We were told. Kill all or we would be killed instead. I did not want to do this, but I was threatened with a pistol. What would you have done?'

Märt grew angrier. The man was showing limited compassion and now trapped, felt there was no time for remorse. Märt knew the farming family had perished and the man was aware of this and that his life now hung on a thread.

The single rifle shot echoed around the glade, echoing in Märt's mind like a tombstone falling. He closed his eyes to let the tears fall and then opened them at the sound of sobbing. Liisbet's gun still smoked faintly with the wisps of cordite.

'What have we all become?' she whispered. 'We are Estonians, not criminals. What have we all become?'

Märt looked around, but Harry had not re-appeared. He put his arms around her.

'Liisbet, courage girl. We do what we must.'

'That's what he said,' she said. 'Are we any better?'

Märt had no answer.

'There are others approaching,' Peeter said, quickly raising his rifle. 'Soldiers'

Märt spun round to see two grey uniformed men approaching from the forest with a group of other men.

'Russians!' Liisbet said.

Märt's eyes narrowed. 'I don't know, I would almost have them for Finns or Germans. What the hell are Finns doing here?'

He was intrigued by the ordinary looking men accompanying them. He had a rifle, but the soldiers appeared to be carrying no more than handguns.

'Cover me,' Märt said. He shouldered his rifle and slowly picked his way to meet the newcomers. Fear thrilled through him, but he welcomed the feeling, despite the potential consequences of his action. The soldiers stopped and the leader called out.

'You have done well with the destroyers, who are you?'

'Friends of this farm,' Märt called back. 'I helped build it.'

'He did,' the other soldier said. 'I know this man. Märt was in *Kaitseliit*, Sergeant Raio.'

Märt gazed at the sergeant's almost white hair and steel-blue eyes. *Old before his time*, he thought. *Just like me.*

'*Tere*, Anton,' Märt said to the soldier, who acknowledged with a nod. 'What are you doing here?'

'Finnish Boys, Erna battalion' Anton replied with a proud smile. 'Come to keep an eye on our Russian friends, now Germany has begun to fight them.'

'What? When?' Märt's composure crumbled at the news.

'I will tell you more,' Raio said. 'But not here. Tell your friends to come out of their hiding and we will go to our camp.'

Märt sized up the situation slowly.

'Your colleague vouched for you immediately,' Raio said. 'Would you not do the same to him?'

'I am sorry,' Märt replied. 'We have been through a lot recently. It makes you forget how to trust. We will take our rifles with us.'

'That's fine with me,' Raio said. 'We need the firepower. We'll take them off the dead also. We will talk more when we get to camp.'

'Who are these with you?'

'Local *Metsavennad*. Come, we waste time.'

'I want to bury my friends.'

Raio sighed. 'Do you want to see them? There is not much left of them. You can still smell the burnt flesh in the air.

I am sorry to be so blunt, but as you can see with the welcome you had there, destroyers are everywhere. Standing out of the forest, as we are now, makes us easy targets for anyone. Come on, let's move.'

They made a swift departure and quite soon Märt found it difficult to keep up with the soldiers.

Having spending so long on the road, his legs now felt slow and unresponsive. Harry was nowhere to be seen and although Liisbet looked troubled, there appeared no chance for Märt to stop and see what had happened. He elected to keep quiet; Harry may have had his reasons to disappear and it may work to their advantage.

They eventually stopped deep within the forest and Märt caught his breath, whilst using the time to interrogate the new arrivals. The soldiers stayed around him, whilst their Forest Brother companions melted into the woodlands to keep guard.

'You do not appear surprised at our coming,' Märt said and Raio pulled a face.

'No, we were forewarned.'

Märt shook his head at what he saw as Harry's continual ingenuity, even though Märt was sure the man had not left the group at any point, he had somehow managed to contact the Finnish unit.

'Are we on your side?'

Raio shrugged. 'You have been named by people who are *on our side*, as you say. Anton knows you from *Kaitseliit* and I just watched you battle a group of vicious destroyers I think that is enough for now.'

'Anton said you were Finnish Boys, but Germany has attacked also.'

'Come, we walk and talk. There are fewer problems in the trees, as the Reds have proven quite scared to follow us. Anton? Sort out the others.'

The other soldier acknowledged and disappeared.

'Why are the Reds scared,' Märt asked.

'There are nearly two thousand people here now. They see us as a threat.'

'You have an army?' Märt was almost speechless.

'Yes, an army of women and children and old men. It is an army of forest brothers, willing to fight but lacking in weaponry or tactics. It is an army of expectation, but no decent supply of provisions or ammunition.

'What do you mean?'

'There are sixty of us from Finland. Finnish Boys trained for reconnaissance and radio work. Close quarter fighting and small arms, that's Erna. We were to come here and observe, report and assist the Germans if they get this far.'

Märt grabbed a branch the size of his lower arm and pulled out a hunting knife he had got from the farms. Raio arched his eyebrows with a question, until Märt showed his intention was to whittle the stick.

'It helps me think.'

'It helps you stay alive if you warn people first,' Raio replied.

'So, you are a reconnaissance unit?' Märt asked.

'Yes, nothing more, armed with handguns, grenades and radios. We were supposed to be located all over the country, but then we heard that the Reds were beginning to make things rough in Kõrvemaa, so we called everyone into the Kautla forest.'

They walked past a shred of cloth and Raio picked it up,

Märt noted the blue, black and white stripes of the Estonian flag.

'A long time since I have seen that,' he observed, Raio handed it to him.

'In this area, the locals got tired of the Reds actions and threw them out. They call it the republic of Kõrvemaa now. The Reds would dearly love to wipe this stain off their red universe. '

'And you came to help the locals?'

'Our mission quickly became a disaster. Only half the force landed by sea, most had to retreat due to enemy fire. Since then, the rest of us have had to parachute in every so often. The German *Oberleutnant* who is supposed to be in charge, has not tried to join us since the aborted landing. My Colonel has no specific orders from this German, so he does what he thinks is right. To protect the people of Kõrvemaa.'

'*Oberleutnant*? So you are of the German army, even though you wear the uniform of the Finns?'

Raio gave a thin smile followed by a snort of derision at the thought. 'Appearances are deceptive, Märt.'

'What does that mean? You just told me you have a German in charge.'

'Yes, true, but we are not the German Army. Those damn shorties wanted us to swear allegiance to their beloved *führer* and we told them to stuff it. We went to Finland to fight for Estonia. They took us in and trained us and the Finns are who we fight for.'

Märt looked at the white-haired sergeant and noted his pride. He was broad shouldered enough for Märt to believe the man would not be pushed around too easily anyway.

He began liking Raio's matter-of-fact practical attitude and strong personality. His lack of stiff formal army mannerisms was welcome.

'So, you are Finnish Army, then.'

'Yes, and proud to be part of the army of our northern cousins. But we can fight like a forest brother. I just chose to wear the uniform today to make sure that you did not shoot me without thinking.' Raio finished with a wink.

'Well, with that helmet, I had you for a shorty.'

'Finland cannot afford to go to full war with the Reds, even if Germany is a huge distraction for Stalin. The 'Winter war' wiped that chance out. So, the Finns are allies, although most of the army is protecting its own borders.'

Märt looked around to see Peeter and Liisbet were quite a way back. Peeter was arguing with Anton, who tried to smile away the tension. He knew both men, they would work things out, even if it took a few blows about their heads first.

'So, there are what? Sixty men defending two thousand? What is this, the bloody Spartans or something?'

The analogy was lost on Raio and he shook his head. 'There's sixty-three here in this area, roughly,' he replied. 'There's about two hundred spread all over the place on reconnaissance somewhere.'

'And what am I being expected to do?'

'Find your spy.'

Märt dropped the stick and just about held onto the knife, as Raio continued.

'You nearly brought him to us, but he ran when he saw me. Come and let's talk at camp. You need to meet some people.'

The camp was basic and functional. Some camouflaged tarpaulin had created some protection, but most shelters were made from wood and branches. The place was buzzing with activity. Raio took his charges through the bustle, past people cooking at fires, sharpening weapons, and repairing clothes. The atmosphere was relaxed, but people looked ready to move at a moment's notice. Raio strode through totally unworried, until he found a group of grey-clad officers standing around a man who was drawing in the dirt.

'Colonel, these are some of the men you wanted,' Raio said.

The man looked up from his drawing and nodded in reply, then turning to his officers, said 'You know your instructions, now go to carry them out. Good luck!'

He stood and stretched, kicking dirt over the lines on the ground.

'You are the baker?'

Märt nodded. 'I was, when the world was sane.'

'They tell me you were once *Kaitseliit* here. Can you tell me a quick way to Ardu?'

'If you have a map, I can show you what landmarks I can remember,' Märt replied. 'The trees will change the appearance of the land.'

'Huh,' the colonel grunted in disgust. 'The German insisted on keeping the maps,' he said, his contempt quite obvious. 'And he hasn't bothered to show his face here yet.'

The Colonel sighed, 'In the meantime, I will do what I see fit. If I draw the map on the ground, perhaps you can add some detail?'

Märt quickly did so and the Colonel nodded in satisfaction. 'As I thought. So, are you a good Estonian, Märt the baker?'

I am an Estonian,' Märt replied stiffly at having his loyalty challenged. 'That is enough.'

'Good enough for me. My men ambushed a convoy on our way over to this forest. It was carrying a Soviet judge coming to sentence some of the locals.

They never got to step out of their car. Since then, we have been felling trees across that road and mining bridges. The Reds are getting a bit upset about us, as we are spoiling their party.'

'You want me to go also?'

The Colonel shook his head. 'No, I have few men and need to stretch the resource to keep everyone safe in this forest. Many are already out on reconnaissance, so I cannot spare anyone except those who come in. Take your friends and Raio and go and find me that spy.'

'The English spy?' Märt blurted out the question. He was not ready for the sudden reference. It had not been discussed, but it was as if Harry was the most famous fugitive in Finland.

'He is not English.'

'Who says this?'

'I do,' said a familiar woman's voice. Märt spun round in shock to see Maarja walk towards him, Juhan following with a broad smile.

'Tell me what is going on,' Märt managed to stumble over the simplest of questions, whilst the ghost of a smile played on Maarja's lips, even if her tone did not change.

'Saving your skin again. I have been told about your friend, Märt. He is not English or at least, he is not working for them.'

'And how do you know that Maarja?'

Her nostrils flared with impatience, even though Märt found the frown on her face did not look displeasing to him.

'From when I was with the forest brothers near Pärnu.'

'You were going back to Märjamaa?' Märt's tone grew accusatory and she sighed.

'Just listen. The farm was empty, my family are dead. I went to my cousins in the south.'

Juhan was eager to take up the tale. 'A nearby town was in trouble as the local reds were about to massacre all their opponents. We went in and destroyed them.'

Maarja tried to shut out the memory of the whimpering from the men and women, lined up to be taken for execution.

'The Russian tanks came in and blew up a few houses, but we withdrew and then the Germans arrived. They are well within our borders, pushing back the Reds. Soon we will be free again!'

Märt raised his eyebrows in surprise.

'This is good news, but tell me why the Reds are here in Kõrvemaa, when the Germans are moving so fast from the south?'

'We don't know,' the Colonel replied. 'Either they do not know this information or are pig-headed enough to take out revenge on Estonians at all costs. Stalin more than likely wants to scorch the earth as his soldier's retreat, so the attacking army cannot forage as it goes.

The problem we have is they tend to want to kill anyone they catch. But if they spend their forces dearly on us, they have less to fight the Germans with. If we stop them breaking Kõrvemaa, we could save Estonia.'

Märt shook his head. 'There are too many, I have seen the columns of men, they are building up an attack.'

'Then we will lead them a chase as we let our people escape and this is where my talk to you about the spy is important.'

The colonel crouched down and started drawing lines around Märt's map to Ardu.

'I know about these columns; they seem to be coming in from three sides. If they continue, they will try to encircle us or force us out.

I want to break us out to the west if it comes to it. Get a clean run back to the Germans. There is a chance that the Reds will be told this by the English spy.

The Russians have already tried sending their Estonian Reds to us to learn about our position and defences, but this Harry is different.'

'The Germans are keen to find him,' Maarja said. 'Find him

and stop him. They say he is not with the English at all, but one of Stalin's men – and one of his best.'

'What are you talking about?' Märt said. 'He was on the list for deportations. I saw it'

'Who wrote the list?' Maarja replied coldly. 'Did it have any official seal?'

'Then why does he want to escape back to Finland?'

'Finland or Russia?' said the Colonel. 'He just needed a guide to get him north.'

Märt shook his head. 'I don't agree. He is in Red occupied lands, why did he not just flag down the nearest soldier and commandeer his own transport? It doesn't make sense.'

The Colonel looked thoughtful and Maarja scowled as Märt stood waiting for a reply.

'He may need to not break his cover. I have radioed Helsinki, this man is wanted and we are to stop him. I do not know whether this is German hands tapping the Morse code. I have no men at my disposal to do this. I cannot really afford to lose Raio as it is, but they say you are a good woodsman and hunter and you brought the spy up here, so he's your problem.'

'Find him if you can, here in the forest. He won't go far while we have his woman. Find him and find out what he is doing. Too much of this does not make sense.'

'Peeter will come with me, but what are you doing with Liisbet?'

'I have put her under guard.'

'I swear to you she is no threat. I have seen her and watched how she behaved on our trip, especially when we met other Reds.'

'I have no time to decide now,' the Colonel said rising. 'But I will think on your words. Go and take food and rest.'

'See that Maarja and Juhan are made safe here also,' Märt said curtly, then a little more politely. 'As best as you are able under the circumstances.'

The Colonel nodded. 'This is the least that I can do.'

He walked away towards the camp. Maarja made to leave, but Märt stopped her by holding her arm.

'Maarja, you came to my aid.' He struggled for words. 'Thank you,'

She slowly looked at him; her blonde hair still made her an angel in Märt's mind. He knew it would never be over for him. There was hardness behind her eyes now.

'So it would seem, Märt, but then you do have a habit of getting into these problems.'

Märt glared in response to the dig, but at that moment he felt a wave of exhaustion wash over him and he felt he needed to scale down the skirmish. 'It was a dangerous journey to come this far.'

'I am resourceful, and I still have friends.' Maarja replied tartly, Märt knew she was spoiling for a fight and he still tried not to provide one.

'Where is Juhan?'

Maarja made no indication where, but replied, 'Nearby, he is a help also. A very clever boy, even though some would have him as a fool.'

'I want to see him. He can tell me his tale.' The words were spoken evenly, but the hidden meaning was not lost on Maarja.

'What will you do now?' He said.

She shrugged and her lips twitched. 'Go home if I can. At least there are no Reds left there.'

'You saved me by coming here.'

Märt's memory spun back to an earlier time, prompted by his own words.

'Maarja, those days are past, and you must now look forward. I can be there by your side. I could be with you always if you wanted me to be.'

Her beautiful mouth opened slightly with surprise, before she sighed and her glorious blue eyes half-closed as she leaned forward to kiss him. Even within the kiss, he could feel her lower lip tremble with emotion.

'I have not saved you,' Maarja said, the emotion of the past drained from her face. 'Only you can do this. It is up to you, if you can, to save yourself.'

CHAPTER FOURTEEN

Kautla (August 1941)

M ärt was woken by a series of cries in the woodland. He quickly rose and looked to where he thought Maarja lay. There was a rustling noise, and a figure was by his side.

'It is your friends,' Juhan said.

'Show me,' Märt replied and he rose quickly to follow him further down the camp.

Peeter sat rubbing his neck, whilst Liisbet was nowhere to be seen.

'He's a strange one, your friend,' Peeter said. 'All smiles and then he leaves a present.' He rubbed his neck again.

'Where is Liisbet?' Märt said. Peeter shrugged.

'Obviously, she had a better offer.'

'Your spy has been in and taken his red girlfriend away with him.' Raio said as he approached, his hunting knife was drawn, and he gripped it tightly.

'She is not a red and he is not my spy,' Märt said, the venom sizzling in his words.

'What is going on?' Peeter said.

'Harry has been annoying the Germans. They want him caught and I am to do it as I brought him here.'

'Were you to know about his actions?'

Märt itched to whittle a branch but resisted the temptation. As Raio had said, drawing knives at this point could be taken the wrong way. 'Not important. He is desperate to get to.'

'So why not stop here, with the Finnish army?' Raio said.

'I don't know. The Germans have told the Finns to give him to them, perhaps.'

'Why do the Germans want him?'

'Well, they sent Maarja to find me and they are in charge of this enterprise.'

'We fight for Estonia and the Finnish army,' Raio said flatly.

'That is so, but the Germans are still influencing what is going on here. Harry wants to get to Finland. He avoids the Reds and Germans and won't talk to you probably because you have a German in charge of your unit. I don't know what is going on, so I would like to find the man just to ask him myself.'

Märt clasped Peeter's shoulder. 'I want you to come with me.'

'Why?'

'Because you can deal with my moods.'

Peeter smiled and rubbed his neck again. 'You mean I am as grumpy as you?'

Märt shrugged. 'Yes, I meant that. Sergeant, I think you have been ordered to come with us. I could do with your fighting ability.'

'And me?' Juhan said.

'I don't know, 'Märt replied truthfully. 'Your mother wants to return south. At least you need to get to the German lines first.'

'So where do we start?' Raio asked.

'No idea. Follow Liisbet's trail in the forest at first light, I suppose. That is if the forest brothers haven't walked over it too much.'

'I like you boys,' Raio said. 'I like the way you have such a fun attitude to life. Maybe I should come with you.'

'Bring vodka,' Peeter muttered. 'For more than my neck.'

'Ah, I like you boys a lot,' Raio said. 'When you are around, the sun is always shining. My men will keep watch, get some sleep. In the morning, we will see what signs there are of flight.'

At the first break of daylight, Märt was up, quizzing people in the camp about what they had heard and seen that night. Where they had been and when they could remember being awoken. At first, people were slow to answer, but with the help of Raio, Märt began to piece together a picture.

'My God, Raio, these people are not as alert as they should be. If an old Englishman can walk in unannounced, then what about one of Stalin's bastards?'

'They are tired, Märt,' Raio said. He looked as if he had aged overnight himself. 'Do not judge them too harshly.'

Märt crouched on the ground to check a small bush for damage.

'We are all tired, Raio. Perhaps if we can keep the tired people away from this trail, I can find out where they went.'

After a day of fruitless searching, Juhan brought over some food for Märt to eat.

'This is a great adventure,' he said.

Märt wasn't sure if the young man was being cynical or not, so he took the comment at face value. He tried so hard to not sound impatient. He really wanted to get to know Juhan, after all the lost years.

'I can think of better ways to keep busy,' he muttered.

The attempt at humour was lost in the tone on all but Juhan, who turned up his smile.

'Like baking bread?'

Märt nodded with a semblance of a smile. 'Much safer.'

'Will you take me with you when you go to hunt the man? I am used to hunting in the forest, my uncle taught me well.'

'I...'

Märt's words caught in his throat. He wanted to keep Juhan safe from the danger that seemed to surround them, but also wanted him around, so he could see how Juhan had grown into the young man that stood in front of him. Finally, he took a deep breath. 'Do you have a rifle?'

Juhan gave a broad grin. 'And plenty of ammunition.'

There was a commotion in the camp that drew Märt's attention. Men were rushing to grab their weapons. Raio came rushing over, rifle already slung on his shoulder.

'There is a report that the Reds are on the move to us. A large column is heading through the forest by Kautla.'

'How large?'

'They say a thousand men, maybe more.'

'How would they use so many soldiers when the Germans are knocking on the door,' Juhan asked.

'They improvise,' Raio replied. 'Destroyers, NKVD, Estonian and Latvian red brigades. Whatever they can use, shove a rifle and a couple of rounds of ammunition in their hand and send them out with a gun at their backs. They mean to hunt us down, whoever they are. The colonel has decided we have to hit them fast before they get a foothold in the forest. Everyone who can hold a rifle. All of us Finnish Boys and forest brothers,.'

'You fight a thousand with mainly pistols?' Peeter said as he sat close by, listening to the conversation.

'And grenades, some rifles, some old, knackered machine guns and whatever we can take off the reds.' Raio gave a grim smile. 'It is going to be entertaining.'

'Remind me again what you define as entertainment,' Märt muttered and Raio laughed, then clapped Juhan on the shoulder.

'You also, young one and the farmer, then he moved on. Maarja came running towards them.

'What is happening, Märt?'

'We have to go, Maarja, the Reds have sent about a thousand men to the forest to destroy us. Juhan needs to come also.'

'But he's still a boy!' Maarja said, a flash of fear in her eyes.

'I think he's shown himself more resourceful than that already, Maarja. We can't shelter him from this one, there's nowhere to hide.'

His stare burned into Maarja and she gave him a hurt look for a long time, before she bit her lip to stop it trembling and turned away, giving a curt nod. 'Just be careful.'

'Maarja?' Märt gasped at the words.

'Because I know you will protect Juhan at all costs. Also, I know what these Reds are like. You saw that farm after it had been burnt. I could only watch when they shut the people in and set the house on fire. I still hear the soldiers laughing. I still hear the screams of the farm people.'

'I will be careful; Maarja and I will look out for Juhan. I will remember what the Reds did, for I helped build that farm.' Maarja nodded and turned back to walk to the fire, her bold expression began to crumple as she turned.

Märt watched her back for a while, then grabbed his rifle and chased after Peeter, who he could just see ahead. Juhan was by his side and turned to give a boyish grin.

Peeter turned to Märt as they jogged and held out a grenade. 'Have you used one of these before?'

'Once,' Märt said. Peeter tossed it over to him.

'One more than me, so perhaps you should have it. Does that boy always smile?'

'Just about,' Märt said.

There was little need for any directions, the sound of a group of motor vehicles now hung in the air. It was beginning to override the noise of the forest and was getting closer.

Märt could feel his heart pumping, the throb of blood appeared around his temple, his lungs burnt, his mouth felt dry. There was a sudden urge to pee, he knew it was from fear. He also was fully aware he had no choice. Kill or be hunted down like pigs. Face the enemy down and give the camp time to gather and retreat. The memory of the burning ruins of the farm came back to him. He was fully aware of what these people could do.

He felt anger and a need for revenge. It gnawed away at him, as he struggled to keep it under control. At his core, he felt that the freedom to be Estonian, was worth fighting for.

He cast a nervous glance at Peeter and for once the farmer gave him a smile, although it was akin to that of a wolf about to hunt. Even as they ran, Peeter still continued to talk, between breaths.

'You scared also? Sometimes it is good to be. But if I am going down, I am going to take the whole bloody lot with me. This is personal. This is for my family.'

Märt looked to Juhan and for once the young man's smile was nervous. *Yes, I have family too*, he thought, thinking of the tall teenager and his mother. *And I will keep them alive.*

'You are right, Peeter. This is personal. It always will be for us.'

There was a shout ahead, followed by an explosion that made them check their pace. A cacophony of noise followed, a combination of engines labouring and gun fire. A machine gun had started to fire short bursts. There was another explosion and the staccato stopped.

'If you boys have finished your talking, you may like to join in the fight,' Raio shouted, pointing to where they should go. 'Take out what you can. Don't take risks.'

146

Märt turned to shout for Peeter and Juhan to stay low, to be careful. There was no time, a bullet thudded itself into a nearby tree and they all dropped to the floor by instinct.

There was no time to dwell on the anguish of the past; it was pushed aside by the urgency of the present.

Märt signalled for the others to crouch down and then indicated with his hand where they should go. It had all come back now, the years of *Kaitseliit*, the years of trying to forget his past. He had joined up in the hope he would find some conflict in which he could die with purpose.

Now he had found it and it had changed his mind. There could be a future if he was with people who were prepared to fight for it. He felt angry at those who were trying to take away the land he knew. If he was going to go, he'd give them more than a bloody nose on the way.

He could see the shadows of a convoy of vehicles, through the brush of the forest perimeter. Many trucks were there, which he assumed would have soldiers on board.

The front few vehicles had been damaged to a standstill by grenade attacks. As he neared the scene, he could make out figures in the debris, hiding under whatever cover they could find. Some wore army uniform, but most did not. There were already a few bodies beyond mortal help. One dead man hung through the open window of his truck.

'Be mean with your bullets, we have not many to spare,' Märt called to the others, trying desperately not to shout and draw attention to them. He spied a group trying to use a truck as a platform for a small machine gun. They had crept forward with a box of ammunition, ready to feed.

One knelt down, fitting the bullet belt into the gun, but spun back in a short spurt of blood. Another went to crouch in his place.

Without a second thought, Märt lobbed his grenade. It fell into the truck's cab, rather than the platform. There was a shout and a rush of activity before it exploded. A man flew out of the cab, some were tipped over the side with the machine gun and lay still. The gun hit the ground and rolled onto its side. The belt of ammunition hung loosely from the truck, waving like an angry snake.

'Good start!' Juhan shouted.

'Keep alert!' Märt shouted back. 'Let's stop the Reds getting our boys.'

There was a scream behind them, and they turned to see Anton fall forward from his position clutching his throat. Raio was following up after him, but a warning shout from Märt made him retreat.

It felt like hours, although Märt knew it had only been minutes. They chose their shots carefully as they advanced. Many were successful and men were lying motionless in testament to this. Others were wild, but the attack had succeeded to pin back the enemy.

'I feel sorry for these men,' Peeter shouted. 'They are being driven forward with a gun to their backs, as if they are looking to die.'

'Don't get too fond of them,' Märt said. 'How is your ammunition?'

'Short.'

'Me too. Juhan?'

There was no reply, and then they heard a shot. Juhan cried out happily. 'That's it, I'm out. But they are all pinned back.'

'Not for long if we are out,' Märt said. 'Okay, I'm going to try something. Cover me, Peeter.'

Märt crouched low and ran in a loping motion towards the truck and its machine gun. He grabbed one of the gun handles as he slid to the ground. He prayed his momentum would tip the gun back over onto the wheels of its tripod.

His luck was in, as the adrenalin nearly spun the gun back a full circle. He lay down and slowly edged towards the wreckage of the truck. It was then he realised how heavy the gun actually was. It took longer to pull it back to the ammunition ribbon drooping down from the truck.

He quickly checked behind and for a moment stopped to look through the gap. On the other side of the ruined column, he could make out two figures that appeared to be running away. For a fleeting second, Märt was sure one was a woman, the other looked familiar. At least it could have been Harry. Märt was certain, but he became distracted by the impact of a man jumping down to his side

'Here,' Juhan's voice rang out and a box of ammunition was plonked next to the gun.

'Do you know how to fit this in?'

Märt quickly adjusted to the arrival and fitted the start of the ribbon.

'You've got to hold it in a way that the bullets feed in straight and flat or it will jam.'

'No problem,' Juhan said.

'You know you are totally mad, boy,' Märt snapped. 'You could have got killed with that move.'

'For sure,' Juhan said. 'But you just did the same. I only copied.'

Märt gave a fleeting smile and patted Juhan's arm. Then they heard Peeter's shout.

'When you two boys have finished, I can't hold these bastards back forever.'

Märt turned the gun down the column, mouthed a rare prayer to God and then squeezed the trigger. The machine gun roared to life. The soldiers, courageous with the lull in the firing, had begun to creep forward ready for an assault. A few fell from the burst, whilst the rest dived for cover. A shot hit the small protective shield of the gun and Märt ducked further behind it.

'Strange,' Raio shouted from the forest. 'They must be used

to having the gun at their backs, not facing it. You boys keep firing, but don't be heroes for too long, when I say retreat, you run like your life depended on it. It will.'

As he fired, Märt's realised his mind had begun to filter out the swear words that accompanied the conversation. Most of the shouts were drowned out by explosions or gunfire. Märt fired the machine gun and the world seemed enveloped in the cacophony of its lethal bursts.

He did not know that much about the gun, but he could almost swear the barrel was glowing red with the heat of continuous use. There was a click and then the firing stopped.

'Run out of ammunition?' Märt asked

'Bloody thing is jammed,' Juhan said. 'I'll just sort it out now.'

'There's no time,' Märt said. 'Those we have pinned down are beginning to realise we have no more bullets.'

As if his thoughts had been read there was a rush of air from a bullet that pinged as it ricocheted around the wreckage of vehicles behind him.

'Right you two, get the hell away from there and back to camp. We've done as much as we can for now.' Raio's voice came clearly through the branches. 'Get out of there, we'll hold them back.'

'Peeter!' Märt shouted.

The farmer looked up from the depths of a vehicle, then raised his rifle and fired into the wreckage beyond Märt.

'What?'

'Get back to the forest. Juhan, you also.'

Peeter rose up carrying a few rifles. He threw Juhan a semi-automatic with a round cartridge.

'Go on boy, have some fun,' he said.

Juhan fired and yelped at the rate of the shots that came out. They edged towards Märt's position and then they all sprinted for the forest. A final grenade blast was heard nearby.

'I thought you would never come,' Raio was quickly at Märt's side to chide him.

'Thanks for waiting,' Märt said.

'You boys are getting too useful, now run!'

Spits of soil began to be thrown up around them and Märt was cut by splinter from a nearby tree. It was clear their adversaries had not given up the pursuit. He dived behind a bush to take quick stock of where their pursuers were.

'Will they follow?' Märt asked.

Raio cursed. 'They would be fools to come, but nothing about the Reds would surprise me. They appear to be firing blindly into the forest for now. You did good work with that machine gun.'

'That heap of junk?' Märt said. 'Jammed far too easily and weighed a ton.'

'I suggest we get back to base,' Raio replied, looking at his three companions with a weary smile. 'You boys are good - mad, but good.'

'Anton?' Märt said.

Raio's face clouded. 'It was quick.'

'Pity.'

'Yes, we parachuted in together only a few weeks ago. Let's go to the main camp, there is no use to split up now, especially as we are low on weaponry.'

'Have the Germans helped with supplies?' Peeter asked.

'No,' Raio replied then turned to jog away.

They ran on in silence, giving Märt time to recall the battle and the fleeting image of a couple escaping from the convoy. He was sure it was Harry and Liisbet, but how did they get there? Had they been in the convoy? As prisoners or fighters?

From what he had seen recently, the Reds would not have taken prisoners. Something within him clung to the belief that Harry was not a threat, yet his mind could not disassociate the man from the ensuing red horde. He needed time to think things through properly and being on the run was not the easiest time to do it.

Raio called out to the camp as they approached. Märt guessed that the word used was Finnish – not one similar to his native Estonian tongue. He didn't mind, better the security of a code word than a shot to the chest. Even then, he wondered if anybody actually had ammunition left.

A man stepped out from his hiding place brandishing a hunting knife ready. Seeing Raio, he lowered it. They approached the centre of the camp to find that everything that could be packed had been stowed into portable packages. Wooden shelters were left intact, some older weapons lay discarded.

'Why leave these?' Peeter asked as they walked through. Raio shook his head.

'The chance of getting ammunition for them is limited. What parachute drops we have had from Finland have not always been successful, many supplies were lost where they fell to the Reds or in their descent.

We have asked our allies, but they have not been so willing to help.'

'What, the shorties?' Peeter asked. 'I thought Hitler had tanks coming out of his arse.'

'For sure,' Raio replied as they carried on into the camp. 'They are getting closer every day. It is only malicious spite that the Reds kill off our people every day, yet our allies seem unwilling to help us with guns.'

'Maybe they have the same problems?' Juhan said.

'Maybe, or maybe they don't want us off the leash. Or maybe they don't want us around in the future. Here's your woman, Märt.'

Maarja was sitting on a fallen tree waiting and on seeing the group approach, she ran to Juhan's arms in relief. Märt kept walking without turning back.

'It is a story worth telling, Märt,' Peeter said.

Märt gave him a hard stare. 'One day, when we are not on the run, I may tell you the full tale if you are desperate for gossip. What next, Raio?'

'Rest here a moment and I will find out,' came the reply and Raio headed off towards a group of Finnish soldiers that included the colonel. He quickly returned.

'We are breaking for the German lines, but fighting at the rear of the column, to give our people time to escape to the forests.'

'Where will they go?' Juhan asked.

To their forest camps or make new camps. Some will take paths to the German lines in the south, others will go west towards Haapsalu. The rest will stay and take their chances with us.

The Germans are moving fast through Estonia according to Helsinki. If we draw the attention of the reds with their petty revenge games, then our people will escape. With luck, we will also lead the wolves to the den of the hunter.'

'What do you want us to do?' Märt asked. He fully expected to be told to fend for himself and disappear into the forest.

'I want you to come with me and guard the north flank of the Erna group. We will be the closest to Tallinn, we may even see its beautiful spires. It will take a few days I think and then we will be amongst friends.'

'Can we hold the Reds?' Peeter asked.

Raio spat. 'Those pigs? We could hold them for a lifetime using toothpicks.'

CHAPTER FIFTEEN

Retreat

On the second night, Märt settled down for what he hoped for once would be a long bout of sleep. It felt like each time they began to rest; they had spied movement. Or a faint noise of moving vehicles had cut through the passive sounds of branches swaying in the breeze, with their rustling leaves.

Now there was a mid-summer downpour of rain. Even in the dense forest, the rain found its way through the trees. It came as small droplets and invariably found the back of their necks and gave a cold chill down their spine.

For the umpteenth time, Märt shifted to a new area, his rest being disturbed by a single drop to the forehead. Close by, Peeter came to with a start.

'Easy Peeter, you are with friends,' Märt said.

He could not really see his companion but heard him sigh and the thump as Peeter sat back against a tree trunk.

'Those bastard Reds. I still wake up with them in my house. In the dusk, I see them walking in shadows, black on white, like a movie. Am I going mad?'

'No, you are only tired,' Juhan's voice came out of the gloom.

'Maybe you should respect your elders,' Peeter snapped like the snarl of a cornered lion.

'Perhaps we should all leave the fighting to the Reds, they deserve more attention,' Märt said.

To him, Peeter's outburst was a release of tension from one who had faced down death.

Much to his relief, they fell into a sullen silence. Märt closed his eyes and tried to think of better times, hoping the dream would reward him with a loss of the heavy feeling around his shoulders.

A hand shook him gently and Juhan's voice cut through the dark.

'They are coming.'

Märt quickly opened his eyes and roused himself, although his body felt tied to lead weights with the fatigue. He crept forward to try and look ahead and found Peeter standing behind a broad oak tree. Raio was nearby under cover. Märt found a bush to hide in and soon Juhan was by his side. Raio signalled to the young man and Märt picked up the meaning.

'Juhan, move swiftly, but keep low. Go back and warn the main party. Go now, be careful.'

Märt looked at the forest straight ahead and at first saw nothing. Then he realised there was a slight flickering of shadows in the hypnotic staggered lines of trees ahead.

He saw a patch of blueberries ahead and slowly stretched forward to pick some to eat. For luck, he convinced himself – even though his mouth still felt dry, despite their sweet taste.

The new arrivals moved slowly, looking around them as they went. Märt thought the actions of some gave the impression they were scared. As if their shadows were Finnish Boys, ready to pounce.

Märt looked around for a good hand-sized stone. There were none on the sandy leaf strewn ground. The men were getting closer and began to spread themselves into a line.

'Fools!' Märt mocked them. He would have been hugging the tree cover.

The men were closer now. His breath was shallow , making the blood pump faster in his ears. They did not have enough ammunition to defeat this group. All they could do was fire off their rounds and hope it would scare them off.

There was a rustling move behind the advancing enemy. Märt spied a sudden darting movement of an animal of sorts. A cry came and the soldiers turned to face the attack. Then another cry happened from behind them, this one Märt understood.

'Grenade!'

He ducked as his instincts cut in. The grenade exploded and Märt heard screams of pain. The remaining troops still moved forward closer to him. Then one fell with a cry, shot from behind.

'Ambush!' A cry went up, before the men beat a hasty retreat. Peeter let off a shot that injured one of them.

It made the rest retreat faster. Some started shooting wildly into the brush, but they were now too far from Märt and his comrades.

'Inspired move, throwing that stone,' Peeter said walking across to Märt.

'Wish I had,' Märt replied. 'Can you see any stones around here?'

Then he decided to keep his thoughts to himself. Those last few shots had not come from his group, perhaps another Finnish unit or forest brothers? Märt gave a shrug.

'We will find out who it was, I am sure.'

Juhan ran back, 'Retreat back to camp. We are heading west again.'

As Märt turned to go, he realised that someone was following Juhan. Maarja approached tentatively. Whilst not being a soldier, she had found clothing that was more practical. She had donned trousers and her long curly hair now was topped by a beret. She shouldered a rifle that Märt knew she could use in anger.

'You need men,' she said sweetly. 'And they were short, so they asked me.'

'Juhan is old enough to look after himself,' Märt replied and she snorted her derision.

'Yes, but together you are all fools.'

'Welcome sister,' Peeter said. 'I, at least feel better for your presence.'

Maarja gave a small nod of thanks, then she whipped round to face Märt.

'I can also sew you up when you get yourself shot. For the Colonel thinks that you are all wishing your life away with the risks that you are taking.'

'What choice do we have?' Raio asked, not showing any sign of acknowledging the tension between the two of them.

'There is always choice,' Maarja replied.

'I am trained, and these so-called red warriors are not,' Raio said and walked off.

'We survive, Maarja, as long as the bullets are there to help us keep them at bay.' Peeter said.

'True,' she replied sadly. 'While we have bullets. The Germans cannot come fast enough.'

They had to fend off two similar attacks. The last one had seen the enemy appear at the last minute. Märt ran out of ammunition and wondered how long he would last, fighting with his rifle as a club and a hunting knife.

The flight finally took them out of the forest and into a small settlement, which Märt was surprised to find still occupied. A few of the farm buildings looked deserted. Märt noted those people he could see looked older, tending their farms as if nothing had changed.

Juhan had been sent to the nearest farm and came trotting back looking quite pleased.

'Old mother and father will let us rest for the night.'

'Do they have food?' Raio asked.

'They have milk and eggs, nothing more.'

Raio smiled. 'Milk and eggs are more than enough – and a hayloft to rest? This is good news, for once to be warm and dry at night.'

They settled down and made their small nests to settle in the hay. In time, the old farmer shuffled in with a bucket of milk and a bag.

'Here, my wife boiled them for you,' he said. 'Raw and it would be hard on your stomachs.'

'Our thanks, my friend,' Peeter replied. 'But where are the young?'

The old man shrugged. 'Those that did not run away were taken by the Russians to fight in their army.'

'The Germans will come through soon. It will make things easier,' Juhan shouted from the top of the hayloft.

'Yes?' The old man replied. 'And when do the Estonians come?'

'We are here, old father,' Juhan replied cheerfully.

'We will be back,' Raio said, taking the eggs from the man. 'With the help of our Finnish brothers and the Germans.'

'Perhaps,' the man said. 'Although I believed Päts when he said he would restore democracy. Why should I believe you?'

Maarja was watching the doorway, but the conversation made her pace around in frustration.

'Päts was a fool, old man. He believed that taking control would solve all Estonia's problems. In the end he took away everything. First our democracy and then our fight.

We let Stalin's men just walk in. Now they travel our land without fear, even though they are losing the fight. Be wary of those who chase us, for they are murderers.'

'Then they are not Estonians.'

Maarja gave a cold smile. 'They are mostly outsiders, although some Estonians are there, proving you wrong, old father. They have no ties of loyalty. Tread carefully when they are around.'

The old man shook his head. 'My father built this farm. Nobody will take it from me.'

Peeter gave an anguished look to Märt, which made him put down the stick he was shaving and walk to the old farmer.

'Old man, please. Listen to us. We have seen a few places destroyed for no reason but spite. Keep one eye to the east and if the Reds do come, go to the forest.'

The man shook his head. 'This is my land, and I will fight them for it. Enjoy the eggs.' He got up to walk out, Raio watched the large barn door closing slowly after him.

'I don't get it, Märt. Why can he not see?'

'Because he is a slave to the land,' Peeter replied bitterly. 'It is a part of him, and he is part of it. He would perish before giving up his birthright. I once too felt this way.'

'Get some rest,' Märt said. 'Let's all think about our own future.'

'Surely we have to stay and help them fight?' Maarja asked.

'With what?' Märt replied. He could not meet here eyes, he knew the question, his soul burned with it.

'Our best weapon is to draw the Reds along to the Germans,' Juhan said from above.

There was no disagreement.

Märt was awoken from his sleep by a sharp pain at his neck and a hand over his mouth.

'Easy laddie,' the voice soothed softly enough for Märt's ears only. 'I am holding a knife, so don't speak too loudly.'

It was as dark as tar. Märt could not see the others, which made the situation feel surreal. He wasn't sure if he was in a dream or if it was real.

'Harry,' he finally whispered. 'What are you doing here?'

'Passing through,' came the reply. 'Needed to call in and

see my family.'

'I thought you would be well on your way to Moscow,' Märt spluttered louder than he meant. The knife tightened to stop him but there was an almost silent chuckle of laughter.

'Not I, I'm not going close to them lot. Don't care much for the Russians or their measure of justice.'

'So, what are you doing?'

'Trying to get to Finland, I told you at the start.'

'Why?'

'I have something to show them.'

Only Harry could put such emotion into a breath , Märt thought.

'What about coming back with us? The Finnish Boys have a radio at base.'

'This I have to deliver by hand. The Colonel has been given instructions to catch me. The Germans are making it difficult for me to reach my destination, as they want me stopped.'

'What is it you have?'

The knife point came off Märt's neck.

'It's too much to explain here, but there will be a time later, I'm sure. Believe me, it is in all our interests to let me leave now.'

'So, go.'

There was a pat on Märt's shoulder. 'I still have need of you and when the time comes, you will understand. For now, go along with the Colonel, he at least is a good man. Be wary of Germans.'

'They at least are liberating our country.'

'If you say so,' Harry whispered. A metal container found its way into Märt's hand. 'Two clips for the semi. If the Russians are coming, they will be early. So be ready. Until later.'

There was a rustle of movement and Märt said. 'Wait! What about Liisbet?'

'She is safe. She is always safe with me.'

'Tell her thanks for shooting the destroyers,' Märt murmured. There was no reply.

Märt woke with a start. Had he been asleep the whole time? He felt his way gingerly to where Raio stood watch and whispered his name.

'Raio, have you seen anything strange?'

'Not I,' Raio replied too quickly. Märt knew the man had been sleeping, though he did not blame him.

'Okay, I'll take over. It's dawn in a few hours, so get some rest.'

The morning was grey, but as Märt went to look outside the barn, he was pleased to see the sun begin to gently caress the fields. He wished he had a change of clothing, he felt he had lived in what he wore for far too long. Perhaps he could swim somewhere? He went to the fence boundary to stretch his legs and take stock of the situation. Looking down the fence, he admired the way the stakes seem set perfectly at forty-five degrees to the ground, cut at an angle to make the rain run off and not gather to rot the inside. It was the old way and good practice.

He turned around as he heard footsteps, but relaxed as he saw it was Raio coming to greet him.

'You are taking a lot of chances, friend Märt,' he began.

Märt frowned. 'What do you mean?'

Raio indicated with his hand. 'You stand around exposed to any watching the farm. Not only do you announce our presence, but you make yourself a target for a decent sniper.'

'I'm sorry Sergeant. It's been a long time since I had to think about anything military.'

Raio pulled a face, but all the time looking around the land for the slightest movement. 'I don't think that's true, Märt. You do things automatically that say otherwise. And you must call me Raio. Unless you are in the Finnish Army, then you do it when the officers are out of earshot.'

'I can manage that, Raio,'

Raio lit a cigarette and stood taking in the smoke.

'So, no chance of snipers then?' Märt said looking at the cigarette.

Raio exhaled. 'No, it was bullshit, we are out of range and reasonably hidden. I just wanted to push you. You know you are playing a dangerous game, Märt.'

'What do you mean?'

'Last night. I heard some of it.'

It was Märt's turn to shrug. 'What did you want me to do? The man held a knife against my throat.'

'I guessed as much.'

'I am not here to betray you, Raio,'

'No, I see that. I watched you fight that column in Kautla Wald. My problem is I don't know what that Englishman is doing.'

'He's a spy, Raio. I know that much at least. The way he reacts to what he has seen the Reds do. He's not a sympathiser. He says he needs to go to Finland to give something by hand.

Something is stopping him from going to your Colonel - the link with the Germans, I think.'

'So, we are tainted by Hitler.'

'Look, if I was English, with my country allied to Comrade Stalin and I had need to get something to somewhere other than the Russians, maybe I would be careful who I trusted.'

Raio leant on the fence and looked across the field. 'True. And the girl?'

'His Achilles heel. She is a passenger. She stole him from you because she had been declared a Red and he may not trust what your Colonel might have done. The man doesn't understand.'

'Understand what, Märt?'

'That this land has gone mad since you boys ran across the sea to bed the Finnish girls.'

Raio gave a wolfish grin and rubbed his lower teeth. 'There was just the one in my case. It's as well I like you, Märt, just don't let me down.'

They both stopped as they heard a sound, faint at first, a rumbling in the forest. Raio swore and threw away his cigarette.

'Tanks! The bastards. Get everyone up and out.'

Märt did not need to be told twice, he ran to the barn to be met by a half awake Maarja.

'We've got to go,' he said, watching her face move from incomprehension to urgency.

'I will raise everyone. There are tanks coming. Go over and persuade the farmer to come now. There is no security left here and the war won't pass him by if he just sticks his head in the sand and pretends nothing is happening.'

'It's their home,' Maarja protested. Märt grabbed her arm, he tried to be light and wasn't sure if the frown was annoyance or pain.

'We both went to a farm like this in Kautla. They were burnt alive, remember? Tell them I still smell the charred flesh if you need them to move.'

Märt ran off wishing he hadn't snapped like that to her. Maarja looked at the farm and wished she hadn't left her to give the bad news. But then she had the skill of persuasion, she had a way with people that Märt had never got close to mastering. Not Märt, impetuous, headstrong Märt.

Juhan ran up to her. 'They want me to go. A diversionary attack to make them think we are moving in another direction.'

Maarja stroked his cheek. 'Just be careful.'

Juhan ran off and Maarja sighed. 'All of you, be careful.'

'Did we lose them?' Peeter asked between deep breaths.

'As long as we keep to the forests, we will always lose the tanks,' Raio replied. 'Just make sure we don't pick somewhere they can surround us.'

'Do you think the Germans are close?'

'I don't know, a day perhaps from where we knew they were the last time we found the main camp.'

Märt had followed the other two but had kept his own counsel. The presence of Maarja still made him feel awkward and almost paralysed.

He wanted to shake his head and get on with things, but his focus had left him. Juhan was walking by his side and the calm that oozed from the young man was Märt's saving grace.

'You are planning, I hope,' Juhan said.

After a few seconds, Märt realised he was expected to answer. He tried to think of the words.

'I am listening, Juhan. I don't trust anything around me anymore. I think Raio is right about the tanks, but I no longer feel we are safe by just hiding in the forest. The Reds have tried to infiltrate Erna in Kautla, they are not afraid to send their people into the trees.'

Raio stopped to wait for them to arrive. 'You are right, they do want Erna, but I think those who stay in the forest and keep their heads down will have a chance. The soviet machine wants to destroy all military opposition. If we are bleeding away resource that could be used against the Germans, that's fine by me.'

'They must really hate us,' Juhan said.

Raio chuckled. 'In the war of independence, we drove them back to St Petersburg. We cleared them south and then pushed the Germans back to Riga. They might still be feeling sorry for themselves. It may be that you and your mother should take shelter here with a forest brother group, whilst we draw the Reds away.

CHAPTER SIXTEEN

Liisbet

Maarja's heart skipped a beat. She wanted to be free of pursuit, but she had made a promise to help find Harry. The key to that was Märt and if she wanted to continue, she had to be near him.

Everyone was looking at Märt as if he needed to make the decision. He looked at the group one at a time, before his gaze rested on Maarja. The look she returned was neither hostile nor pleading. He turned and walked on muttering under his breath.

'Remind me never to get into a card game with you.'

He was relieved that nobody acted as if he had been heard. 'If they want to travel with us and they are not in any danger of getting in the way, we should make them welcome.'

Raio nodded. 'Okay, but this might change. We have no space for carrying passengers.'

They continued, but to Märt every step felt heavy. He stopped to shift his pack and Maarja brushed past him.

'Carrying passengers,' were the only words she said. She moved off before Märt could reply.

The words were not required, her body showed exactly how she felt. Märt moved over to Peeter, at least he felt a kindred spirit there.

'Where is the rest of the unit?' he asked and Peeter shrugged.

'No idea, I was just asked to keep watch over us and report of any approaching enemy. I'm sure Raio knows.'

'I don't think he does,' Märt replied. 'We don't have a radio, so he can't check where the main force is, or the Germans, or the Reds. We are just one of their outlying units steadily pushed away by hostile forces.'

'Well, I wish he did know, if only to keep this small band happy.'

'That would include us Märt,' Peeter chuckled. 'When are we ever happy?' Then it was like a cloud passed over his face. 'I am hoping the Reds come. I haven't killed enough for what they did to my family.'

Märt looked at the anguish on his friend's face. 'Courage, Peeter. You keep the memory of your family alive by staying alive yourself.'

'Go away, friend Märt,' Peeter said softly.

'We are all here?' Märt whispered.

'No idea.'

'Who's that? Raio?'

'Yes.'

'Peeter?'

'Yes, Märt.'

'Juhan?'

'*Tere Homikust!*'

Peeter groaned. 'Why do you always have to be so bloody cheerful? We've been on the run for three days. We've had over a dozen skirmishes and we have one bullet between us.'

'I have six,' Juhan replied

'One bullet each then. Don't you understand fear, boy?'

'Only when I need to, old man,'

'Juhan, stop.' Maarja's gentle reproof floated over the air.

'There's another column. Listen.' Raio said.

'Where is it? Behind us?' Märt asked.

'Think so,' Raio replied. 'The Germans cannot be far. I keep looking for signs, I think ...'

There was a burst of artillery quite far off.

'I wonder where it is,' Peeter remarked.

'What is it?' Juhan asked.

'The sound of our salvation,' Peeter snapped and muttered an oath.

'Let's make for it,' Märt said. 'Come on, it's not too far away and we are the locals, so should have better ideas of where to go. We know this land better than the Reds or the shorties.'

'It's my turn to guard the rear,' Maarja said. 'You carry on.'

There was no argument and they set off in the darkness.

'That woman of yours is a godsend,' Raio muttered to Märt. 'I tell you if you weren't around, I would...'

'What?'

'Nothing.'

'She's not my woman,' Märt replied.

'Even so.'

'Your loss,' Märt replied moving on.

Their progress was slow in the darkness that cloaked the forest. The day had been long in time and long in action. They had kept moving as much as they could to gain extra space from their pursuers. Märt hoped they could gain a bit more space. A bit more time to rest, regroup and work out where they were and where they were going.

'It's no use, Märt said. 'We are falling over tree stumps in the dark. There is little sound of pursuit and we are deep in the forest. I say we rest and take it in turns to keep watch. Say thirty minutes each.'

'I will be first,' said Peeter. 'You all need some time.'

'I won't argue,' Maarja muttered.

It was nearly morning when Märt was roused from his sleep. There was a dim edge to the rays of light and the shadows appeared to be slowly melting with each blink of his tired eyes.

A fine mist hung in the forest ahead, like a ghost. Märt tried to peer through it, rubbing his eyes for focus. Märt tensed as he heard the crack of a branch, whilst hoping it was just another of the many sounds of the forest morning. Was that a shape forming in the mist? He wasn't sure, the image ahead was fuzzy.

A bird flew frantically away from the branches of a nearby tree. Then there was another crack of a broken branch and he knew for certain someone was approaching.

Their outline was still faint and Märt could not work out how far away they were. A warning shot would certainly announce Märt's presence to the pursuers – it was foolish to think this person was alone. The different shades of grey in the shadows were mesmerising. Märt knelt down and tried to focus his eyes ahead. He could tell that Maarja had moved to his side. Her scent would always be unforgettable to him.

'We've got company,' he whispered. 'Rouse the rest but be quiet and keep out of sight.'

He tried to judge the figure's approach once again. Were they armed? Should he fire off a precious warning shot? Should they run or hide? The figure was nearing and Märt was surprised that they still appeared alone. Perhaps someone desperate to catch up with the retreat? Maybe he should use his hunting knife?

There was a gentle but firm downward pressure on the front of the rifle. He looked to see it was Maarja, pushing it down. He looked with horror at her for a second until she replied to the unanswered question.

'She is no threat. And she is alone.'

'Don't shoot!'

The feminine voice was small and soft and very familiar. The tone trembled with fear.

'Liisbet?' He called softly.

'Märt?' She replied hopefully, her voice wavering.

'Come forward, Liisbet, slowly. Keep your hands where I can see them.'

The shape appeared stronger now and he could see her clearly.

'Are you alone?'

'Yes, Märt,' she sobbed. 'Don't shoot.'

'Are you armed?'

'No.'

He could see that she looked exhausted, her clothes a bit broken and dishevelled. She almost stumbled and he raised his rifle in instinct. She raised her hands quickly, and nervously came to a halt. Then he moved forward to her side.

'*Tere*,' she said, her lips quivering with fear. 'I thought you were going to shoot me.'

'So did I,' Märt replied. 'Where's Harry?'

Her eyes filled with tears and she suddenly became the frightened doe that he remembered watching the cattle trucks full of people. For once his stiff demeanour crumbled and he drew her into an embrace. She shuddered for a while and then returned it fiercely. Märt could not see Maarja, but even the thought of her watching made him flush.

'I meant to say that had I known it was you, I would not have raised my rifle.'

She nodded and gave a nervous smile, though her lips still trembled from the shock.

'Harry has gone, Märt. He… we have been tracking you for days. We have been slightly ahead of you for a while.'

'Why?' Raio asked, showing a clear air of suspicion in his tone.

'Märt is family,' she replied with a glare of indignation. 'We even came to your aid once. Now you are close to German lines, Harry decided to go alone and send me to shelter. He wants you to take me to Rapla, Märt.'

'Where is he?' Märt asked again. She shook her head, ignoring a tear running down her face.

'He's gone, Märt. Off towards Tallinn. He is trying to find an old friend. A Swedish-Estonian called Sven, a fisherman who lives just outside Pirita.'

'Why has he gone to the Reds, girl?' Raio demanded.

Liisbet stiffened at the blunt tone and her reply came out as if carved on tablets of stone.

'There are no boats in Estonia. The Russians destroyed them all to stop us running away, remember? After you had gone to Finland, of course. He needs a boat to go to Finland and his only option is to steal one from the Russians.'

'He is no Red, Raio,' Peeter's voice came from the bushes, as he approached the group. 'I trust him as he has trusted us with his little angel.'

Liisbet's face relaxed into a smile, as she heard the words.

'I am glad you are here with us, farmer.'

'I also am pleased you have come. Raio, you are a soldier. To you, the world is black and white. In this land, there is as much grey as a morning mist. I do not trust many,'

He nodded to the group. 'They are all here; Märt, Raio, Liisbet and the fool. Märt, if you do not protect her, I will. If you do not take her to Rapla, I will.'

'Let's cross the German lines first,' Märt replied. 'We should start now before our pursuers get closer. If we are lucky, we find the Wehrmacht today.'

'It is not far,' Liisbet said. 'I will show you.'

Maarja was standing back from the group but listening, as Märt walked past her she sounded almost disapproving.

'Should we trust her?'

Märt shrugged. 'I trust her and she is leading us into the right direction. We are almost surrounded and have no means to really defend ourselves if we fall into a trap anyway. We have no means to defend ourselves if we stay.'

'Well I'm not sure...' she began, but Märt cut her short.

'The decision has been made. You can stay if you wish.'

She recoiled from the bluntness, then the fire in her eyes returned.

'Come on Märt, how is he supposed to steal a boat from the Russian Army? And why if he needs to get a message to the Finns, does he not cross over to the Germans now. Or even just talk to one of these Finnish Boys?'

Her voice had carried, and the men stopped to look at her. Juhan was close by, relaxed, but for once quite protective of his mother.

'Perhaps we can talk about this when we have more leisure to do so,' Peeter replied. 'And you can tell us of how you got here also.'

'Stop this now,' Märt snapped. 'We have all stayed alive so far by keeping together and looking out for each other's safety. We are tired and hungry, but our goal is close. We should not be falling into petty bickering when we need to be focusing on our escape.'

There was a silence, as everyone appeared paralysed, not knowing what to do next.

'There is movement in the trees,' Juhan said. 'Far enough away for now, but we need to get going.'

'Lead on,' Peeter replied, looking at Liisbet, before sending a dark glance at Maarja.

'It's not far,' Liisbet said. 'Just move through this forest and cross the road through it.'

They started off again. Märt was happy to trust Liisbet, but he knew the land itself could easily throw its own issues back and change the situation. It had happened enough times already, that he was sure there was at least one more twist waiting for them.

They made good pace and soon saw the gloom lift ahead, indicating the edge of the woodland. Märt brought them to a standstill at the fringe and they looked with dismay at the scene on the road.

A small column of trucks had stopped about a hundred metres down from them. Across it, the woodland continued, with its dark pockets calling to them for their freedom.

'It's a trap,' Maarja hissed.

'No,' Liisbet replied. 'I have not led you to this. They were not here before.'

Raio crept forward as close as could without being seen, before crawling back on his belly.

'Mostly trucks carrying soldiers or destroyers, I think. Not many people. They are up to something, but I'm damned if I know what.'

'Either way, our journey has to be across this road.' Märt replied.

'We should look to move further up and cross where we cannot be seen.'

'There is a sound of vehicles further up also,' Peeter muttered. 'And we are definitely being followed.'

'Let's calm down,' Märt replied. 'We can still succeed. We just need to move further up the road as far as we can and then make a break across. Maybe the other vehicles will drive past and we can get across easily. Let's save our energy for one final burst. We are nearly there.'

'Shit!' Raio whispered. 'Where did that lot come from?'

Märt turned and saw shadows in the forest.

'No choice then, we move up the road now. If we are seen, we cross on my signal.'

They started to make their cautious way up, keeping low and trying desperately not to do anything that may give their position away. They kept each tree as a shield to their backs. Märt hoped that the broken light streaming through the branches could help camouflage them. He quickened the pace, his throat now parched with fear. Was this the end?

Liisbet was close and she looked terrified. Her eyes were large and wide, as she stumbled forward, nervously looking from side to side.

'It's not your fault,' Märt whispered to her.

She gave no indication that she had heard him; he just hoped it had somehow sunk through the barriers. He couldn't remember when he had started to lead the group; it just seemed to have passed naturally. Echoes of his past in *Kaitseliit* had helped him assume the role quite easily. With that knowledge however came the weight of responsibility that he had not felt for years. One thing was certain, he was going to survive – and he would drag them all through with him.

A cry rang out, followed by another.

'They are too bloody close,' Peeter muttered.

'Don't worry old farmer, we can outrun them,' Juhan whispered.

'Idiot!' Peeter hissed in reply.

Märt looked for Maarja and saw her skirting around low bushes nearby. She returned the glance but showed no emotion.

He tried to smile, though he knew it probably looked like a grimace these days, so he stopped quickly.

They either trust me or they don't. If it's the former, I can keep us all alive.

A shot rang out and clipped a tree nearby.

'Faster,' Märt warned and stopped worrying about stealth.

Ahead, the forest appeared to pinch the road.

If they could just get there, the break of cover would be so much less, it just may be enough.

The next shot caused shavings of tree bark to spit back and graze his cheek. *Close, so close.* A lot of shouting seemed to come from all around him.

The forest seemed to bulge out into the road ahead. There was a stream running under the road, he realised. They could not cross it and keep their pace. He took a deep breath.

'Now!' he screamed and launched himself out of the forest. Shots rang out all around him. He prayed they were out of range. He tried to focus straight ahead on his goal. The tree branches seemed to be open in welcome as he stumbled onto the gravel road.

Blood was now pumping in his ears and time seemed to slow down for him. He was sure there was a roar of engines, but Märt did not dare to look. He had made his run it was now up to the Gods whether it meant success or death.

The land fell away below the road and Märt half-stumbled down the bank, before flinging himself into the forest.

The noise around him now seemed to be punctuated by flashes and he felt he had stumbled on a large firework display. He continued to run, praying the others had followed. His face felt warm by a flash of flame and he began to tense, waiting for the final white-hot bullet to cut him down with a searing pain in the back.

In his haste, he lost his footing and crashed to the ground, frantically trying to scramble himself back on his feet. Märt looked straight ahead and froze at the sight. A grey-clad man crouched close ahead of him. He wore a helmet and had his rifle in the firing position. He looked straight at Märt for a second and gently shook his head.

'Get down!' Märt screamed and fell to lie as flat as possible on the ground. There was a cry and the sound of rifle fire increased, although this time it was from the front. Märt tried to feel as small as he could and prayed for his own safety. Then it all went silent and soon Märt felt a gun prod his back.

'*Aufstehen!*' a voice shouted. It took Märt a while to realise the man was speaking German.

Doubting the miracle, Märt looked up to find he was staring into the face of a German soldier. He slowly got up, as the soldier stood ready for any action.

The surge of the fight coursed through the man's veins. He panted with the exertion and even his rifle still quivered reflecting the adrenalin rush.

Märt made sure his arms were away from his body and hands out. He remained very still.

'We are Estonians in the Finnish Army. *Estlanders!*' Märt could hear Raio shouting. 'We are escaping the Reds, rejoining Colonel Kurg's unit. Finnish Boys.'

The soldier in front of Märt did not move, although Märt was convinced there was a hint of confusion in his eyes.

'Yes, these men are with us,' Märt heard a voice to the side of him.

'Thank god you are here, Toomas,' Raio shouted.

'Making sure we all came back, Sergeant' the man replied.

'That is good to hear and see.'

'There are six of us,' Märt said to the German soldier in pigeon German. 'Four men, two women.'

The man stared back for what seemed like a long time and Märt began to feel as if he would be shot. Then the soldier blinked.

'Quickly, come.'

Märt gathered his rifle and quickly looked around. Peeter was getting up from the ground. Juhan was already standing and helping his mother up.

Only Liisbet was missing. He found her lying on the floor. She shrieked when Märt touched her.

'It's alright, little one, we are safe. The Germans have found us, come with me.'

Her face turned to stare at him, and he saw a lack of comprehension. Gently, he lifted her up.

He avoided Maarja's gaze, although he could feel her eyes on him. In the background, he could hear Toomas talking to Raio.

'You were damn lucky, the Reds were right on your backs. Another minute and they would have had you. We need to move back in case they return. There were enough of them, but they were only destroyer scum.'

'Perhaps we should go back and check for ammunition,' Juhan said and Märt looked around behind them. He could see at least one human form crumpled on the ground. One hand was held up, clutching the sky in pain.

'I wouldn't,' Toomas said. 'We are only a reconnaissance unit. We are a few miles from the front line. Let's go.'

Märt looked down at Liisbet, as she still held him tightly for support.

'We made it, little one,' Märt soothed. There was no reply, but her grip tightened momentarily.

Maarja looked on impassively or she at least tried to give that impression. There was much to do, she knew. Too much to get distracted by the scene of Liisbet clinging to Märt. She turned to suppress the wave of jealousy that flowed through her, it made her feel sullen. A German soldier was by her side and she muttered to him.

'I need to speak to your commanding officer. I need to find an *Oberleutnant* Schulz at the earliest opportunity. I have important news for him.'

CHAPTER SEVENTEEN

All roads lead to Tallinn

M ärt stared out of the temporary base and sighed. He felt frustrated that the world had conspired to trap him at a German Army camp. It was difficult to suppress the urge just to break out.

Raio came to his side. Like the faithful hound, Märt thought. *He knows when to avoid me and when to be close.*

'It is good to have food, a wash, clean clothes and a blanket at least, Lieutenant.'

Märt grimaced. 'That is a field commission only, Raio and your fault. I am hardly a graduate of the military academy, passed out with General Laidoner's blessing.'

The sun was rising, making the morning dew sparkle, as life in the camp began to pick up.

'I can understand the need to rest, <u>sergeant</u>,' Märt said with unbridled irony. 'And I have just slept a long time both before and after I washed and scrubbed the bugs from my clothes. I have even grown to like the taste of food once more. But now I am fully rested, we are kept here.'

Raio handed him a steaming mug of coffee. Märt sipped it slowly and welcomed the warmth of the brew as it began to wake his body.

He stretched and looked on jealously at the German soldiers who came into view armed and fully kitted out. He was jealous mostly about their boots. They looked warm and comfortable.

'We need to regroup,' Raio said. The faint aroma of cigarette smoke came to Märt's nose, which he wrinkled in distaste. 'We are exhausted and have lost many men.'

'Peeter has gone,' Märt said vaguely. He felt sad at the words.

'I know, Märt. He was a good solid man to have in a fight. Very handy, but he was going to kill Juhan, because the boy drove him mad. It was better to let him take Liisbet away. She wanted to go home, there was nothing left with Harry gone.'

'What will be left for her in Rapla? There's certainly nothing for me to consider back there. There's bound to be some left who were sympathetic to the Reds and people will link her to the deportations.'

A soldier had moved to a large half-track vehicle. It coughed into life sending a cloud of blue smoke above it.

'What do you think happens now?' Raio asked, the wistful look not hidden from his face. Märt shook his head.

'You really want this, don't you?'

Raio took a long drag and shrugged. 'I'm keen to get Estonia back from outsiders - that is worth fighting for. Half of those we picked up.

at Kautla have gone back to the forest.

They see the job done, but my Tallinn is still not free. Those Estonians who came over from Finland, those of us who joined the Finnish Army, that's who is left.'

'And me,' Märt reminded him. 'And Juhan.'

The half-track was now full of German soldiers and it powered away. The large vehicle roared its way down the road, smoke still coughing from its exhaust like some overgrown tractor. A row of blue helmeted heads could be seen in the toast rack seats.

'There's no subtlety, is there?' Märt asked. Raio took a long drag and threw the cigarette butt away.

'There isn't in war.'

Juhan joined them, still smiling, but now with a definite frown of concern on his face.

'I talked to them, we'll be getting new weapons soon – or at least ammunition for the old guns.'

'You had better keep your rifle clean then, young man,' Raio replied. The stiff manner of the sergeant came back quickly, but it did not knock the smile from Juhan's face.

'Yes, that's true.'

'Any sign of your mother?' Märt asked, trying to be as non-chalant as possible.

'No, she spoke to someone and they took her away. She did not look worried but said she would be back soon.'

It was a mixed blessing for Märt. His concern for her was real, but her absence was a breath of fresh air, allowing him to focus.

'Right then,' he said. 'I had better go and make sure we get that ammunition.'

A German soldier came running up carrying a piece of folded paper, which he presented to Raio. He got a withering look for his trouble and followed the direction of the curt nod, before moving to Märt.

He opened the letter and read the contents. He then took out a lighter to burn it, before thinking better of it and putting it in his pocket.

'We march,' he said. 'The Germans are being a bit more successful than we thought, it would seem. We should get that ammunition a bit earlier.'

'You had better get a uniform too,' Raio said.

'If it's not Finnish, I'm not wearing it,' Märt said walking off.

Maarja was fed up with walking. Whether in the forest or not, her body felt worn out from the constant flight of the past few months. Schulz's soldiers had left her with few words. She was grateful, for she had no need of conversation.

A month ago, I was by Pärnu , she thought, *the month before back in Märjamaa. Why does it feel longer?*

She thought of her long-lost love, he was a good caring man. She was always happy around him. Then there was Märt, always there for her.

Two burning stars in her life that had lifted her and brought her strength and warmth. Now they were gone, the stars had been no more than meteorites in the sky.

She worried about Juhan. She knew Märt would look after him, she had made sure of that, but would Juhan look after himself?

Why had she been sent to Tallinn to find one man? It seemed ridiculous that she would stand a chance. Where could she even start to look? There were a few Swedish Estonians, or at least there were before the war. Pirita was a start, the other side of Tallinn Bay to her beloved city. Possibly less busy, as the Germans would be focusing on the capital. She knew the way, for she had loved being taken to the ruined abbey as a child.

She had loved sitting down as her father told her the legend of the abbey. How the villagers rose up to sack the place and defeat the wicked Abbess. How the young novice had led the way, by showing the hero a secret tunnel to get inside. It was a great tale.

She wished she was the novice, leading the people forward to right the wrongs in the world.

Maarja felt as if she would spend the rest of her life walking through forests. The morning damp still hung in the air and she was convinced her clothes already smelt stale from it. She pulled her shawl closer around her shoulders.

She would find this man, Maarja was now certain of this fact. How she would get the man back? She had no idea. Would she have to kill him? Could she?

She took a deep breath. *If that was what it took.* She paused and allowed herself to rest a while. She was sweating, this was not good. She would soon cool down or her odour would be bad. How could she ever use her persuasive charm when she smelt like old rope?

She hardly knew Harry, but it was what he represented that killed him in her eyes, for he portrayed change. Her younger life was one of ease and affluence. Then the war of independence came and changed everything. It spread over the land and in it her heart was taken. Emotion was washed away to become a life of simplicity and labour. She never complained, even when her great love was taken from her and her heart was broken, even then she carried on. Then war returned and changed it all again and she now no longer knew where her heart lay. The change was brutal, and Harry represented it. It was enough to condemn the man.

Maarja moved on, she was well behind the lines now and needed to be careful. A stranger would stand out in the ruins of the land, easy pickings for summary justice by a revengeful occupier.

She tried to think of her encounter the previous night with warmth. Schulz was so patient and gentle, until the passion rose within him. She tried to feel emotion, but she knew that all she had left was shame.

Tallinn was shattered, a pall of smoke cloaking the old town on Toompea hill, as it rose from the more modern hinterlands. She dreaded to think what the city had left to offer.

From her experiences in Märjamaa, she knew it would be hard to avoid detection. She desperately hoped that her false papers were good enough to stand under scrutiny. Märt's image swam into view, that and the British Navy officer, Huw. Why had it always gone so wrong?

Her heart felt as if it was tied to a stone, dragging her

down. When she had returned from Schulz, she found the Finnish Boys had already left. Märt and Juhan were nowhere to be seen. In desperation, she searched the camp, asking questions, looking for clues. Then she found a note pinned to a board by a small knife. Juhan had cheerfully scribbled:

We are moving north. See you at Piik Hermann when we get to Tallinn.

She hoped it would happen. She could not lose her son and live. The thought made her shudder, but it was enough to spur her on.

'It's up to me then,' she muttered to herself. 'To make sure it all happens.'

◆ ◆ ◆

Peeter looked at the line of people stumbling down the road southwards. Some were lucky to have handcarts, most carried what belongings they could on their shoulders and heads. They all looked as if they had not washed in months.

He wondered how badly he would look also. He slipped back into the forest to where Liisbet sat, leaning against a tree trunk. The girl looked up at his approach and tried to smile.

'Don't tell me, there's no room for us.'

Peeter slumped by her side with a sigh and leant against the tree.

'You would have thought that with all the deportations and murders, there would not be enough people left to cause a traffic jam. The problem is when the Germans want to send a unit through, everything going away from the front just stops and it all causes a great mess.'

There was no reply, except Liisbet tapped her hand impatiently on her leg looking troubled.

'I have said something, little one.'

Liisbet shook her head. 'I still remember watching the train, seeing the people inside fighting for air as they were taken. I see it many times in my dreams.'

Peeter patted her arm. 'I still see my family,' he said softly, almost as if in a trance. 'We are all haunted by this war. People are coming out of the forests now. The men still want to fight, whilst the women want to return home.'

'I think you will find there are some women who want to fight also and some men who want to return.'

'True, I'm sorry Liisbet.'

'Why are you here? With me?'

Peeter gave a hollow laugh. 'Those people who sat at my table and drank vodka with me are the only family I have left. Märt can look after himself. The Englishman has gone, you need protecting.'

She looked across and patted his arm.

'I'm not here to screw you or anything like that,' he said trying to make light of the words.

'No, but you would kill those who try. I remember you shot that Red at your farm.'

'Yes, although I took no pleasure from it.'

In the distance, the snarl of diesel engines echoed around the woodland. A German Kubelwagen passed into view, the passenger standing, holding onto the wind deflector. His other hand waved wildly as he yelled instructions for the masses to get out of the way. Then quite soon, a column of tanks rumbled past. Anyone who was too stubborn or slow to the command quickly moved when faced with the oncoming mass of steel monsters, and they quickly swept up the road. The lead tank's officer was standing half out of the turret, looking around the area. He looked as if he was surveying his kingdom.

'If I was a diplomat, I would say these short, cursed Germans are acting like they are here to stay, like the landlords of old.' Peeter muttered.

'Harry thought so,' Liisbet replied. 'Certainly, they will live on the land whilst Stalin still wags his tail.'

'Why did Harry leave you?'

Peeter knew his tone was too sharp, and he cursed himself for the rush of emotion. He held his hand up in apology.

'He said he needed to go where it would be too dangerous for me,' Liisbet replied. 'I said it would look better if we went as a couple, but he said no... the age difference...' she swallowed. 'He had to go into Tallinn to find a boat.'

'Any boat or a specific boat?' Peeter ran his hands through his hair in frustration. 'I want to believe you girl, because if he was a Red, he could have betrayed us at any point, but why not the Germans?'

'He is British, I think he only wants to talk to the Finns.'

'Why not talk to the leader of the Finnish Boys?'

Liisbet shrugged. 'The colonel commands his men on the ground, but the Germans wag the tail in Helsinki.'

'Okay, so he wants to talk to the Finns, without being caught by their allies or their enemies. What the hell does that mean?'

Liisbet suddenly slammed her fist to the ground. 'How should I know?' she shouted. 'He would not say. How many times do I have to tell you people? None of you listen, it's as if you don't believe me. You are all arseholes!'

Peeter looked sadly on at the frustration and anger that Liisbet now showed in her expression. She looked even lovelier with her reddened cheeks and widened eyes.

But he would never tell her. He would never again give himself the luxury of letting someone know. He would lock his own emotions within himself.

'I mean no harm, Liisbet, I was just thinking out loud. There is something going on here that is bigger and deeper than Hitler against Stalin and poor little Estonia. I wish Harry had had the balls to tell us. He damn well needs our help now.'

He stood back up and dragged his pack to his shoulder. 'Come on, let's do it.'

Liisbet looked on in confusion, still trembling with receding anger. She didn't know whether to shout or cry.

'What do you mean?'

'It's simple *kallis*. You don't want to go back to Rapla. I see this. What is there for you anyway? People who think you were Red, or people hiding their Red sympathies and know you turned? I can see what you are thinking. Your heart lies north now, and you will not rest until you find the Englishman again. Besides, there is something he is doing and if it is as big as I feel it may be, everyone will want him dead first. So, let's head for Pirita abbey. We'll get a lift from the Germans, telling them we are *Metsavennad* going to fight. We'll find your Harry, don't worry.'

CHAPTER EIGHTEEN

Separate Journeys

'D o you recognise anywhere?' Juhan asked.

'The lakes. We are on the Tartu road, not too far from Tallinn,' Raio replied.

Märt looked at the woodland around the lake. Sitting in the back of the truck, involved being bounced around like a rock sieve. He looked at the calm lakeside, wishing that he could just fish there and let the world get on with its troubles.

'I wish we were going to Pirita,' he mused.

'We are going to Pirita,' Raio replied. 'God help any Reds standing in our way. There's talk…'

'There's always talk, Sergeant,' Märt snapped, then took a deep breath. 'Sorry, Raio. It's all this stuff with Harry.' *and Maarja*, he thought. 'It's getting in the way of my thinking.'

'Maybe he'll be in Pirita,' Juhan said cheerfully.

Märt wished for a stick to whittle.

'Juhan, maybe there's a young attractive nun waiting for us peasants to lead us by a secret tunnel to Pirita.'

He tried to make light of the tension, although it did not feel right to him.

'I'm worried also,' Juhan said softly. 'But all we can do is carry on and trust in our luck.'

Raio patted his newly issued machine gun.

'I put my trust in Herr *Schmeisser* here, he helps me win any argument.'

Märt went back to watching the forest. He became absorbed with the variation in the types of trees and bushes at the front and the larger evergreens behind. He started to look for silver birches and blueberry bushes; all to take his mind away from the thought of Maarja.

Maarja moved swiftly to the doorway from her hiding place. She had spent so long watching the house that she ran awkwardly through stiffness. She was sure no soldiers were around. It was a strange pool of calm in an occupied territory.

She tapped on the door and waited. There was no sign of life. Mouthing a quick curse, she tapped again. Still there was no reply. She groaned inwardly and whispered to herself.

'Where are you?'

'Who is it?' A brief whisper sounded from the other side of the door and Maarja caught her breath.

'Maarja Tamm.'

The door quickly opened, and a hand reached out. Without any time to think, she let herself be pulled inside.

'Little Maarja, is it really you?'

'Yes Edvard. It has been many years.'

'You cannot stay, it is too dangerous. Every day is filled with the fear of being arrested for working in government.'

'I know, but I have nowhere else to go.'

It was dark in the corridor, but Maarja could make out an outline of the man.

The tiredness of old age was in his voice, old age and resignation. Maarja reached out to clasp the old man's arm.

'I am travelling. I need one night, no-one will know.'

Even though his head was no more than a silhouette, Maarja saw he nodded as he sighed.

'You were a good girl, strong and brave.'

'We all have to be brave now, Edvard.'

'Come, I have a small light in the back and some stew. I try to keep the Reds thinking I am not here. It makes me miss all those trains.'

The stew was watery, with only potatoes and turnips, but Maarja treated it like it was the best meal of her life. She dipped the black bread into it and sucked the broth out. Her stomach felt as if it had swooned.

'I have some water, clean.' Edvard said.

'You are kind.'

She ate in silence, but she knew by the dim, flickering candle-light that he was watching her and sizing her up.

'You remembered where I lived,' he finally said.

'Yes, Edvard, I hoped that you were here.'

'Amongst my trees and lakes - I always liked to escape here from Toompea hill. Though it is a lonely place since Liise died.'

Maarja nodded. She remembered the old man as a shrewd diplomat. A strong father figure in the foreign affairs department.

The man had shrunk in his old age, as he shivered and pulled his coat closer around him.

'Why are you here?' He asked.

'I am seeking a man. He is dangerous.'

'To whom?'

'To everyone, I think. I don't understand it all, but I need to locate him.'

'Where is he?'

'Heading for a Swedish Estonian fishermen in Pirita called Sven, I think.'

'Sven? There is only one Sven who that could be. I believed he had run away already to Finland.'

'Can you tell me where he lived? That would be a start.'

'Yes, I can do that. Perhaps I can help you also. My wife's things are here if you want a change of clothes or shoes.'

In the flickering shadows he looked a tragic figure, haunted by his loss. Maarja could sense the need within him to help.

'You are a good man, Edvard,'

'You always wanted to do well for Estonia,' he replied. 'And you were my favourite.'

'Is there nowhere you can go, to keep you from harm?' Maarja reached out to touch his arm.

He coughed out a laugh. 'Yes, my dear. Sweden. But I am an old man and too tired to run. I certainly cannot outrun the destroyers and Red sympathisers who prowl around every-where. If they want to take me, I will have no defence.'

'Perhaps they will not come.'

'Perhaps. You will want to sleep, so perhaps we should talk some more tomorrow. There is a spare room, you can relax.'

'Thank you, Edvard.'

Peeter was stumbling, cursing everything that made his passage anything but smooth. A horsefly decided to take the moment to land on his arm for a quick taste of blood. With a quick swat and a curse, it was delivered from its life.

'You know, I can hardly keep up with you,' he grumbled.

Liisbet smiled. 'You're not that old.'

'No, but I am tired.'

'Do you want to rest?'

'No, I want to find Pirita.'

She pulled herself up and stretched.

'Then let's go, before the Reds catch us.'

Peeter looked to the heavens. The sky was a patchwork of sea blue, flanked by white clouds. A large dark one hovered menacingly nearby, the blurring at its base spoke of rains to come. The rumble of explosions seemed constant these days, his mind had just become good at accepting them as background noise.

There was a new sound now, the drone of aircraft. Peeter found a break in the tree lines that allowed him to look further ahead. Normally, he would feel exposed at this moment, but he became fascinated by the antics of a plane so far away. It was just a small dot in the sky.

It had lifted its tail to nose-dive straight to the ground. There appeared no reason why it would do this, no sign of damage and the sound of its engine still hung in the air. Then a banshee howl overrode everything else. The scream ever increasing in intensity had Peeter's mouth open, yet just as he thought the plane would crash, the pilot pulled the nose up and it flew away. A tiny speck continued the descent out of view. A puff of smoke was followed by a percussive thump on the ground and the sound of a blast.

'Those Germans sure as hell don't like something,' Peeter muttered.

'The battle line is getting closer to us,' Liisbet said.

'It also means we are closer to our destination,' Peeter replied. 'I think we will see the Baltic Sea soon enough.'

'There's a lorry coming,' Liisbet warned.

'This might be our chance,' Peeter replied. 'Let's get ready and check it out.'

The lorry struggled along the road like a pregnant duck, as it weaved in and out of the potholes. Peeter narrowed his eyes.

'It's slow enough and it looks like it is carrying cargo. Two men in the front, looking bored. Let's try, there's nothing left to lose.'

The olive coloured lorry was level with them now and the two men inside seemed focused on the perils of the road rather than anything peripheral.

As the lorry lurched past, Peeter sprinted out to come directly behind the back. He knew there was no time to worry on whether he was seen in the rear mirrors or not, this was their only chance. He grabbed the tail and scrambled up to get a foothold. It was enough to hold on with one hand and loosen the canvas with the other. Having succeeded in his task, he rolled over the tailgate and turned in time to yank Liisbet on board as she made her lunge. They rolled over together, coming to stop against a pile of wooden boxes.

A soldier inside shook himself from his slumber and stumbled forward, shielding his eyes from the daylight that was breaking through. Peeter scrambled to his feet and launched himself at the man, sweeping him off his feet. He grabbed him by the tunic and punched him.

The jab sent the man's head back and cracking against the side of the lorry, where he lay still. Peeter grabbed hold of him, lifting him up towards the end of the lorry. The man was quickly dropped out of the back and Peeter noted with satisfaction that the man still did not move on the ground as the lorry ambled away.

The vehicle continued its lumbering journey without stopping, lurching side to side and causing Peeter to stumble before he righted himself.

'Do you know this part of Estonia, Liisbet?' he asked. She shook her head.

'We had better keep the flap open and keep an eye out for landmarks – if there is anything left of them.'

CHAPTER NINETEEN

Movement

T hey were moved to another camp in the forest and it made them more restless. Märt was simply happy to find somewhere dry and warm, especially as he could smell food. He slumped back to the floor of the truck. Like all the other stops, they would be kept waiting.

Raio was still by his side. 'Another forest. Another day of nothing. Are we their allies or prisoners?'

'Patience Sergeant. They do not know us, or our strengths. We fight for Finland, their ally. Why would they want to capture us?'

'Why can't they use us then? We know this land so much better than they.'

'Patience, Raio.'

'Some are already doing reconnaissance work for the Germans.' Juhan chipped in. 'There's talk of the Finnish Boys regrouping under a new banner to go free the islands.'

'They had better take us, that's all I am saying,' Raio grumbled. 'I don't see us getting any work otherwise in a hurry.'

'Seems as if your prayers may be answered,' Märt replied. 'They seem to be grouping us with others. Either they will prepare us for a new challenge or shoot us, but until then, I want my sleep.'

'Maarja, wake up!' Edvard was rousing her, by shaking her shoulder. 'You have to go. There are soldiers outside and they are coming for me.'

The fog of waking quickly rolled away, as Maarja shook away the confusion from her head. For a second, her tiredness had stopped her remembering where she was, who he was and even what she was doing. Then it was gone, and she was rolling out of bed, only stopping as the blood rushed from her head giving her a feeling of floating. She held her head for a moment.

'Edvard, is there an escape?'

'If you go out the back door, there are smallholding buildings and a small smoke sauna. Between the two is a gap, you can get behind the buildings and use them as cover. Good luck.'

'Come with me,' she looked at the old man and wondered how he could move fast, but she did not want to leave him to the wolves. He shook his head.

'It's too late, now go!'

She stared for a moment, before kissing his cheek and squeezing his arm, she moved outside and seeing nobody in her way, ran for the outhouses.

She felt bad for leaving him, but there did not seem to be much else that she could do. As she reached the buildings, she could hear somebody beating the door.

Maarja moved herself through the long grasses behind the buildings, she realised in her haste that she had aimed for the wrong end. The sauna still stood away from her reach. She had no clue about the area, except the road led to Tallinn.

Glancing back to the house, she could now see a Soviet jeep outside. The engine was still running, although the occupants had left it. They had obviously no fear of trouble. There was a small gap to the small smoke sauna lodge, which was slightly closer to the house. Maarja tensed and held her breath, then made a short sprint to reach it. She grabbed the stone chimney to slow herself and stop overshooting. Her heart was in her throat as she desperately tried to control her breathing.

With great caution, she looked around the corner, moving back straight away at the sight of two soldiers at the house door. One was returning from the jeep, carrying a rifle, held as if ready to break the door down.

Maarja looked around, the grassy garden offered no shelter, but it was bordered by a slatted wooden fence. Part of this was covered by a bush, stretching towards the entrance, partially hiding the jeep. Maarja thanked the foresight of choosing earthy colours from the clothes of Edvard's wife.

The bush would offer her protection, as long as nobody looked too closely at the shadows behind.

It gave Maarja an opportunity to make her escape, but perhaps to divert attention from the soldiers and give Edvard time to hide.

She thought of all the things she had learnt on the farm and how they could be put to good use. Creeping slowly forward, she reached the line of bushes. The soldiers seemed totally focused on the house and cursing the lack of response. As she looked around to ensure she was not being watched, she caught sight of a face staring from the window of the house opposite. It watched her without a flicker of emotion, showing neither encouragement nor alarm. There was no effort to move, they just stayed still, like a doll.

Maarja decided she had no choice but to continue, moving faster towards the jeep. She jumped in and positioned herself with gear stick and clutch at the ready. Holding the steering wheel, she double de-clutched the jeep, the groan made the soldiers turn and they cried out in anger. The car gave a nervous lurch forward in response and she was off on a jerking pace down the road.

The soldiers sprinted after her in pursuit. One stopped to fire on her. Broken glass sprayed past, slicing her hand. She winced in pain and stopped wiping it, when she realised the glass was still in it. She would need time and tweezers. Now was hardly the time for vanity.

The soldiers had stopped running, and she cursed as she checked the rear mirror, slowing down to try and entice them further away from the house. Both fired their rifles, their accuracy being better than Maarja hoped.

She had really thought they would come further, giving Edvard more time to run. Even if he would probably not, she had given him a chance.

She could not loiter now and stay safe. Her sigh of resignation lost in the groaning engine, she moved off. As she did, she caught a faint movement in her mirror. Behind the soldiers and towards the doorway of the house opposite. It did not look smooth, but it was definitely a person. She hoped it was Edvard, being hidden by his neighbour. She prayed there was still kindness left in this broken land.

Maarja drove on, thanking her uncle for teaching her how to drive a tractor. She would not get far driving the jeep, for she would never pass as a soldier. However, this was the land of her childhood. With her knowledge of the minor roads, perhaps she could get herself closer to Pirita and save her exhausted legs. Could she find those roads? All the landmarks of the past seemed to have turned to shattered piles of stone.

It did not matter. All Maarja wanted to do was to drive as far from the house as possible.

Peeter cursed himself for staying in the lorry far too long. He had been too comfortable and now he realised they were in trouble. They had stopped at a checkpoint. Peeter could hear the driver shouting in Russian at someone, and a reply came back which he did not understand.

He should have paid more attention to his Russian in school, but he only ever wanted to work the family farm. Now there was something in the tone that made him send Liisbet hiding under sacking behind the boxes.

No sooner had he done this and sat down, then the canvas flap was thrown back. Peeter tried to look as if he had been roused from sleep, as he shook his head and gazed towards the soldier. Nothing was said and the soldier seemed to gaze at him for ever, then just as quickly the flap was slammed shut and the soldier slapped the side of the lorry with a shout. The driver set off and Peeter breathed out. It would have taken just one question for the bluff to have failed.

With great caution, he peered out of the back and groaned at the sight. In spite of the piles of debris at the roadside, marking the site of old buildings, the lorry seemed to have picked up its pace.

'We are heading for the city.' Liisbet said, coming to look.

'Are you sure?' Peeter asked. 'It's all ruins out there.'

'The soldier talked about the roads. Left was to Tallinn, so we turned left.'

'We have to get off, Liisbet. Soon.'

The lorry turned again and slowed down before finally stopping. People were coming towards the back. They weren't soldiers but civilians, either helping or being made to help, Peeter thought sourly.

They looked uninterested and disheartened. Quickly, he undid the back flap and dropped the tail. Then he handed a box to the first arrival. The man took it without a word and headed off. Peeter found another and handed it to the next. In the brief seconds he had before the next offload, he whispered to Liisbet.

'Quick, drop out the back and go hide in the shadows. We're not in a base, but they won't be expecting a woman, certainly not a civilian. Go hide and I will come after you as quick as I can.'

The first man returned and Peeter gave him a box. As he turned, Liisbet caught his look and she dropped out of the lorry and was gone. There was no outcry, the soldiers were out of sight. Peeter had no idea where she had gone but hoped she was safe and that he could find her – if he could get out of this mess.

A soldier appeared, Peeter guessed it was the driver. He barked a question. Peeter shrugged his shoulders and looked indifferent. The man called another who came over and asked in Estonian.

'Where is the man who was guarding this?'

Peeter shrugged again. 'No idea. I'm just here to unload.'

He picked up another box and handed it to one of the returning civilians. The soldiers looked confused and started calling out a name. Peeter knew he could not keep this up for ever, another came to get a box. Peeter jumped down to the ground.

'Get the boxes out for me for a minute, comrade. I need a piss. I'll be back soon, but I'm bursting.'

Without looking, he picked up the box and moved off. His brain screamed for him to run, but he kept walking an even pace, no matter how awkward it felt. He stacked the box with others and looked at the soldier observing it. The man looked bored. Peeter gave a curt nod and moved back. He started to walk a longer arc back and when he was ready, rushed into the shadows, hoping for he would melt into the night like ice on a fire. He quickly found a side street to take himself out of any potential line of sight. He heard footsteps following him and tensed, ready for battle. At the last moment he turned, fists raised. He took a step forward and then stopped and relaxed. It was Liisbet.

'You're a cool one,' she said.

'Everyone just has their orders, and they follow them,' he replied.

'Let's move to the coast.'

'Perhaps we should just focus on getting away quickly

now,' Peeter replied.

'From the sounds over there, it appears they have woken up to what I have just done.'

They quickened their pace down the shattered street. Peeter took deep breaths and looked at the strange look on her face.

'What?'

Liisbet replied with a lop-sided grin.

'What?'

'That was the most ridiculous thing I have ever seen,' she replied.

He looked at her and then saw the twinkle in her eye. He began to chuckle. Sniggering, they both moved off.

'I am hungry,' Peeter finally said.

'Yes,' Liisbet's fatigue and hunger restricted her conversation. She looked to reply as he had expected. Now he had to find food for them and then Pirita and then the elusive Harry.

'We will have to forage. If we can find a house that doesn't look like it has already been stripped.'

'Not all houses are ruins,' Liisbet observed.

Yes, God is selective,' he replied.

A few shattered streets further on, Peeter found a house he felt was worth trying. Liisbet frowned at the house and complained it looked tiny. Peeter shrugged.

'I don't care, compared to the others it is undamaged. If you look very carefully at the door, the lock is broken. The window is smashed, but you can't see it in this light. The garden has cover, check nobody is around.'

The street seemed deserted and they quickly moved to the shadows created by vegetation. Peeter closed the door behind them, placing a chair against it.

What happened here?' Liisbet said, as she stared at the carnage inside. Furniture was tipped over, plates smashed and left on the stone floors and drawers were left hanging open.

'Looters,' Peeter spat with contempt.

Liisbet shook her head. 'No, I think this was a deportation.'

'They may have tins,' Peeter said, wading through the broken crockery to start opening cupboards. He missed his step and stumbled on top of a suitcase, stepping on it for balance.

'Peeter, have you no heart?' Liisbet whispered, as she looked at a battered suitcase. 'Don't you see the heartache here?'

'I do, and my heart grieves for them. But my stomach has a voice also and one I must obey.'

He found potatoes and a tin of meat. Liisbet had even found some old dried black bread. By soaking it in water, they had managed to add flavour to the feast.

Peeter waited until dusk and then started to heat a meal. He had found some water bottled for storage and eventually, they sat back on chairs, drowsy as the hunger receded in their bodies.

'What do we do now?' Liisbet asked giving Peeter a dreamy smile.

'Sleep,' Peeter replied. 'And then find Harry in the morning.'

'You are my protective bear,' Liisbet sighed.

'I will always be there for you, little one. If that is what you need.'

'Thank you,' she replied. Her look made him think of a four-legged animal. He wasn't sure if it was a faithful dog or a predator wolf.

CHAPTER TWENTY

To Pirita

M aarja wept as she walked through Tallinn. The shattered buildings, their gardens churned up by bomb blasts and tank tracks were alien to her eyes. She no longer knew the beloved city of her youth or certainly could not recognise what was left of it.

The stolen jeep had helped her, but she had ditched it at the first sign of trouble.

Maarja deliberately ignored the bay and the silhouettes of ships. It reminded her too much of 1919, when the Royal Navy had come to stop the Bolsheviks do what was happening now to Tallinn. It was where she found her greatest love.

Her heart heavy with thoughts of the past and present, she searched for the way to Pirita. It would not be hard to see the ruined abbey, its great north window rose like a buried diamond above the houses. What she needed was to find the house of the Sven the fisherman within Pirita. She thought of the knife in her boot, would it be enough protection?

For the hundredth time she hoped Juhan was safe. He would always survive by some bizarre twist of luck, but her mind did not want to acknowledge this for fear of cursing the reality. She just prayed that somewhere in this mess, she would meet him again alive.

She had been given a map, all those days ago, to allow her to memorise the streets of Pirita and Maardu. One of those was the location of the street where the fisherman lived. There did not look to be many houses marked in these villages, so she thought there would not be a problem finding it. Once again, she practiced her story in her head if she was stopped. If they were prepared to listen to her, that was.

Why was she there? Her story was that her only son had gone to fight for the glorious Red Army against the fascists. She travelled to find him, to know he was still alive. It was a simple ruse; defend the borders, embrace the flag. Tell them what they want to hear.

The tram line would have ended close by, the road edging a large green parkland area. Even though the large manor house and the land would probably be teeming with soldiers, the bushes on the perimeter could give her shelter as she skirted the area.

'Maarja'

She froze to the spot at the voice. It was far off, but the name had floated across the wind and seared her very heart. Then she relaxed as she remembered where she was. The large manor house was called Maarjamae Palace. How could she have not thought of this?

It was a false alarm, but also a swift warning for her not to drop her guard. Had she not heard that, she could have walked straight into company.

She moved back into the shattered streets to circle back inland towards Pirita. The house was a bit further up the northern peninsular, close by a small jetty, that's what Edvard had said, not that far - considering how far she had come. She relaxed a tiny amount as there was no-one to be seen. Soon, she would be there. Soon.

'I refuse to swear allegiance to Adolf Hitler,' Märt said slowly, the anger in his voice was barely suppressed. There was no space to argue in his tone.

'That is what the Finnish Boys will do now. You are to regroup, Erna 2 they are calling it already. We need you ready for liberating Tallinn and the islands. You people know it better than us.' The German opened his arms to signify peace. 'I am not saying you will have to. I know you were all asked in Finland and refused. It may be asked of you again. I just ask you to consider it.'

'I am no Nazi. I am not one of the League of Veterans,' Märt replied. His face was red hot with anger now.

The officer's attitude fuelled Märt's anger as he replied.

'Being that you are from a small nation, perhaps you would not understand. The fact that we are freeing this land from the red animals. Well - you should be grateful.'

Märt turned away and looked at his men. Raio caught his gaze and gave a faint shake of the head. Märt turned back and took a deep breath.

'We are all grateful to our German cousins for this. What we have learnt though is that we are no longer the peasants for rich country squires. We are independent of mind and spirit. We make our choices freely and we are grateful, but we are also democratic.'

The German officer shook his head sadly. 'Ah yes. Your democracy in the last twelve years had your president dissolve parliament and run the country himself, yes?'

Quickly seeing the offended reaction, he held up his hand to ease the tension. 'I mean no offence, but maybe this gesture may be the difference between being part of the liberation or part of the reserve. Perhaps even being a prisoner of war. Think about it. Good day.'

His heels clicked as he gave a stiff bow and then a stiff-armed salute. As he turned to go, he gave a parting comment.

'You know, it is perhaps fortunate that it is the Wehrmacht that makes this request and not the SS. They would not be so understanding.'

Märt watched the back of the departing man with distaste. Juhan and Raio came to stand with him.

'Is that what it means to be patronised?' Juhan asked and Raio chuckled.

'A good observation.'

Juhan sighed. 'For now, the forest feels more inviting.'

'Yes, Märt replied. 'I will bear this in mind.'

'And so, we wait,' Raio said.

'And whilst we wait sergeant, you get the men together and keep them fit and battle sharp.'

Raio nodded, as Märt continued.

'And no repeating of this conversation, either of you. I don't want the men to start doubting as I do.'

Maarja had found Sven's house, north of the ruined Abbey and a little inland towards Maardu. There were nets strung to the side of the building, with buoys attached, lobster crates stacked nearby and an overarching smell of old fish. She wondered how people could live with the aroma.

The house looked deserted, but then all houses seemed that way now. Either the people had been taken, had died or were in the forest. In the outbuildings behind the house, one of the doors hung open and was swaying with the wind, the joint creaking in complaint. It was the only sharp noise here, the explosions and aircraft noise from Tallinn seemed strangely muted. She went to the house and found it was unlocked.

Inside, the place was dark and oozing a hollow emptiness. She knew that she daren't show any light, for fear of being spotted. Even though she had seen many houses like this, actually being in this one put her on edge and the atmosphere made her tremble with fear.

She went to a door to a side room and holding her breath, stepped through it, moving towards the shadows.

Her arm was caught, she tried to step back but was yanked in. Maarja felt she was being strangled, making her head explode in white light. She tried to scream in terror, but a hand clasped over her mouth. She struggled desperately, until a sharp blade pricked her neck and she fell as still as her fear would let her.

'What do you want?' A voice whispered harshly. It was familiar and slowly she tried to regain her composure. Her reply still felt like a little voice had come from within her.

'You, Harry.'

She was shoved to the other wall. Even though she could not see him, she could make out his silhouette and there was a dull glint of a knife.

'Who sent you?' He asked.

'The Germans. They want to speak with you.' She was past playing games. She was tired and wanted an end to this, one way or another.

'I bet they do. Who sent you?' Harry's voice was still urgent and harsh, but then he stopped. 'You're Märt's woman, aren't you?'

'I'm not Märt's woman,' she snapped, the thought of the young British officer came into her head once more. He let out a snort of derision.

'The only reason that you are alive is that you are Märt's woman.'

His animosity made her bold in return, she was fed up of being pushed around.

'Whose side are you on?'

Harry moved slightly out of shadow, so she could see his features. He still looked more like a bank manager than a spy.

'Whose side are you on, Maarja Tamm?'

'Estonia's.'

'Then let me go,' he moved to the doorway and was through it before she drew breath. She let out a long sigh and noticed she was shaking. She resisted the urge to succumb to the fear, drew the knife in her boot and followed him to the kitchen.

His back was turned to her, as he retrieved bread and sausage from a shelf, placing it on a plate. Without looking up, he spoke.

'If you've come to kill me, now is your chance to try. Otherwise, sit down.'

She was frozen to the spot. In past years, violence had been alien to her, killing had been unthinkable up to now. She has committed herself to this mission, but now she was faced with the task, her mind asked the single question. Why?

He had turned around to face her and in the grey light, she looked into his eyes for the first time. The dark discs appeared bottomless. He held out a plate of food.

'Too late. Sit down and eat, you must be starving.'

He tipped water into a glass and put it in front of her.

'Eat slowly, savour every bite. Make sure your stomach feels full.'

'You are a cool one,' she replied. Harry took a drink and sat down.

'Lady, I could kill you without breaking sweat. It's my training, so let's talk instead.'

Maarja stared at the food. Her stomach begged her to take it. In the end, her stomach won the argument.

'Where's Sven the fisherman?' She asked between chews.

'Gone. Being useful somewhere else, I'll wager. I'm waiting for his return.'

'From where?'

'Where do you think, Maarja Tamm?'

She carried on eating and looked at him thoughtfully.

'Märt trusted you and he doesn't make many friends. But you scare me because I don't know what your plan is. Whose side are you on?'

Harry stared at her for a while and then retrieved a glass and poured himself some water, which he downed.

'I am not your enemy.'

'But you are British.'

'Yes, my dear.'

'So, you must support the Reds.'

'Stalin has his own agenda. He only comes to the West when he needs something. We only ally with him, so he can distract the Germans.'

'So, you support him?' She insisted. Harry shook his head.

'But you clearly do not support the Germans.'

'True,' he replied. Maarja could see he was not going to give away anything unless asked directly.

'So, you want to flee to Finland, Harry. Will this help Estonia?'

He sighed again and looked at his glass. 'You want honesty? It doesn't matter. Estonia is finished. Whoever wins here won't be restoring an independent country. Forget any dreams of the state you won in the 20's. Look for how you can survive under your new masters.'

'That's not true!' She shouted, the pain and frustration getting the better of her. 'The Germans will free us.'

'Like they did before? The Germans were the wealthy landowners. Brought in by the Tsar. You were the serfs, the common people, worthless and used. It will be the same. All those who fled before the Russian advance will return and expect life to carry on as if nothing had changed.'

Contempt washed through her.

'If Estonia is finished as you claim, what are you doing? You are trying to talk to Finns. A British man going directly to Germany's ally? You are trying to take Finland out of the war. You are trying to weaken our liberators!'

Harry shook his head. 'Do you really believe this? Go upstairs and look out to your beloved Tallinn and see what your liberators are doing. Go!'

She scowled, but obeyed. The windows in the front room were already taped up with cracks. Cautiously she peered out from behind the curtain.

The view across the bay was commanding. The long strand swept across to the capital, towards the medieval buildings on Toompea hill and the church spires she loved to look at. She thought of the cobbled streets in the old town and the markets in happier times that sold fresh food and fine cloth. She thought of the long summers, strolling around the Toompea, looking down on the people struggling up the Long Leg.

Now the city looked broken. There were still houses standing, yet many looked half-built with no roofs and sometimes a jagged end of a wall. The windows looked dark and foreboding with their lack of glass. A pall of smoke hung over the city and the harbour, where ships appeared to jostle for space. Above, aeroplanes flew past in loose formation. The tiny specks of black falling from them signified bombs being dropped in a crazy formation. They were creating grey clouds of smoke to rise in awful slow motion. The scene was desperate and Maarja's heart sank at the view of her home.

She headed back down to Harry. In peacetime, she would have thought him to have a kindly look. Very thoughtful, like a benevolent teacher. Maybe that is what he once was. Now all she saw was danger around him and hardness behind his eyes.

'Your city is all but taken and the Reds will soon be gone or dead,' Harry said. 'Then the Germans come back in and run the place like the Hansa of old.'

'So, what would you want to do?' Maarja asked. 'Split Germany from its allies and you weaken her. The Reds get a chance to draw breath and fight back. If you weaken them enough, perhaps even Stalin will rise again. What good is all this for

Estonia?'

'It gives Finland a choice,' he replied slowly.

'Which helps the British, not the Estonians,' Maarja snapped.

The sound of footsteps came from outside and Harry held up his hand.

'Quiet! Listen!'

The sound was of someone approaching the door and Harry rushed to a full-sized cupboard.

'Quick! Get in now!'

Maarja hesitated and Harry's look was blacker.

'Don't mess around woman, do you want to live or not?'

She was in and the door shut, just as the front door banged open. Some rough voices started shouting.

'Don't shoot!' Harry said quickly. His voice nervous, a total contrast to before.

'What are you doing here?' A man asked.

'I'm with a destruction battalion. We were told to clear the houses. I was looking for people and food.'

'Well that's finished now. We've been ordered to get every-one ready, we are leaving this shit-hole and sailing back to Kronstadt.'

'I am an old man,' Harry replied hesitantly.

'Not at all,' came the reply. 'Are you a coward?' Have you been hiding?'

'Not at all.'

'Then get out now. Are you alone?'

'Yes, my group were wiped out by bandits north of here.'

'Well now is your chance to fight back. We go back to Mother Russia to regroup, get more weapons. Then we come back and wipe this place off the map. Into the truck with you, now!'

There was a shuffle of boots. Then Maarja caught her

breath at the soldier's next words.

'Shall we burn the place down?'

'No point,' another replied. 'No time. Let's move on and find some more of these pathetic Estonian scum.'

The front door banged again and then she heard nothing. She waited, desperately trying to hold her breath in the now over warm and claustrophobic cupboard. Then, with her nerves jangling, she levered the door gently open.

Cold air rushed through, making her brow feel cool with damp sweat. She ran for the stairs, as she heard the front door open again.

It was too late to do anything but hide in the front room and hope to God they believed the place empty. Hoping that the floorboards did not creak was just one of many wishes.

Below, she could hear movement, then a clink of bottles and a man's voice barked out an earthy request for someone to get into the lorry and the door banged again.

Soldiers looking for vodka, she thought. On her hands and knees, she crept to the window and peered down to see the truck begin to move off. Sitting in the back, surrounded by soldiers was Harry. She shuddered as she felt his gaze on her, then someone dug him in the ribs and said something to him. He nodded and looked straight ahead, as the lorry disappeared down the road.

The pain in Peeter's back had got too much to bear, as he grudgingly moved from a drifting slumber to being awake. He tried to move, but realised, the weight against his left shoulder was Liisbet. His left arm had curled around her in sleep without thinking. He liked the feeling of closeness and persevered with managing his lower back pain.

In the end, it got too much, he tried to marginally shift his pelvis, but even though the relief rippled through him, Liisbet stirred. She snuggled closer, her left hand reaching for his shoulder. Then she stopped and slowly her eyes opened. She looked up and then moved back slightly to stare at him.

'*Tere*,' he said softly.

'*Tere*,' she whispered.

They didn't move for a while until he gently reached out to straighten a wayward lock of her hair. Liisbet gasped and looked away and Peeter sighed.

'I am sorry.'

'No, I am sorry,' she replied. 'I was cold and a bit scared.'

'It's alright,' he replied. 'I understand, you are for another and I am still in mourning. I would not be good company.'

He tried a light tone to ease the tension, but Liisbet shuddered with cold and moved away. She stood and rubbed her arms to warm them. Peeter sighed again. What had he been thinking?

Yet the feeling of her closeness was soothing to his raw emotion. It felt like a lifetime since he had last embraced a woman, given the turmoil of the world. When he closed his eyes, he still saw his wife smiling at him. Yet the feeling of holding Liisbet close to him had been beautiful.

His back complained as he moved, and he gasped at the sensation of feeling flooding back into his arms and legs. It would take a lot of massaging, walking, and stretching, before his hips felt part of him. He wished he could do the same for his troubled heart.

'Dried meat,' Liisbet said, bringing in food from the kitchen as if nothing had happened. 'I could not find any water. I think this is vodka.'

Peeter joined her in the kitchen. He had found a small pot of home made jam.

'It is fluid, there is some water in it at least,' he said.

'There are plum trees in the garden,' she replied. 'Maybe

some are ripe. Let's fill our pockets and we can go.'

They moved out from the back of the house, but immediately found that none of the fruit could be taken from the ground.

Peeter found a small ladder in a shed and they were soon harvesting the plums. He picked a few and started dropping them down to Liisbet. It was a light moment and Liisbet could not help laughing as one plum bounced off a tree branch away from her. She reached for it and her momentum sent her tumbling to the floor, where she sat and giggled at Peeter. A shout from the street put Peeter on alert. Two men quickly made for them. They were not soldiers - and Peeter immediately distrusted them. Probably auxiliaries, destroyers at the worst. Undisciplined, erratic irregular animals. Stuck in the tree as he was, he had no defence.

'What are you doing,' the first man arrival said.

'Picking plums. There is no water around here, although there is some vodka in the house. Have it if you want.'

'I think we will,' came the reply, as the man signalled to his colleague to go. 'And we will have some plums also. Are they any good?'

'Decide yourself,' Peeter said, casually tossing one down. The man caught it in one hand and bit into it.

'A bit sour, but not bad.'

'There are cherries over on that tree also,' Peeter said as he passed some plums to Liisbet. As the man turned, he gave a quick flick of his head.

'What is your business here?' The man asked.

'Surviving,' Peeter replied. 'Now the damn Germans have cut off all the roads, we have to find what we can from those who are unfortunate not to be with us.'

He moved down the branches, to a point where he could jump next to the man.

'Hey, where's the damned vodka?' The other soldier's

voice rang out from the house.

'In the kitchen,' Peeter shouted.

'The woman can show you,' the leader said, pointing at Liisbet, eyes still trained on Peeter.

'She can bloody go get it herself,' his colleague snapped. 'And quickly, as we are in a hurry.'

Liisbet looked at Peeter, who nodded. The look was long lasting. Then she was gone. Peeter closed his eyes and took a deep breath. Holding the plums to his chest and jumped down. The man stepped back and pulled out a pistol.

'Easy now,' Peeter said. 'Plums, remember?'

The man relaxed and smiled. 'Yes, but you know there is more to it than that.'

Peeter shrugged. 'For sure, what do you have in mind?'

'Well you are lucky. They are evacuating everyone able to carry a rifle back East. We have a number of people to find. Congratulations, you just joined the Red Army. A ship awaits at the harbour.'

'Where's that vodka?' The other man shouted and went inside. He was gone for a while. The leader looked at Peeter who nodded. His reward was a pistol blow to the head that made him fall to the floor.

'Yes, she's gone,' he said as he gently dabbed the cut on his cheek. 'She's not stupid, but you still have me and the fruit and I will find you that vodka. Those will be enough.' Peeter satisfaction was limited as he felt the size of the cut.

'You are lucky we have orders,' the man snapped. 'You had better find me that vodka.'

CHAPTER TWENTY-ONE

Arrivals and Departures

A young German private ran towards Märt with a note. He stood to attention and handed it over. Then with a stiff-armed salute and 'Heil Hitler', he was gone. Märt did not bother responding. He read the note and then crushed it in his fist, his face showed a rare smile, although it was close to a grimace.

'Raio, get the men ready. We move out.'

'Where are we going?' Juhan asked.

'Young man, you are not supposed to eavesdrop on officers,' Raio said sternly as he walked by. 'It does not matter how long you have known them.'

'Don't worry, he will know soon enough,' Märt said. 'Get them ready, we are taking Tallinn. All of the Finnish Boys are going.'

Perhaps this would be a new start for this land, Märt thought. Perhaps for him, it would mean a new start and a brave future, as he pushed behind him the pain of the past. Maybe life could get better, cleansed of all his troubles. With people ready to start the new journey with him.

The men cheered when the trucks arrived finally, late in the evening. Märt was last to get on, and rank rewarded him with a seat in the cab.

'Ten weeks ago, I was baking bread,' he mused.

Toomas, the young Finnish Boy who had saved them in the forests, sat next to him and smiled.

'Now you are a hero of Estonia, lieutenant. Not a bad change of fortune.'

◆ ◆ ◆

Peeter looked around the dark hold of the ship that he had been put in. He was lucky to have found a corner to lean against the hull, close enough to the doorway to get dim light, although he wondered how long it would be before the cold seeped through his clothing. A man slumped next to him and broke into a fit of coughing. He looked dirty, untidy, and rough, but Peeter was sure he was hardly a virtue of personal hygiene himself. The man held a coat which he draped over him, flicking the sleeve into Peeter's face. The newcomer then placed his hat over his eyes and tried to sleep. Peeter pretended to ignore the man.

He had no desire to talk to anyone. Although many had been conscripted like him, some believed in the cause and would be distasteful to listen to.

The man was making himself comfortable and digging his elbows into Peeter's ribs. Peeter pushed back in irritation and the man sighed then sat back and looked up from underneath the brim of a flat cap.

'Bloody place smells of fish. Finest herring boat in the Baltic, the *Eestirand,* and now we are caught on it, Peeter. Nice scar that, very dashing.'

Peeter's irritation at the intrusion into his own thoughts meant it took a short while before the words sunk in.

'Who the hell are you that knows me?'

'We're family, you and I,' the man murmured.

'Harry? How the hell did you get on this heap of junk?'

'I got captured same as you, so it would seem?' Harry raised his hat and gave a small smile. 'Outflanked for once. Were you alone?'

'No, Liisbet was with me. She was trying to reach you in Pirita when we got jumped by some destroyer bastards,'

Peeter quickly patted Harry's arm as for once the man's

face showed a flicker of emotion.

'Don't worry, I made sure she escaped.'

'I hope so. Where is she now, do you think?'

'Pirita, trying to find an Estonian Swede called Sven.'

'Well, hopefully Maarja will get her to the German lines.'

'Maarja? Why not Märt?'

Harry smiled. 'Maarja was trying to find me for the Germans. Märt is probably with the Finnish Boys.'

'I should have stayed,' Peeter cursed. 'There were only two of them who caught me.'

'Right, well wear this coat and walk with me,' Harry said, unfolding the garment he was carrying.

'I reckon the Soviets have crammed in as many people as they can on this ship. That will be in the thousands. Cannon fodder for the defence of Leningrad. I'm not staying if I can, but I thought you may be interested in escaping with me.'

He stood up and walked across to the stairwell, which was guarded by a pair of armed men. Their guns were raised and pointed at Harry before he got within ten paces of them.

'Sit down!' One commanded. Harry smiled in return and raised his hands to prove he was unarmed. Pinned into the palm of one hand by his thumb was a small clutch of banknotes. The men became interested in Harry's hand and he used the opportunity to move closer to them.

'Comrade, we are poor farmers and not used to the sea. I will get sick here and the men around will kill me for the mess and the smell. I just want to journey on deck, my friend here is worse.'

'It's a long journey and I don't want it smelling of puke,' the other guard muttered, still eyeing the money. 'Come on. Where are they going to run to?'

The first guard grabbed the money and glared at Harry, before pointing at some cans. 'Right you two, go and empty those piss-pots. Spill any and you will be drinking the rest. Now go!

Peeter went over towards them, taking care not to stand on the mass of jumbled outstretched legs.

He picked up the cans, relieved that both were not full and made his way back. At one point, he stepped too close to a leg and received a torrent of abuse in return.

'You want this over you?' Peeter snapped back. 'Do you? Then sit back and make room.'

He reached the doorway, to find Harry stood ready the other side of the guards. He walked straight past his captors without a word and handed the pots to Harry.

'They are only half full and you've just given me the officer's greatcoat, so you had better carry these.'

'Fair enough,' Harry replied. 'Just hope I don't slip on my way.'

The movement up the stairwell was haphazard, because even there, people were sitting down. Harry was left shouting 'Clear the way! Do you want some of this? Well you'd better make room then!'

As they reached the first landing, Peeter tried a door. A soldier blocked them and barked an order. Harry replied in Russian. 'Out of the way!'

Peeter just fixed him with a cold stare and the man stood back.

They found themselves in the engine room. A cacophony of noise from the machinery and choking diesel fumes assaulted them.

Harry closed the door, and they surveyed the site. The crank was in full flow, meaning the ship was on the move.

Below, they could see movement from the stokers, as they fed the furnace that blew heat back in their faces.

Ahead was a walkway of metal mesh with steps leading down and up a deck. Without thinking, Peeter took his coat off in the warmth and Harry quickly put the pots down and took it from him.

'It's better I am the officer,' he said. 'I speak Russian and won't take the coat off unless I really have to do it. Another thing.' He reached down the front of his trousers and produced a revolver.

'Where the hell did you keep that? No, I don't want to know...' Peeter spluttered.

Harry grinned and started for the walkway stairs. Peeter made to pick up the pot, but the look from Harry was enough to stop him. He shrugged, what was the point now?

'There's a lot of Russian soldiers here, some destroyers – Russian and Latvian. The majority is hundreds, maybe thousands of Estonians called up into the Red Army, some like you and me. I don't think it will reach its destination and I sure as hell don't want to be on it if it does. Come on.'

They made their way up to the top level of the engine chamber, finding another door to exit. Their stay had been as swift and unobtrusive as possible, so as not to invite attention from the engine crew.

They were quick to step through the door and back into the busy mass of people along the staircase Only one looked up, a young boy who acted as if he had been plucked off the streets.

His expression was beyond hope, but Harry gave him a quick wink and his face changed with a ghost of a smile and a spark of defiance in his eyes.

They reached the doorway to the deck and Peeter could at last breathe cool salt air for the first time in hours. He gave a gasp of pleasure and relaxed. An officer quickly came up to them and started shouting at Peeter, Harry stood in his way.

'Where have you come from?' The man yelled.

'We were told to come up. There's no room down there,' Harry replied in a firm voice, challenging the man to doubt him.

'Like we have space,' the officer replied and stormed off

through the crowd.

'The secret, friend Peeter, is to keep the coat buttoned up, so they don't realise there is no uniform underneath. Speak Russian at all times. Oh, and never be defensive.'

Peeter looked up and down the boat, it was a large cargo ship, with a tower of decks with the bridge on top in the middle and hatches at either end with rigging.

'I'd like to stay close to the bridge,' he said. 'There is more shelter.'

'So, does everyone else,' Harry replied.

'That's why we should go towards the hatch. There's too many soldiers around Tallinn harbour. Let's look for an opportunity to jump when we get a bit further out and then swim to the beach.'

'Good idea, Harry, but I think they have already thought of that.'

'Why do you say this?'

Peeter sighed and pointed. 'By the way they have lined up the ships either side of us. I take it that if you jump, you'll be run down by one of these boats. Looks like we are in convoy and by the time they spread out, we'll be away from swimming distance. They thought of this, they know we don't want to be here.'

'Well, I suppose it was too obvious even for them,' Harry replied. 'Keep alert for other opportunities – if we sail close to the islands or something.'

'Do you think anyone would notice?' Peeter asked dryly.

'I don't care. I'm dead if I get to Leningrad. I'd rather drown first, but I'll not throw my life away unless I have to do so.'

They were were beginning to pass the other ships. Many sailors lined their decks shouting insults at their captive audience. There were a lot of insults traded by those on board *Eestirand* until the ship started pulling away past a Navy destroyer.

Peeter caught a sob in his throat, but a man close to them was already weeping as he looked.

'It's the beach,' he sobbed. 'All our people, all our women-folk are on the beach. It's heartbreaking...'

At that moment, the destroyer fired its guns, sending a salvo of shells into the city.

'Hope they miss, you Red...' The man screamed; the words drowned in another volley of fire from the Navy ship.

'Don't worry,' Peeter said. 'They are Reds. Probably firing blanks, or the shells will land in Lake Peipsi.'

The explosion sent tremors through the ground and plumes of dust, smoke, and rock floated high into the air, like some macabre death dance. Märt was sure that nobody had been standing there, but he began to doubt his memory.

'Everyone take cover! He shouted.' 'Move for shelter, any-where away from the open, let's think safety.'

What the hell do these Germans want of us, lieutenant?' Toomas shouted. 'We should be involved in the fighting in the city. We know the damned place. Why are they keeping us here?

'Keep your concerns to yourself and get decent cover,' Raio called out. 'If you get wounded through stupidity, I'll go finish you off myself.'

'Easy, sergeant,' Märt said. 'That was a big gun, probably from a ship. The Luftwaffe will be off after that one.

He had found cover in a collapsed building, where the con-crete beams left a gap. There was a large void big enough to hide in. Yet again, a shot fired close to him and Märt ducked.

Toomas was right. Why were they just left sitting there? There was only one reason Märt could think of. The Nazis wanted the swastika flying over the capital. If that was true, would they ever take it down? Did this mean that they would renege on the agreement?'

Yet again, Märt wondered if there was a method of getting to Pirita, finding Maarja and heading into the northern woodland to join the Forest Brothers. He shook his head, there was too much going on. For now, he would have to just bide his time.

Another salvo of shells hit nearby. Märt kept his head down and closed his eyes as a trickle of grey dust fell on his head and seeped down his neck. There was a scuffing sound and Raio slid in from the street.

'You have coloured your hair to be like mine,' he said. Now how will they tell us apart?'

'The least of their worries at the moment,' Märt replied with a smile.

'I could swear that last lot was further away,'

'God, I hope so,' Märt whispered.

'Isn't that the Captain?' Raio asked, watching a man racing towards them, running from cover to cover. 'He's not going to beat off those guns by waving his pistol as he goes.'

'He's hardly in uniform.' Märt replied.

'You're hardly in uniform.'

The slim man was quite athletic, as he moved quickly from haven to haven. Märt called out to him and he ran over to them.

'*Tervist*,' the man said between breaths. 'How is it?'

'It's a bit warm here, sir,' Märt replied. 'Even for August.'

'Perhaps the Reds are making it warmer. They certainly have a sting in their tail. We're stuck here, but I've got to send check the area, report back and make sure that we are not surprised by the Reds coming to us from another flank.'

'Aren't they on the run?'

'And at their most dangerous, we would be exposed if they

arrived without warning.'

'What about liberating the city? My men know this place, the Germans don't.'

There was a moment's silence as the two men locked gazes. Even the artillery seemed to oblige by a lull. Märt slowly nodded.

'I would like the East flank. If there are still radios available, we can set up at the point and watch the west and east bays of the peninsular.'

'That's settled then,' the captain replied. 'Better than waiting for Ivan to get lucky with his random shots.'

'Get the men together,' Märt said to Raio. 'I will address them.'

'In this current barrage, I would suggest we just pass the word down the ranks. The men are good, they will obey. I think they have grown to realise that the Germans were not planning to use us. Besides, it will be good to get away from this shellfire.'

Märt nodded and looked across the shattered buildings of the city. Palls of smoke still rose from many and the acrid smell of carbonised wood was everywhere.

Perhaps he should not have been so eager, but his was a small unit, only a dozen men. He could see the opportunity to go to Pirita and try and solve the mystery about Harry.

'Raio, get them started towards the tip of the peninsular. Establish good vantage points at north, west and east. Keep good communication links with each other and Colonel Kurg's HQ. I will follow, but I need to do some investigation first.'

'The spy?'

Märt nodded. 'I will try and finally get an end to it.'

'Take Juhan. He's the joker in the pack. No, I don't mean a clown. He's a maverick, things happen around him and he makes the difference.'

Märt rolled his eyes. 'I suppose you could say that. Make your base North, close to the top.'

'Don't be too long.'

'I won't. I'm going to commandeer a car and an Estonian flag to show the world the locals are back and here to stay.'

Maarja still could not take her eyes off the view from the window, as she waited for Tallinn's imminent fall. She knew it would only be a matter of time before she saw one of the church spires collapse or Toompea breached. She dreaded the moment and yet was transfixed by the picture before her. She had watched the Soviet destroyer begin to bombard the city.

She wondered about the groups of people on the beach. At first, they had looked like evacuees, certainly not soldiers.

Then she realised there was a convoy moving out of the city harbour. One ship in particular seemed to be passing through the others. Maarja quickly scanned the room. This was a fisherman's house. He may have a telescope.

She found one by the bed and held it up, struggling at first to adjust the focus and hitting the window, before she realised how to zoom in. The ship seemed to be crawling with people. This one seemed different from the others. The other boats had people in uniform, this did not. It was as if the whole city was covering the deck.

She had once seen an ant hill and the scene before her made her think of it. The difference being that the ant hill was teeming with activity but here, the men seemed to be static and re-signed, almost as if they were on a journey to oblivion.

She quickly scanned the boat and gasped as realisation hit her.

'You!'

Maarja turned in alarm at the sound of a voice from the doorway.

'Liisbet.'

'What have you done? Where is he?' The young girl took a step forward.

'You're too late,' Maarja replied.

Liisbet drew a knife and rushed forward. Maarja put up her arm in desperate defence. It swept under and knocked the knife hand up. The knife was dropped and Liisbet lunged for Maarja's face. Maarja blocked in fury and desperation, then delivered a backhanded slap that left Liisbet staggering to collapse on the bed. Liisbet felt her lip and shakily raised herself up.

'He was taken by the Reds, Liisbet. He hid me from them.'

'What?'

'He was here. He was waiting for a way to get to Finland. A soldier patrol came by, rounding up all the men and they got him.'

'Where have they taken him?'

'On that boat,' she indicated and offered the telescope. Liisbet snatched it away.

'Then that is where Peeter is also. Where do you think it is going?'

'Back to the motherland, the Reds are pulling out and they are stripping the land of all its assets. But I don't see them getting there.'

'Why's that?'

'The flag. I saw them take down the hammer and sickle. I don't know what's going on, but that boat is flying the blue, black and white of Estonia.'

CHAPTER TWENTY-TWO

Eestirand

'**S**omething's going on,' Harry muttered as they sat with their backs to the forward hatch.

'Why do you say that?' Peeter said, refusing to open his eyes.

'There is something missing.'

'Like what?'

Harry stood up and looked around. 'I'm not sure. It's that people are talking more and...' he drew breath. 'well, well, well...'

'What?' Peeter opened his eyes and squinted upwards. Seeing Harry's expression, he stood up. Harry gave a thin smile as he looked at the masts.

'Here's a lesson for the Red Army. When you are conscripting Estonians for cannon fodder, don't use an Estonian boat, with an Estonian captain. Looks as if there's been a rebellion.'

As realisation dawned on Peeter, there was a commotion at the front of the hold. Two soldiers appeared running up from the stairs that led from the lower decks. They held their rifles ready to use. Harry moved up behind them and as the first turned, he slammed the rifle down and jabbed his elbow into the man's solar plexus.

The man whooshed as his breath exploded and he doubled up into the back of Harry's rising fist. As the man staggered forwards, Harry punched him.

The other soldier had been trying to bring his rifle to the

ready, but instead raised it to use the butt as a club. Harry quickly stepped to the side and blocked the leading arm of the soldier. Pulling it down, he landed a blow with his elbow on the man's back. There was a sickening crack around the man's shoulder blade, as he screamed with agony. Without needing to be asked, Peeter grabbed the two rifles, now loose on the deck.

'You have done this sort of thing before?' He casually asked Harry who gave back a dirty look in reply.

They turned to face more hurried footsteps coming from the stairway, but this time the man showed he was not holding a weapon.

'Ah, good, you sorted them out.'

'You are a Red officer?' Peeter asked.

'I am Estonian,' the man replied. 'I was in Laidoner's officer corps until the Reds came. Then I was pressed into this damned army.'

'You still wear the coat.'

'Yes, it is a warm coat. I am cold. Look, you two seem to know how to keep busy. Try and keep order on deck around here. The Captain may look to take off to Finland or force land at Estonia. We'll know soon enough, but I don't need panic on the deck.'

Without waiting for an answer, he moved off towards the bridge.

'Well, I don't know where he's expecting us to go. I would expect Finland.' Peeter said.

'Depends on whether the Red Navy would let us,' Harry replied.' Apart from the destroyer they may have a sub protecting this convoy. Don't take anything for granted. The flag will make them realise soon enough they have lost the ship.'

*****

'Truce?' Liisbet said, offering Maarja a plate. 'I found this in the cellar. Smoked sausage. Wild boar I think.'

'Thank you,' Maarja replied and took a small bite of the proffered slice.

'What do we do now?' Liisbet asked, offering a drink. Maarja sipped it and then took a swig. She had not realised before this how thirsty she had become. Then she shook her head.

'I don't know any more. I thought I did, but...' she tailed off and stared out of the window.

'Who is this Sven anyway?'

'Just a man that can get Harry over to Finland,' Liisbet said.

'So how is he able to do that - when the Reds destroyed all the Estonian boats?'

'Harry didn't really say, but the impression given is he is in Finland now and will come over.'

'So how does anyone get hold of him?'

They stared at each other and slowly the realisation dawned on them.

'Radio!'

Liisbet began to rummage through the wardrobe and then stopped to look curiously at Maarja, who was standing in the middle of the room, eyes slightly closed and frowning.

'What's the matter?' Liisbet asked. Maarja held up a hand to indicate she needed silence.

'If I had a radio set and I didn't want people to know. Where would I hide it?'

'In the cellar?' Liisbet asked. Maarja shook her head.

'Too cold. Too damp. No, it would have to be upstairs, where the heat of the house gathers. The attic would be too cold again, as the heat went through the roof. It would need to be on this level and the best reception is a room facing the sea, nothing blocking the signal...'

She walked past Liisbet to the bed, having to press against the bedstead to get by. As she did, her foot stood on a floorboard that gave a mournful squeak. She stopped and tapped the floor with the toe of her foot.

'Here,' she dug her nails into the edge of the floorboards but couldn't lift them.

Looking wildly for something to provide leverage, her gaze fell on a metal shoehorn. She reached to grab it and shoved the bed away from the area, flipping back a rug to create a puff of dust in the air.

'Wait!' Liisbet said. 'Surely the floorboards that have been raised will not look so set in the floor.'

'Yes, I see them,' Maarja ran her fingers around a group of boards where the join looked hollow. She quickly raise it to find that it was only enough to put her arm in. She rummaged around.

'This can't be enough... wait.'

There was a click, as she raised a whole section of floor, below which lay a battered suitcase. The two women grinned at each other, then Liisbet frowned.

'Now what? Do you know how to use one?'

'A good point.'

Maarja looked at the rows of dials and knobs.

'Maybe I start with the headset.'

She jumped as the noise of radio interference crackled through them with great volume. A quick adjustment of the knobs made her locate the volume and tuning.

'Come on, you can help me.'

Holding one earphone to her ear, she beckoned to Liisbet to come and they sat side by side as Maarja slowly tried to tune the radio. She moved the knob as far as she could, but there was no let up in the static noise that besieged her eardrums. She slowly began to move back, then suddenly heard a snatch of a voice.

'That's Estonian,' she shouted, knocking a switch in her excitement.

'Who said that?' The man's voice said.

Maarja looked stunned, then pulled the lever again.

'My name is Maarja Tamm. I am looking for Estonian units nearby to Pirita.

There was silence, she realised she needed to flick the switch back and the world was drowned in static. Then the voice came back.

'*Ema*? Is that you?'

'Juhan?' In her excitement, she missed the switch and had to repeat herself. 'We are at Sven's.'

There was a crackle of response, and then the voice came back. 'Stay. We are coming.'

'How come everyone knows where this is?' Liisbet muttered.

'Please confirm, your location,' the radio crackled.

Maarja covered her smile well, although the relief of hearing Juhan once more almost overwhelmed her.

'But how does this get us Harry back?' Liisbet asked.

'If the ship is flying the Estonian flag, it would seem to indicate they do not think they will go anywhere but Finland or Estonia. Either way we can get to him through the Germans or the Finnish Boys. Märt...' *Or Schulz*, she thought.

There was a sound of footsteps downstairs and Maarja got up with images of Juhan in her mind. As she came down the stairs, her smile bright in anticipation, she was stopped in her tracks by the sight of the man who greeted her.

The man was not the slim, raven haired youth of her womb. Neither was it the grey flecked hair of morose Märt.

The man was grey haired, but it fringed his curly hair all the way to his beard. He stood ever much the sailor in boots, trousers and a polo neck sweater. His face looked as if he had faced every Baltic storm that had ever been in Estonia.

'But how will we get Harry on the radio...' Liisbet was saying, continuing the conversation. She stopped on the stairs, when she realised that they were not alone.

For the first time, Maarja noticed the man had drawn a luger pistol, which he kept pointed towards the two women.

'So, two questions,' he said with a strong accent, almost Scandinavian in tone. 'What are you doing in my house and where is Harry?'

'You are Sven?' Maarja asked.

'Yes, I am Sven,' he replied. 'Who the hell are you?'

*****

The tree lined silhouettes of the smaller islands were now more than a dream, as *Eestirand* left Tallinn Bay. Peeter looked across enviously at them, wishing he could lose himself in their dark shadows, walking with the soft spring of the soil under his feet. He wondered if he would ever have the chance to visit such natural places again in peace.

He had never spent much time on a ship before. True, he had been fishing many times on the lake, but that was a tiny craft. There, the waters were benign and placid.

Here, the boat rocked forward as it breached each wave and then rolled from side to side. He felt uneasy about it and a cold sweat formed on his brow. It made him clamp his mouth shut and breathe slowly through his nose, focusing on the cold air as if it was the cure to his unease.

He found focusing on the islands afar was much more comfortable than watching the waves. Then, he spied something and nudged Harry.

'Look on the horizon; I think there are aeroplanes coming. Many of them.'

Harry raised his hand to shield his eyes.

'They may be coming for us. We had better find ourselves some protection.'

'Why would they come for us when we fly the Estonian flag?'

GERAINT ROBERTS

'Because they won't see the flag whilst we stay in a convoy of Russian ships. Come on, I think we should head for the middle of the ship, use the bridge to shelter us. Stand away from the approaching aircraft.'

'Close to the lifebelts then,' Peeter replied. 'Just in case.'

Harry gave wry smile and Peeter shrugged.

'I will be on this ship as long as I can. I can't swim.'

They began to move their way through, the massed people on deck. Harry drew his pistol. Whilst it grudgingly cleared a path, the trail was laden with curses and dirty looks.

'This will do,' Harry said. 'But do not discuss anything with our neighbours.'

From the looks on people's faces, Peeter decided there was little chance of conversation. He closed his eyes and waited, listening to the rush of the sea as the boat ploughed through the Baltic.

He noted the rhythm of the boat's engines and the smell of coal smoke as the exhaust blew back across him. Somewhere in the background, there was a faint drone of aircraft engines. Soon, they would be over them like an angry swarm of wasps. Then the drone would be accompanied by the whistle of descending bombs and the screaming of injured and panicking men.

He took a deep breath and images of his family came to his mind. Perhaps it would not be long before he joined them? The thought was as if a load had been taken off his shoulders and for the first time in a long while, he smiled.

'Something amusing?' Harry asked.

'No, I'm just looking forward to the next journey.'

'If there's a chance to stay alive, you should take it.'

Peeter nodded. 'If there's a chance, my best idea would be to stay with you. You are a born survivor.'

Harry nodded. 'Good man.'

Men had now begun to observe the aircraft. There was

more animation on deck, an increase in the buzz of conversation and the air was thick with fear.

Peeter sat down and tried to keep his eyes closed, falling back into the images of better times.

She had been so beautiful, why did they have to take her from him?

The whistle of bombs was in the background, as Peeter dreamt of his daughter's happy giggling face, as she ran around the gooseberry bushes. He felt the initial shudder and the ship lost its rhythm in the wake of an explosion. A fine spray washed over, the bomb had missed. Then there was a large bang, followed by another. He was thrown to the side and covered in spray. There was no way of avoiding the reality and he opened his eyes to look on the scene of confusion.

Men were now pushing and shoving, screaming all around them. People were trying to push past him. One shoved him out of the way to reach for the lifebelt another tried to snatch it and they wrestled together. An arm pulled at him.

'Stay calm and stay where you are,' Harry shouted. 'Don't get lost in this panic.'

'People are jumping off the boat, what's going on?'

'We got hit. It went straight through the hatch. I think the ship is taking water.'

'Well, shouldn't we be jumping too?'

'Peeter, stay calm the Captain has changed direction. He's heading straight for that large island. Is there a port there?'

'Probably not, but it is land. People are jumping Harry! There's a lot of talk around here of being caught in the suction when a ship sinks to the bottom. We should go.'

As he made to move, Harry grabbed hold of him.

'Look Peeter, be patient. The Captain is running for port or a beach. The engines are at full pelt. If you jump now, you'll get sucked into the propellers in the wake and get chopped up.

Do you want that? The longer we leave it, the less we have to swim. Stay calm, a ship takes time to sink.'

The deck was like a maelstrom of panic as people fought around the pair to get free. Peeter tried to block out all the shouting, crying and screams that were all around him. He looked Harry and as their gazes locked, he saw the calmness within. Peeter gave a curt nod and took a deep breath. Voices started changing around him, stronger tones.

'Stand firm, we will survive. Stand firm and don't jump!'

He sighed as all the frustration left his body. It was better this than being sent into a battle for a cause he did not believe in. If he was to die, at least it would be in sight of Estonia.

CHAPTER TWENTY-THREE

Prangli

'I asked you a question,' Sven's tone had not changed, but his face showed his irritation.

'We are Harry's friends,' Maarja said.

'I am Harry's woman,' Liisbet said, slowly moving down the stairs.

'I know nothing about any friends,' Sven replied.

'I am not trying to hide things,'Liisbet said. 'We have spent weeks trying to find him. He said he would be here.'

Maarja looked at her and then sighed. 'No, enough of this. Harry was taken by the Reds. He hid me so I could escape them. I think he was on a ship in the convoy that just left Tallinn.'

'So why did you stay here?' Sven demanded.

Maarja shrugged. 'It's dry and warm. There is food and the owner had gone. Besides, where is there to go?'

'You can come back with me and talk with my superiors,' Sven said. 'They can decide what to do with you.'

'Drop your weapon!' A voice from the doorway commanded. Sven froze and looked across at Maarja, before slowly lowering the gun. Maarja sighed with relief as she looked at the figure at the door.

'Märt, it is alright. Don't shoot. This is Sven.'

'Sven? Where's Harry?' Märt snapped, although Maarja could see the gun was still a threat the way as Märt would not put it away. She tried to calm things down.

'He's gone, Märt. The Reds took him. They were rounding

up men to ship out. I think he was on one being used as a troop ship. It was flying an Estonian flag.'

Märt relaxed, even though he still held his pistol ready.

'That's Harry buggered then. I take it that Sven was here to pick him up.'

There was no reply.

'Okay, I will take that as a yes.'

'Märt, I think Peeter is on there also,' Maarja said.

'Russian bastards! Okay Sven, I think I need to know what you will be doing next.'

'Go back.' The reply was nonchalant and brief.

'To Finland I take it? Sven, we are with the Finnish Boys. The Reds have been squeezed out of this area. You have to trust us.'

Sven looked across slowly. 'You talk of trust, but you are the one holding the pistol.'

Märt gave a grim smile, then slowly put the safety catch on and place his pistol in his pocket.

'Sven, if you are going back to Finland, take these women with you. They need to escape this madness.'

Footsteps sounded from outside and Juhan rushed into the room. He beamed as Maarja ran to embrace him with a sob. He returned the hug and then quickly broke off.

'Märt, I talked to Raio. He has reached the top of the peninsula at Rohuneeme. They saw a convoy of ships from Tallinn. It was attacked by aeroplanes. Oh, hello!' he finished, having seen Sven for the first time.

'Juhan, what else?' Märt snapped.

'One ship was badly hit; it's heading for the main island.'

'Prangli,' Sven said.

'What kind of ship?' Märt demanded, an edge creeping into his voice.

'He said something about a cargo boat. He called it *Ee-*

stirand. It was the biggest commercial boat in Tallinn.'

'*Eestirand*?' Sven said. 'Good Estonian herring boat. Strong.'

'That will be the boat I saw flying the Estonian flag,' Maarja said and Märt frowned and cursed.

'Then I need to go and find them. Sven?'

'Yes, I will take you Märt,' Sven said. 'My boat is hidden a few kilometres from here on the other bay.'

Märt bit his lip and then nodded. 'Juhan, stay with the women and keep them safe. If I am not back in two days, take them south.'

Maarja watched Märt and Sven depart from the upstairs window. She knew that Märt had the same desire for the truth that burned in her heart. She was worried that he would just accept Harry's story and send him to Finland.

She was convinced that this was not in Estonia's interest. Maarja watched as Liisbet helped Juhan unload his jeep. There was not a moment to lose, there was a wavelength given to her in case of the unlikely event it was needed.

It was her good fortune that she had the opportunity. She rushed to open up the radio again. The static crackled as she moved the dial to the correct wavelength, then pressed transmit.

'Message for Schulz, message for Schulz.'

'Proceed,' came the reply.

*****

Märt followed Sven along the deserted roads and lanes of the area. He was thankful that the cloud cover was thin enough for the moon to provide some small illumination, giving the whole cloud base a silvery sheen.

'*The clouds are probably all smoke from the bombing and fires,*' Märt thought. '*God knows there's been enough.*'

For a large man, Sven was very quick on his feet. Märt was finding it difficult to keep up, meaning he had little time to think of anything else but where the man was and to keep his eyes and ears open for any danger.

'Here,' said Sven after a while.

Märt looked at the path that ran past empty shattered houses. He could see no difference to any part of the journey so far. A very quick thought flashed through his mind. Was this a ruse? Mentally, he was exhausted. The past two months had caught up with him and he no longer felt the energy to fight through on this journey. Besides, he had made safe the people he cared about - as safe as anyone could be in this land. Sven stopped and indicated for Märt to wait, before disappearing into the shadows. He soon returned, carrying a jerrycan. Märt could hear some liquid sloshing about inside.

'Not far,' Sven said and carried on walking.

They were now a few kilometres from the house and Märt wondered if he could ever retrace his steps if the need arose. The sea breeze blew across his face and he knew from the taste in the air that they were quite close to the shore. Sven took them towards a bank of reeds. They had grown to the height of a man and now stood like thin, ghostly sentinels in the night.

Sven moved into them, double backing on his path at an angle. He then quickly changed direction again and continued to zigzag. Märt saw it as an attempt to hide the trail. Their progress had slowed because of this, but Märt knew they were close. It became obvious to him when he accidentally strayed from the path that Sven was taking and got a boot full of water for his trouble.

Sven put the jerrycan down and moved into the thicker reeds, his boots now made a noise as they moved like stepping on wood floating in water. It was the boat, Märt realised quickly. The way the water sloshed around the boat as Sven moved was enough. Märt passed the jerrycan to him and Sven gave a quick flick of his hand.

'Push.'

Märt quickly cast the boat off and jumped in. Sven gave him a helpful pull to send him sprawling to the front of the boat. He took out a small paddle and began to slowly use it to send the boat further out of the reeds.

As they got into deeper water, Sven pulled the cord on the engine. It turned over a few times before spluttering to a stop with an almost wounded tone. In Märt's ears, the noise seemed to echo all around the marsh.

The engine coughed again and then spluttered before taking hold. Sven opened the throttle and the boat began to glide slowly away from the reeds, towards the shadows of rocky boulders that stood sentinel in the water. Then he opened the throttle and the placid ride became more agitated as they moved out from the coastline.

'How do you know where you are going?' Märt shouted over the engine noise.

'I know,' Sven replied.

The noise of the engine stopped any serious conversation and Märt began to study the lines of breakers that decorated the tops of the waves.

Even in the dim light, there was an almost luminous glow to the water. It was mesmerising to him.

The horizon was dark and appeared to grow steadily as they moved towards it. Märt began to see the shape was not linear and hoped it was an island. It was a long journey and Märt had begun to doze from the movement of the boat. Sven finally cut the throttle, making the prow sink back into the water and leant forward to Märt.

'I go slowly around here, for we do not know what we will find. There may still be Reds and I have not travelled this coast so much in the past year to remember it well. We may have to wait until daybreak.'

Märt gazed at the island that now cast a significant shadow

ahead of them. He observed the wash of submerged reefs and noted how Sven was taking a circuitous road to avoid them. After a while he spotted a glimmer of light on the horizon.

'It may be a boat,' Sven said. 'But we need to get closer to see if she's moving or sinking or just beached. Be cautious, the coast is not shallow but there are still many boulders. They will damage us if we stray too close.'

He opened the throttle a little bit and Märt kept an eye on their goal, whilst checking for hazards ahead of them. The illumination now appeared to be more than one light.

They were in a straight line and appeared to be away from the island's coast. The land began to cast a more pronounced shadow on the sea. Märt decided it was undoubtedly a ship, but then the lights disappeared.

'Either she has sunk or they realise there is a war on,' Sven said. Once more he cut the engine. 'If we go closer at speed, they may be alerted to us. We must make for the shore a fair way off.'

'What if they need our help?' Märt asked

'What if it is not *Eestirand*?' was the blunt reply.

'If they are sinking, does it matter?'

'Okay, I'll not stop here. The bay is wide with too many small islands and rocks. We go in close and berth on the island. Then you can go look and decide.'

They took a wide berth around a headland and then coasted to the bay. Märt could now see the beach ahead and realised that dawn was rising. He imagined the seabed looked close enough to touch, although it could just be the reflection of the sea. Now he knew why Sven was so keen to beach.

The ship was obvious in the early morning light. It looked grounded amongst rocks, slightly lower at the stern. They were still too far away to see individual people, as Sven headed for an outcrop behind a headland.

'This is as far as I go. I will be waiting here.'

Märt had no energy to argue. It was a place where the boat could easily blend in with its surrounds, possibly even be pulled onto shore. The forest was remarkably close to the short shingle beach, making the boat easy to camouflage.

Märt jumped out of the boat and waded to shore, quickly moving to the tree line. He spied a white sandy path that led through the needle-strewn forest floor, that looked lit up in the early morning light. On an impulse, he jumped onto a rocky outcrop and took off his boots to pour the water out and wring the socks. He needed a moment's rest and time to think, so he lay back and closed his eyes to focus.

He woke to the sound of voices and the noise of vegetation being trampled. A group was nearby and as Märt rolled over to look, he spied five men nearby picking berries from the hundreds of bushes that paved the forest floor. He jumped up quickly and made his way over to them, trying to push aside the worry that they may still be Reds and that this island may still be hostile. The answer was to engage them quickly in conversation and avoid any awkward questions.

'Good berry patch this,' he said. 'Better than further up.'

'Where have you been?' a man with a sleeve missing on his tunic piped up. From his arm muscles, he could have easily passed as a stoker.

'Are you with the duty looking for shellfish?'

'Someone's got to,' Märt shrugged. 'But the rocks are rubbish here. Wrong side of the bay.'

'Yes, I saw your lot further down. At least you are further away from the horseflies.'

'Not really, they still bite you, even when you are standing in the sea. I had better go back and join them.'

Märt set off for the beach, choosing a path that would quickly take him out of view. He vowed not to appear so obvious in future. There were another three foraging groups as he made his way around the coastline. Two he managed to slip past, but the third was unavoidable. However, he was not treated with suspicion.

The group was a mix of men in uniform and civilian clothing. Märt chose to speak to the leader, judged by his bearing.

'It is as well, Prangli is where it is,'

'What do you mean?' the man replied.

'I mean the boat was sinking, I don't fancy Russia with the cold months approaching.'

'True, perhaps I don't fancy Russia for other reasons,' the man admitted. 'Mainly I don't want to be cannon fodder for Stalin. I was thinking the Captain should have turned back for Tallinn.'

'Maybe he did not think that there was enough time left for the ship.'

'There is that also. Not enough berries to go round though. They must take us off soon or we will starve.'

'I am sure the Germans would want us back soon,' Märt said, lifting a hand in farewell and getting a knowing laugh in reply.

Märt had learnt a lot from observation and the discussions. The people he had met were conscripts and not volunteers and most were openly hostile to the Soviet Army. He at least could relax in the knowledge he was among friends.

On an impulse, he chose a tree to climb as a vantage point and in a short amount of time was looking at the beach beyond the headland.

It was a sea of men, huddled in small groups or standing in line to ferry supplies to and from a rowing boat that moved between the stricken ship and the shore. Makeshift shelters appeared to have been made with canvas and were dotted around at the beach edge and in the trees. The stricken freighter was not too far offshore and from the way it sat in the water, Märt could see the stern had shipped water. The captain could not have done a better job in making sure it was grounded, he decided.

One problem remained for Märt. There were hundreds of men; some would be on the island foraging, whilst many still appeared on the ship, implying it was stable. That brought up a dilemma he had suppressed for a while. In the middle of such numbers, how was he going to find Harry?

Märt descended the branches and strode for the beach. Nobody had seen to challenge him up to now. He could have been Josef Stalin for all they had seemed to care. As he reached the shore another sight greeted him with dismay.

There appeared to be bodies floating in the surf and a party of men were retrieving them. He moved to the first group sitting on the beach, aimlessly staring at the activity.

'Are you the Kautla men?' Märt asked. There was no reply and Märt had to repeat himself three times before one gave a sullen shake of head.

He moved on and the next group proved even less responsive. As he moved on, he heard one mutter.

'Try Kõrvemaa,' followed by a snort of derision from another.

Märt carried on systematically walking up the beach. Most were not interested, but once or twice he was asked questions back. One man became very inquisitive.

'I don't give a stuff about Kautla,' he said. 'When are we due a shift at unloading? The man did not even bother looking up from the small fire at which he warmed his hands. 'It's bloody exposed here and we are all bloody starving.'

'You know they are aware of this,' Märt replied, moving on.

Yes, but what about getting off this place and back to Estonia? We must be in the German territory by now?'

'All in good time, soldier,' Märt replied over his shoulder.

'They'll come and get us, but they are still fighting for Tallinn.'

'Crap,' the man snapped. 'If that was the case, why were we on that bloody boat?'

The man had begun to get overly aggressive. Märt turned to see he had jumped up and started to walk towards him.

'No, you haven't answered my questions. Who...?'

'You were looking for Kautla men?' A voice said behind him, cutting through the argument. 'Come, I will take you to them.'

Märt spun round to look at a stocky man, with a flat hat pulled down so that his eyes peered from under the brim. They gleamed with blue fire, as if ready for the owner to dispense justice. They always had done, Märt thought.

'Thank you, please show me the way.'

The man at the fire cursed at Märt's back as he walked away. Märt ignored the taunts and instead focused on his saviour.

'Maybe I should have known you would find me in this group, Harry. There's only, what? A thousand here?'

'I heard nearer three altogether. We had a few more, but they jumped too early and drowned. I was hoping you might pop over, Märt.'

'I suppose your training makes you always keep your eyes and ears open to opportunities?' Harry shrugged and then in a quieter voice said.

'Peeter is here also.'

'Good, we are getting you both off the island now.'

'We'll see, let's get Peeter first.'

The farmer was sitting on the beach, looking out to sea. A rare smile crossed his face as he rose to greet Märt.

'I knew you would come, or someone would. Have you seen any of the others?'

'I left Liisbet and Maarja with Juhan. You are coming back

with me.'

Peeter shook his head in disbelief.

'This is all madness. How did you manage it?'

'It is of no worry,' Harry said, drawing the other two further away from any of the small groups on the beach. He sat and beckoned the others to join him.

'I'm not going back to the Germans. The Russians nearly just had me and I am not jumping from one camp to another.'

'Harry needs to get to Finland,' Peeter said.

'Why?'

Harry tapped his nose.

'So how am I supposed to trust you?'

'Why should I trust you?' Harry replied.

'I just came to save you and I spent a long time taking you up the country,' Märt replied.

'And you have just come from Maarja, who would sell me to the Germans for the 'greater good' of Estonia. What else can you tell me that would convince me?'

'Sven brought me here.'

Harry looked at Märt thoughtfully for a while.

'This Sven really exists?' Peeter said. 'And he has a boat? Brilliant.'

'Take me to him and then we talk some more,' Harry replied.

'We need to go without being watched,' Märt replied. 'Wait until nearer dark.'

'You men. We need help,' a man called. Although speaking Estonian, he wore a Red Army officer's cap.

'An unwilling conscript to the cause,' Harry said, as if reading their minds. 'We will talk later.'

Dusk had fallen and the men on the beach had retired to

whatever shelter they had. Even in mid August, the open sky nights were cold. A few small beach fires littered the sands, but fuel was scarce. Märt waited for most activities to slow before he led Harry and Peeter into the woods. He was relying on his memory now as to where he had come from, although he had tried to ensure that his path had few twists and turns on the way down. He soon returned them to the large boulder, from whence he had started.

'Harry, we need to talk now before we go any further. Sven will be waiting for us, so we won't have too long. Tell me what is going on.'

'I need to get to Finland,' Harry replied.

'I know this,' Märt replied. 'But why not just come to the Finnish Boys in Kautla?'

'I have to speak directly to Finland's government. The army is too locked up with the Wehrmacht.'

Peeter frowned. 'Why don't you want to talk to the Germans? They have liberated us.'

'Do you think so? You are free now, you think, to do what you will?'

'Not whilst the Reds are around, but in time.' Peeter replied.

Harry smiled. 'You are wrong. The Reich wants to create a new country in the Baltic called Ostland. They want to make it a new colony for Germanic people. The squires will be returning and in time you will be moved away unless you are of good German stock.'

'What are you saying?' Märt gasped.

'The German New Order. They want to create a Greater Germany, stocked with their master race of blue-eyed blonde Aryan people.'

'So where do we all go?' Peeter asked.

'Where indeed?'

'And what of Finland?' Märt asked.

'The long-term plan would be to annex Finland into Greater Germany.'

'That is ridiculous! They are allies.'

'Finland has resources. Metals like iron and nickel. And an Aryan people. Do not look at me as if I am mad. If Finland is treated as an equal, why were the Wehrmacht trying to insist that the army swore allegiance to Adolf Hitler?'

Peeter shook his head. 'So what you are saying is, if Stalin gets us, Estonia is dead. If Hitler gets us, Estonia is dead. What else is there?'

'The British and Americans have been working on an agreement. It is something along the lines of the last war, where peoples were allowed their own self determination and occupied countries would have their boundaries restored.'

'So, we just wait for the Americans to just walk in and free us?'

'I don't know, Märt. But it is worth hoping for and if I provide the Finns with this evidence, they will not be so happy to give such blind obedience. They will be looking over their shoulder and looking at possible alternatives.'

'You know that would weaken the Germans here. The Reds might then even win - and Finland would be overrun.'

'We would never let Finland go under. The nickel mines are too important to give to Stalin. Yes, Germany relies on its allies in the East; Finland, Hungary, Romania. If they have less support, they will need to fill the gap with their own men – by taking troops from the west.'

Märt rubbed his eyes.

'What you are saying is that you risk your life to deliver some documents that may or may not put a flicker of doubt in somebody's mind?'

Harry shrugged. 'It's what I do.'

'And why should we help you?'

'Because you cannot do anything else. What you have now leaves you nothing. My mission may not seem much, but it will lead to a better future. We cannot help now, but we will.'

'What do you want from me?' Märt demanded.

'Get me to Finland, I will do the rest.'

There was a pause, the area had become quiet beyond the ever-present rush of waves and the breeze in the trees. It was a sharp contrast of calm to the constant barrage of artillery hammering into Tallinn.

Even their whispering had felt that they were disturbing nature. Märt stared at the sky. There were silvery specks of stars, millions of them. So many stars, each with planets – and there he was on just one of them. A meteor briefly flashed a streak across the sky in its glorious demise. He took a deep breath.

'I will do it. Peeter?'

'Märt, I trust you both. You know I will follow.'

'That's great,' Harry said smoothly, the unmistakeable click rang in the air as he uncocked his pistol.

'Yes,' said Märt, doing the same. Even amongst friends, trust walked a thin tightrope across the abyss.

'You're late,' Sven said, walking out of the reeds, as they began to climb on the boat. He looked the group up and down and finally fixed his eyes on Harry.

'Is he the man then?'

Märt nodded.

'Do you have enough fuel to get to Finland?' Harry asked.

Sven nodded. 'Yes, I have plenty. More in store. I could go to Finland and back if I needed.'

'Then we go to the mainland first.'

'Why?' Peeter asked.

'Liisbet. You know where she is. I am taking her with me. She deserves more than this.'

Sven looked to Märt who nodded. The boatman shrugged. 'Okay. Get in.'

The journey was made without discussion, as everyone seemed lost in their thoughts. Märt was wondering what he had done. Was this the right way forward? What *was* the right way? Was Harry a threat or a saviour? Märt knew the man had never threatened him. He had even helped in the escape from Kautla. Märt's instincts were still to trust him, however bizarre his mission appeared to be.

They had begun to near Viimsi headland and Märt wondered if Raio would pick up the trail in the dark. Thoughts of his companions then went to Maarja. He knew he had never stopped loving her. He was also aware she would never forgive him.

If they were going back for Liisbet, they would take Maarja and Juhan also. It was beyond negotiation. The boat had room and Märt would row them across the sea if that is what was needed.

Sven had slowed down as they entered an area of half submerged boulders. The reed-strewn land ahead looked deserted and still. Märt was grateful for the calm, too much had happened. His bread-making days now felt like a distant memory, although only three months had passed.

The moon was bright enough to work in without a light, he thought. A real hunter's moon. A brief wink of light from the reeds caught his attention. Something had reflected off the moon's rays. Märt scanned the area, although it was waterlogged, there was no way that would have come from water.

'Sven, stop. I think we are being watched.' He shouted.

A shot rang out and Harry fell back and rolled off the boat into the sea. There followed a crescendo of noise, more shouts as shadows began to move on the shore. Someone screamed.

'Halt!'

Märt could hear the German tone of voice and in a split second, he made his mind up.

'Sven, get out of here, now! They want us and Harry.'

Without waiting for an answer, he dived into the sea, heading for where Harry had fallen. The boat's engines revved and began to grow fainter as it moved out to sea.

'Märt, help. I can't swim.'

'Peeter! Where are you, Peeter?'

Märt looked around and found him flailing in the water. Märt quickly swam over and grabbed hold of him, trying to avoid being hit or the farmer dragging him under in his panic.

'I've got you now, so don't panic. Stop struggling! Look, how many times have I let you down?'

'Okay,' Peeter finally said through gritted teeth. He was panting with fear.

'We just kick our legs when I say. Ready? Now.'

Märt's toes came up short, as his foot found the seabed.

'Peeter, you can stand in it. Put your foot down. Peeter!'

Peeter disappeared and then resurfaced with a moan.

'Can you feel the seabed?''

'Yes, just,' Peeter replied.

'*Kommen sie hier*,' a voice commanded from the shore. Märt started to wade across.

'You are an idiot Peeter.'

'You are no better.'

'True.'

As they neared the shore, Märt heard another voice. This time it was female.

'That is not him.'

They were half-dragged out of the sea and flung to the ground. Märt looked up to a line of guns being pointed at him.

An officer stepped forward from the gloom. In peacetime,

he would be thought of as having a kindly face. He barked a question to his men than on reply turned to Märt.

'Where is he?'

'Who?' Märt replied.

The officer shouted again in German and Maarja stepped forward.

'Märt,' she said kneeling down to him. '*Oberleutnant* Schulz wants to know what happened to Harry.'

'I didn't find him. There are three thousand men on that island.'

Maarja translated and Schulz replied.

'Where is the other man in the boat?'

'I told him to go because some arsehole started shooting at us.'

'There was one more.'

'No there wasn't.'

Märt had now got to his feet and stood glaring at Schulz. The air crackled with resentment with his waspish tone as he looked at Maarja.

'You can tell your boyfriend I am a Finnish Army officer and that I only report to General Mannerheim and those in his chain of command.'

Maarja translated and Schulz vented a torrent of angry German words in response.

He wishes to know why you went to Prangli if not to rescue your friend.'

'If you notice, I did rescue my friend,' Märt replied indicating Peeter.

'I am in charge of a reconnaissance unit that is watching the coast on this peninsular. We saw a convoy and watched a ship return and beach at Prangli. I went to see what was happening and have found that nearly three thousand Estonians were being taken by the Reds to Leningrad. I have come back to organise a rescue of them and I expect assistance not hassle.'

Schulz shook his head. Maarja began to plead, but Schulz indicated for them to be taken away.

'What is going on?' Peeter asked.

'They want to ask more questions,' Maarja replied, before continuing her discussion with Schulz. He flicked his hand up with a curt *'nein!'* and strode past her.

'What the hell have you done?' Märt snapped trying to grab Maarja.

A soldier quickly brought up his rifle and hit Märt in the face, then pushed him to stumble forwards. Märt and Peeter were taken to a nearby house and shoved into a lean-to shed and the door was bolted.

'What the hell is your woman doing?' Peeter asked getting to his feet.

Märt waved his hand. 'Perhaps we should not talk so loud when we do not know who listens.'

'Okay,' Peeter whispered. 'What the hell does your woman think she is doing?'

'What she thinks is right,' Märt replied. 'We need to stop her before she is successful.'

He went to the door and lifted the latch slowly, before easing the door open a crack. It was immediately slammed back in his face, making him fall back.

'Well that answers that question,' Peeter said. 'Shall we check the walls and roof to see if there is another way?'

He went around the lean-to, then after a few minutes of pushing and prodding, he gave up.

'A house wall on one side and corrugated iron all around. Too bloody secure, this is.'

'We need to see what happens outside and take our chances when we can,' Märt said lying down.

CHAPTER TWENTY-FOUR

Rebellion

H e was awoken by the sounds of a light scuffle outside. It was over very quickly before the silence returned. Märt put his finger to his lips and went to the door as it began to open. Peeter got ready at the doorway as the door was roughly grabbed and a man stepped in. The man took one look at Märt and focused on the rapidly developing bruise on his face.

'Lieutenant, you tell me which of these short-arsed bastards did this and I will castrate him. '

'Where the hell did you come from, Raio?' Peeter asked.

'Juhan radioed you had gone. We waited for signs of your boat. We've been tracking you since you came back in the bay. Toomas had you marked out straight away. Where's Harry?'

'I don't know, the shorties shot him, and he fell overboard. These bastards are looking for him too. Maarja led them to us.'

'And do we want to give him to them?'

Märt shook his head. 'No, I will explain later.'

'Your word is enough, Märt. What do we do now?'

'Disarm them and tie them up.'

'Maarja?'

'She comes with us. If I have to drag her there myself. She needs the truth - and we need to find Harry.'

The swim had not been a problem, in spite of the bullet wound that created a sharp pain with every other stroke. He had trained for so long that he had no problems with adapting his swimming style to cover any eventuality. However, his arc was getting lower as his arm began to stiffen. He knew speed was of the essence and he needed to get out of the water as quickly as he could - before the adrenalin rush faded and shock set in with the cold.

He had never been shot before. It was bad form and not up to his standards. Now as he sought shelter amongst the rocks, he started thinking of how to stem the bleeding and where to find shelter. At least the cold would have slowed the flow of blood. That was a relief.

Harry gave a wry smile after the agony faded from pulling himself up the beach. It was just another challenge, but wasn't he always looking for a new challenge? The world began to develop white specks in his vision and a fuzzy outline. It wasn't going to end like this. He wouldn't let it happen....

A faint voice caught in his mind as the darkness closed in.

'Ah, so you are Harry...'

'We should take their vehicles.'

'Sergeant, as soon as they are free, the Germans will be looking for those vehicles.' Märt replied and then stopped. 'Where is Toomas?"

'I left him searching the coastline.'

'Okay, go and find him and take Peeter with you and the truck. I will take their Kubelwagen and will meet you where the port is for Prangli.'

'That is Leppneeme, it's on the east side near the top.'

'That's good enough, Maarja!' Märt shouted and his eyes winced as she appeared. 'You are coming with me.'

Without further word he pulled her into the Kubelwagen and started driving. She sat with arms folded and glared ahead before glaring at him.

'Shouldn't you be tying me up?'

'I'm not into those kind of games.'

She scowled at the flippant humour. 'Like you did to the rest of your enemies.'

'You're not my enemy.'

'Then what are we doing now?'

'Going to get Juhan. I take it he is still in Sven's house?'

'Yes, I told him to stay. Why are you doing this?'

'I believe Harry.'

'You are declaring war on the Germans.'

'I don't care about that,' Märt snapped. He slowed the car down, to negotiate around some rocks in the road and then gave her a quick look.

Maarja started at the lack of emotion in his face, but she could see his eyes still burned with desire.

'We pick up Juhan and Liisbet and then we meet the others.'

'And then?'

'Depends on Harry.'

'What? You follow his orders?'

'No,' he stopped the car and switched the engine off. 'It depends on if we have found him and if he is still alive. Now we walk the rest of the way, I will not take this car any further as they will be looking for it.'

He headed off without another word. He knew she would follow, if only for Juhan's sake.

The house felt empty, which made Märt wary. Signalling for Maarja to stay outside, he grabbed the door. The hinges creaked gently as he slowly opened it. Knowing he had lost any element of surprise, he crept into the room and kept to the wall. Looking constantly for any danger, he moved slowly along towards the kitchen.

He could hear a faint resonant noise from above, almost like a metronome. Faint and animal-like, perhaps a cat. Märt could not remember the last time he had seen a cat. He stopped to listen and as the quiet of the room ahead threatened to swallow him up, he realised he was listening to faint snoring.

'Juhan.'

There was a rustle and a sound of footsteps, Liisbet came down the stairway, shouldering her rifle as soon as she saw Märt.

'You are late,' she said.

Märt shrugged. 'I was kept away for a while. Is Juhan ok?'

'I am awake.' Juhan's voice sounded out and he was soon down the stairs and into his mother's arms as she burst through the door.

'It is as well you were not held hostage,' Märt said dryly.

'What now?' Juhan said. 'Did you meet Raio?'

Märt nodded. 'Go get the radio and the car. We are going to meet them.'

'Did Harry survive?' Liisbet asked, the edge on her voice showed her fear.

Märt sighed, seeing the dismay in her face. 'I do not know. But if he did, we will find him - and I want to see those documents of his.'

By now the roads were no longer deserted and there were the occasional passing of military traffic, as the Wehrmacht looked to strengthen its position in Tallinn Bay. According to a brief conversation that Märt had on radio, the city had now finally fallen.

Märt went to the bedroom. He wanted to contact Raio if he

could. He was surprised to find Maarja using the telescope to look across at the city.

'I need you to come with us,'

He tried to sound as gentle as possible, but it was like grasping a nettle and he hoped the sting would not be too painful.

Maarja turned and looked at him with a strange expression.

'You know, you tell me that the Germans are not our saviours. Tell me why the Estonian flag is now flying from Piik Hermann?'

Märt took the offered telescope and looked for himself. The sight was gratifying, but he could not celebrate.

'I spoke to the Finnish Boys, the main unit is on the outskirts of town. They were stopped from taking part in the final assault. The Germans held them back, what happened here probably is that a few Forest Brothers got into the city and got to the tower before the Nazis could plant their swastika.'

'But it *is* there...'

'Yes, but will it be there tomorrow?'

CHAPTER TWENTY-FIVE

Harry's mission

L eppneeme was at the top of the Viimsi peninsular, facing east in a small bay that pointed it in the direction of Prangli. The harbour felt empty, a nondescript grey wall amongst the ubiquitous sunken granite boulders and reed-strewn marshlands. It was not an area that had attracted many houses and was relatively flat. Bland was the word that Märt thought of it. As he pulled up at the port and saw Raio coming towards him, he could see his Sergeant had the same view.

'Were you expecting a ship here?' Raio asked.

'Not really. I just wanted to pick an obvious point to rendezvous, an area that made it easier for you to collect your boys, if we needed them.'

'Come over here.'

Raio took them to the truck and undid the canvas flap at the back. Harry was lying on the floor, shivering and half conscious. Toomas sat with him, trying to keep him warm with a sheet of tarpaulin as cover.

'He was shot, but the sea cleaned most of the wound and sterilised it.'

Raio nodded in acknowledgment. 'We have to get him warm and quickly. We could try taking him back to Sven's house?'

'I suppose it is warm and would provide shelter,' Märt agreed. 'But it is too close to where we were captured. Is there not anything close to where we are now?'

'There's an empty farmhouse up the road,' Toomas said.

'That's where we will go for now.'

Raio frowned. 'Are we making sure that the Germans cut us off?'

Märt stopped for a moment with a smile.

'Is it really the time to start to count our enemies? Yes, probably we are, but we did that when we stopped here to look for Harry. Let's get him some rest and keep up the reconnaissance, as we were ordered. Put an extra group monitoring the road to here to give us plenty of notice of any visitors.'

Harry slept through the rest of the day and by morning, he had begun to sweat. Liisbet now constantly by his side, looked up as Märt approached bearing a hot drink.

'How is he?'

'He has been restless during the night, but his breathing is good now.'

She smiled her thanks and took a sip of the drink. Märt observed she looked grey and drawn.

'You have had no sleep?'

Liisbet shrugged and made no reply.

'This place is old, musty and damp. It has few comforts, but for now it is the best place for him to keep warm and dry. We need medicine from somewhere.'

She gave him an accusatory glare and he could only shrug.

'Don't think we haven't tried. My men have pooled their field medical packs and Toomas is out collecting wood for this fire, like I did in the forest by Peeter's farm when you had the fever.'

There was another silence, save the burning logs which spat their sap out as if in contempt amongst the dancing flames. Märt continued.

'You are right, this is a musty old place, but reasonably

stocked, like this coffee. It looks as if the owners left in a hurry, another family suffering the Reds hospitality.'

She turned swiftly away and started to mop Harry's brow.

'I do not see you as a Red, Liisbet. I never have.'

She nodded and seemed on the verge of tears. Märt looked at her small nose, upturned at the end, her smooth skin and dark eyebrows, in contrast to her sandy coloured hair. In another lifetime, he would have wanted to know her better.

'You are kind, Märt. I am sorry that I said what I said.'

'I believe him, Liisbet and besides, we are all family.'

'Märt, if things happen. Tell Peeter...'

Harry whispered something and they moved to focus on him as his eyelids fluttered open. Märt took out his water canteen and Liisbet took it. Harry took in a sip of water and sighed, then he slowly looked around.

'Hurts like hell,' he croaked. 'Who put salt in the wound?'

'Nobody asked you to fall off the boat,' Märt replied and a faint smile crossed Harry's lips.

'I take it we are still stuck in Estonia?'

'Yes, the Germans extended their welcome to us. Listen Harry, I don't know how to get in touch with Sven or anyone not influenced by our guests. I have not told base about this, but the airwaves are not safe anyway. I need to know what to do, as you need time to heal. The season will turn soon and the sea gets rougher. Before long, the ice will come in until the spring.'

Harry made to get up and Liisbet helped him. He nodded his thanks and reached inside his tunic, wincing at the pain as he moved his shoulder. He recovered a small piece of material that was waxed shut. He carefully prized open the seal and removed paper from inside. With great care he began to unfold it. Märt looked up and spied Maarja looking from the shadows. Her expression was one of fear, for what they may be shown. She looked like a cornered fox, looking for escape. Märt called her.

'Go get Raio and come back here.'

'Why?'

'Because I want you all to see.'

The four of them were now gathered around Harry, as he handed Märt the opened papers. Märt studied the first – which was a map. He then handed it to Maarja.

'What is this?' she said softly.

'Hitler's dream,' Märt replied, whilst reading the other sheet.

'When the war is finished, this is what they want to create.' Harry whispered. 'It was stolen from Berlin.'

'Why are the Baltics marked as Greater Germany?' Maarja asked.

'Because that is what they will be, colonised by the Germans.'

'It is detailed here,' Märt said without looking up. 'Non-aryans would be sent to south of Peipsi, Ukraine or Siberia.'

'What is this document?' Maarja asked.

'It is the New World Order,' Harry replied. 'It has Hitler's stamp on it. This is why I cannot let it fall into German hands. They fear that if it is known, that the Finns may make peace and the Baltics would begin to form a resistance. It cannot fall into Russian hands, for they would use it to let the nations rise on their terms.'

'What is left?' Raio asked.

'The British and Americans,' Harry replied. 'They plan to intervene.'

'America is neutral,' Maarja said. 'And Britain is alone and in no position to do anything but defend itself.'

'For now,' Harry replied. 'But it is only a matter of time before America joins in and then they will be on the attack. Until then, we have to keep alive and get this paper to those in the Finnish government who would listen. Even doing that in Finland is hard, the country relies on Germany to supply it with food and arms. There are many Germans working with the Finnish army. Many airmen with the Luftwaffe fly from their airfields. That is why I will not go to the military.'

He started to fold back the papers, resisting Liisbet's attempt at help, until she passed him a candle to allow him to seal the packet. Finally, he lay back exhausted and let her get the paper back to its hiding place. Märt stood and led Maarja's from the room. She looked dazed.

'Now you understand?'

She looked away. 'Can all this be true?'

'You saw how Schulz reacted when we tried to land. They want him dead.'

'I don't know,' she muttered.

Märt gripped her arm once more. 'What is there not to know? Do you still not see? We are stuck between a wolf and a bear and only the lions will come and help us be what we are.'

She snatched back her hand. 'What there is to see is that I may have condemned a man to death for a noble cause. In doing so I have condemned Estonia to oblivion.'

'There is still time to fix this,' Märt replied. 'Go and find Juhan.'

She moved away, then stopped and turned to look back at him, her eyes now flooded with tears.

'Perhaps now I understand how you feel having betrayed someone. How do you live with this?' She stumbled away.

'There is no comparison,' Märt said although he knew she would not hear. 'You do not have to bear the pain of a love lost.'

Toomas came running into the house, as Märt was trying

to rest. He had failed to settle down totally, every slight sound had made his mind whirr into a trigger-like awareness.

'We have had orders. To stand down and return to the Finnish Boys outside Tallinn.'

Märt shook the sleep from his head and croaked a reply.

'Who was it from, Toomas?'

The stocky man shrugged and wiped the fringe of dark hair away from his eyes. 'I don't know. It was sent in Morse.'

'Try and get to speak to one of Colonel Kurg's men.'

'The Colonel is no longer in charge sir. He resigned after Tallinn fell. He was angry the Finnish Boys were not allowed to liberate it.'

Märt winced. 'Tell Raio to come.'

They soon gathered in the kitchen of the farmhouse. Maarja appeared with Juhan also, which did not surprise Märt as he outlined the message.

'I don't trust this communication,' Märt said. 'I cannot refute they may be trying to get us to move so they can catch us and get Harry.'

'What? You think they...' Peeter started but Märt cut him off.

'This is of no surprise.'

Peeter looked to Raio who shrugged. 'The head of the Finnish Boys is German. The only reason we have managed to operate as we have is that he failed to land with us in the first place.'

'But knowing what you know now...'

'Knowing what I know Märt, I would not wish to remain in the unit,' Raio replied his words like slabs of stone falling in the echoing room. 'We have fulfilled our obligation; we have driven Stalin's dogs from the gates. I feel I am free to go.'

'Where would you go?' Peeter asked.

'To the forest,' Raio replied. 'Toomas knows of a good place north of Rakvere. Good hunting there and he knows the farmsteads.

I will take those who feel the same as me. Harry can come also. It is near the coast and when he is recovered...' he trailed off and looked at Liisbet. 'You come also.'

'There are many who would stay,' Märt replied.

'Saaremaa and Hiiumaa are not free. Some dream of being at the gates of the old St Petersburg, as we were in the War of independence. I will take them back to base and then resign.'

He could see Peeter was about to volunteer to join him and raised his hand.

'Go with Raio, Peeter. You are a clever man, but no soldier.'

'I will go with you,' Juhan said quickly. 'Mother, will you go with the men and wait for us?'

'I will go home,' Maarja said tightly. 'Even if my farm is destroyed, I will return to Märjamaa.'

'Then it is settled,' Märt said. 'Let us prepare.'

He followed Maarja as she stormed outside. He called her name, but she would not stop until he caught up with her.

'Maarja, he's a man now. He makes his own decisions.'

She whirled around to face him. The slap ricocheted off his cheek.

'Don't you dare dress this up for what it is not. You have your revenge now. You have taken him from me, like you take everything from me.'

The anger flared within him, though he tried to suppress it.

'Then go wait with Raio.'

'What choice is that? That Englishman is dying. What do you think his little girl will do when that happens; and she starts looking for the reasons why?'

'Then go home and feel sorry for yourself,' Märt yelled in his frustration. He wished he had the words to save the moment, but the wound within her eyes was already too deep.

'I have done nothing to encourage him. He is his own man and has to follow his own path.

Whilst that path is with me, I will protect him. At the cost of my own life if that is what is needed. Peeter and Raio will do the same.'

He felt short of breath and tried to take in more oxygen.

'As for you, if this is your decision, I pray you are safe. If you need me, send word if you can and I will be there.'

She closed her eyes, screwed them shut to hold the pain. The tears still leaked through as she turned to walk away. He knew he had to say the words at that point or never.

'It has never changed, Maarja. What I feel for you.'

Maarja could not turn but her words were clear.

'Once I felt as you do, but for another. That was long ago. Promise you will bring him back to me alive.'

'I promise.' Märt could not stop the tears. It was all that was left.

CHAPTER TWENTY-SIX

Capture

T he Kübelwagen had given up, its radiator hissed steam and hot water dripped to the ground. Märt looked at the street they had stopped in. In better times, it would have been an exclusive area, only for the rich. Now the houses looked empty and abandoned.

'If it was December, the cold would make the radiator unnecessary,' Juhan was saying. 'Now if I had an egg, I could fix this'

'Where would we find eggs in a shattered city?' Märt replied.

'We could try any house that looks as if it may still have food. The egg will cook in the radiator and plug the hole in it. I did this on the farm before. It works for a while.'

'Well this heap of junk won't go without water; unless we have a direct tap supply from a river.'

'I think we are being watched,' Juhan said quietly.

'Where?'

'On the corner of the street. Two German soldiers.'

Märt cursed. 'Well we had better go down and meet them.'

'Maybe they know of eggs,' Juhan said with a grin.

The soldiers had started to walk towards them and as Märt greeted them, he could see both their wariness and lack of Estonian language.

'We are trying to fix our vehicle,' Märt said.

'Why do you drive this?' One of them asked haltingly.

'We are Finnish army, returning from reconnaissance in

the North. This vehicle was given to us.'

The soldier shrugged his ignorance. 'Papers, *bitte*.'

Märt and Juhan provided the ID given to them. The two soldiers looked very thoughtful and muttered together before one said '*Kommen Sie*.'

There was an old police station being used as a base and as they entered, it was intimated that they should hand over their weapons. They were taken to a room and left with a guard outside.

'What happens now?' Juhan asked.

Märt paced the room and looked up at the small window high up the wall. It was barred.

'My guess is they are sending for someone who speaks Estonian. It is as well that we let the rest of the unit go on ahead.'

They waited for the rest of the day, but there were no visitors. Juhan settled to sleep on the floor. Märt sat on a chair by a table and put his head in his hands to think. Soon his head was resting on the table in slumber.

In the morning, they had two visitors; One to bring in bread and coffee, the other to guard him. By the end of the day, they had not seen anybody else and they settled down to get what rest they could.

In the early hours of the morning light, the same two men re-appeared, both now armed. Märt and Juhan were escorted from the room, where a car was waiting with the engine running. They were wedged into the back with a soldier who was happy when he waved his pistol about. His colleague in the front passenger seat faced them with another cocked pistol in hand. Any attempt at conversation was met with animated displeasure. Märt tried to look around for landmarks but received the same response.

The journey carried on for over an hour. Then they arrived

at a clear area surrounded by barbed wire. The camp, such that it was, revolved around two sheds that Märt thought were good only for chickens. A barbed wire fence divided the two and they were steered towards the larger of the two camps. They could see groups of men sitting aimlessly on the ground, whereas on the other side of the divide, the people seemed to be more animated. Märt heard some shouts and catcalls after him and quickly spoke to his nearest captor.

'*Ich bin Estlander.*'

The man's eyes initially bulged with anger, but subsided as the words sank in.

After a quick consultation, they moved towards the gates of the less populated camp, much to the derisive cheers inside. They were admitted and left alone to their own devices.

'That was lucky,' Juhan said. 'I think they nearly put us in with Russians.'

'Did you not hear what people were shouting?' Märt asked. 'Saying if we were Estonian, we'd better tell them? All the insults from the Russian prisoners?'

Juhan smiled. 'No, I close my mind to that kind of shouting.'

'Well sometimes it pays to listen.'

'Why are we here?'

'My guess, Juhan, is our captors have no idea how to talk to us and could not get anyone who spoke Estonian. So, they dumped us in a prison camp. End of their problem.'

'And the start of ours?'

'If we cannot get out, very possibly.'

They found that the food was better at the camp, although not much of it.

'How are you getting on?' Märt asked Juhan after at the end of the day.

'The German guards do not know the language.'

'Ah, and these captives are Estonians in the Red Army,

most forced to fight. They know nothing also. Juhan, I am worried perhaps. If we get stuck here, it may be for the duration of the war or until they tire of us.'

Juhan looked across at the Russian camp. 'It is worse over there. The Germans treat us as men, those bastards get little food and are treated as dogs. I have watched them get beaten for nothing.'

Märt nodded. 'I feel sorry for them, even though it would probably be the same if the roles were reversed.'

'We should keep alert for chances to escape.' Juhan said.

'Agreed.'

'I wonder how the others fared.'

'One day, Juhan. We may get to find out.'

They were kept there for two weeks before a staff car visited the camp. After a long conversation at the gate, the German officers were let in and the men told to line up. Märt was one of a few chosen for interrogation and queued up for his turn. After an hour, he was taken into a small room where an officer waited with a scribe behind a table. Märt gave his name and unit.

'What unit again?' The officer demanded.

'JG 200, Finnish Army,' the officer looked at Märt over his glasses. 'And what are you doing here?'

'I was returning to my unit south of the city when my Kubelwagen broke down. I let my men go on and then was arrested and taken here.'

'What was your crime?'

'Breaking down. And not speaking German.'

'Where is your unit now?'

'I have no idea. There was word of going to the main islands. It could even be St Petersburg for all I know.'

'You should hope that is not so. Do you have papers?'

'They were taken, sir.'

The man nodded slowly and sighed. 'I will check your story and if it is true, you will be released.'

'My driver also, sir,' Märt added. The officer nodded vaguely and Märt was led out. He hoped this was the final breakthrough of luck that they needed.

A month passed and nothing had changed. Märt could only take his frustrations out by walking around the perimeter. All the while, he kept one eye on the weather and prayed that the winter would come late, for fear of freezing to death in the camp. He wondered how the others were faring. He felt relieved that Maarja hadn't named him to her contacts – whoever it was that she had got caught up with.

He cursed her beautiful face. For being so keen to save her country, that she couldn't see what the Germans had done to her. He wished for a time when it was all less complicated with her, only to realise there had never been such a time.

The officer that had interrogated him returned as Märt was about to give up hope. The meeting was in the same small room, with the same person taking notes.

Märt was pushed in before the man even had time to remove his gloves, let alone his coat.

'Some surprising news, I think.' He said. 'It would appear there are two Finnish army soldiers missing from a transit. One was an officer. It was assumed the people had returned to their homes. You are free to rejoin your unit, they are busy on Saaremaa eradicating the Red problem.'

'How do I do this?'

'We will arrange you transport to the local base where you can clean yourselves up. Then you will get another transport. They will arrange this. Here are your papers. *Heil* Hitler!' The officer gave the stiff-arm salute and without waiting for reply strode out of the room. Märt quickly found Juhan leaning against the hut trying to stay warm.

'It is cold, but it is nearly November,' the young man said with a shivering smile. 'At least the lice are dead.'

'Only resting, come with me, we are leaving. Now.'

'So soon?'

'I don't want them to change their minds.'

The makeshift camp was a twenty-minute truck ride away. They managed to successfully get cleaned, heads shaved and fresh clothing and weapons. Their teeth were sore with the effort of chewing fresh, hot food, but their bellies were full.

A young soldier came up to them with new boots, jackets and helmets.

'My apologies for the delay,' he said offering them to Märt.

He looked at the lapels on the uniforms. And the name 'Ostland' on the badge. Märt remembered the plans Harry had shown him. Any tiny shreds of doubt he had was now gone. There was an SS badge also.

'Why the badge?' Juhan asked.

'The Germans think any foreigner who fights for them believes in all they do.' Märt replied.

'So now we are Nazis,' Juhan said with an edge. 'And Ostland is the Germans new land – Estonia and Latvia. Not what we are fighting for?'

Märt resolved to rip the badge off at the earliest opportunity.

'Sir, one of *Oberleutnant* Schulz's unit will be picking you up to take you to the port.'

Märt nodded his thanks and as the man left, he murmured to Juhan.

'Get dressed quickly, we are going. Schulz was the man chasing Harry. The German who screwed up your mother's ideas.'

'Maybe I should stay and have a word with him,' Juhan replied. His normal shining eyes had gone dull, as grey clouds block sunshine.

'Choose your fight, but choose your timing also,' Märt said. 'We will get out of here and then head north to Tallinn and then take the train east to Rakvere.'

There was a lot of activity with incoming trucks. Märt waited patiently in the shadows away from the guards and as a large half-track rolled by, they briskly walked out at its side.

'So, do you think Harry is still alive?' Juhan asked.

'I don't know, we will have to see.'

'I got some medicines, in case.'

'How? No, don't tell me. Why am I even surprised?'

They both began to laugh, although Märt soon quietened, as his thoughts turned to Maarja. Would she be at camp? After their last parting, he hoped so.

Their paperwork seemed to give them a passport to travel. They managed to get on a train to Rakvere.

The guard was Estonian and from his look, knew that they were not giving a full story. With a nod and a crafty wink, he agreed to let them off at a small station before Rakvere and promised to make the driver aware.

'Where now?' Juhan asked as they watched the taillight of the train disappear into the distance.

'North, to the coast. Toomas talked of the land not being far from a manor house up there. I think we are just west of that point now - but will know better when I see the shore-line.'

'I hope they have a change of clothes,' Juhan said. 'I don't want to be a German soldier and I don't want the lice to come back? They may just be hiding.'

'Don't worry Juhan, we are on the edge of winter now. Soon the snows will come and your lice will freeze to death when you leave the clothes outside overnight.'

'I don't think we're going to stay in a sauna lodge, that I can leave my clothes outside,'

The road was a fairly level gravel path. For them, it was much better than the forest ground, which was now sodden with autumn's rains. Their progress was fast and the effort gave little time for conversation. After they had crossed the main road to the east, Märt stopped and allowed them to break into their rations.

'The main road was empty - do you think the Germans are already in Russia?' Juhan asked.

'Narva fell many days before Tallinn, so I expect so,' Märt replied between bites.

'Do you know where this manor house is?'

'Yes, I was here with the *Kaitseliit*. Toomas said their camp would be east of there.'

'Did you go all over Estonia with *Kaitseliit*?'

Märt shook his head. 'Not all.'

Juhan smiled. 'You would know it if Germany keeps to that plan. That's where all the people who weren't Aryan would be sent.'

'That hasn't happened yet.'

'So, looking for this camp is not a needle in a haystack?' Juhan chuckled.

'But we know which haystack to look in.'

He stretched. 'Let's get some rest. I want to reach the coast early tomorrow and then move along from there.'

'Why the coast?'

'If they still plan to get Harry out, they can only do it across the sea.'

They reached the coast by mid-morning. The forest quickly receded into grass covered sandy ground, before a large steep shingle beach led them down to the shoreline. The boulders in the sea looked as large as a house in places. Ahead of them, a small, wooded island lay to the west of the beach.

'Damned Island,' Märt remarked as the shingle moved under their feet, making them slow their progress. 'Yes, that is its name. The causeway to it is dry at low tide. It was once a lookout post, perhaps we should check it up.'

It was soon obvious the causeway was flooded.

'We could wade across that,' Juhan said. 'Tie our boots around our necks.'

There was a shout from the island and a soldier appeared. He wore a grey uniform and shouted to them in German, whilst waving his gun.

'*Estlander! Finnisher truppe!*' Juhan shouted.

The man raised his gun and shouted some more, there was a rustle and a few men appeared to move to him.

'We need to go now!' Juhan said and turned to run. Märt watched as the newcomers produced a machine gun long enough to need a tripod. One produced a box of ammunition and started loading it.

'*Hande hoch!*' The first soldier cried, letting off a warning shot. Märt needed no second invitation and turned to follow Juhan.

He struggled to wade as he strove desperately for firmer ground. Finally, they were back on the grass and headed for the forest. The crack of bullets raking up the shingle behind them gave them more incentive than ever before to keep going. When they were deep enough in the forest, they stopped to catch their breath.

'When did you learn German?' Märt asked.

'I didn't, I just picked up a few key words. One of them is *überläufer*, which the soldier shouted. It is the word for de-serter or turncoat. Also, he was SS, They don't see grey - every-thing is black or white. I suppose there are no Finnish units around here.'

'Juhan,' Märt gasped between breaths. 'I am so glad that

you are here.'

Juhan grinned. 'Where next?'

'Let's go along a bit, there is a village past the manor house. We may pick up some tracks whilst we get there.'

CHAPTER TWENTY-SEVEN

Schulz

Maarja was surprised by the knock at the door. The shock when she tentatively opened it was even greater.

'Herr Schulz. What are you doing here?'

He smiled and moved towards her, forcing her to step back off the threshold, as he quietly closed the door behind him.

'I perhaps should be asking you the same question, Frau Tamm. I last saw you being taken away by the renegades. Yet you have escaped and now stand before me.'

'Yes, I am staying here with an old friend.'

'It seems you have many friends. Your captor, was he not your former husband? And your son? It seems there are many things that you did not tell me. It is good that I have found out about your friends and contacts.'

His words came very softly, but with great menace and she backed towards the front room of the house and tried to smile.

'There was much that you did not need to know. You wanted Harry, I found him for you. Nobody else needed to be hurt.'

She staggered backwards at the blow, the combination of force and surprise made her legs buckle and she fell to the floor. Gently she put her hand to her face and stared at her blood-covered fingers.

'Yes, they found Harry. He was dying and then they were recalled by the Finnish Boys. That's all I know.'

The slap was backhanded, the ring on his finger drawing

a line of pain across her cheek. She staggered back against a table and he grabbed her hair, bringing her screaming with pain, to a stand.

'There is more that you can tell me - and you *will* tell me much more.'

He screamed in pain and dropped her, as his arms went to touch the stab wound at his side. Maarja held the knife firmly in front of her.

'You will need an army to take me, bastard!' She shouted. 'You shouldn't have left your lackeys in the car.'

'I didn't need to bring anyone,' he snarled. 'And I will kill you, then I will find everyone you ever loved, and I will kill them also.'

His hand scrambled to open the flap of his holster and pull out the luger pistol. His eyes now raged with hatred and contempt, as he stared down Maarja's defiance. Then there was a sickening thud and his eyes glazed as they rolled upwards. He crumpled to the ground and lay still.

Maarja stood shaking as she sucked the air back into her lungs. She did not notice the blood on the knife was thick enough to send small droplets onto Schulz' body. Slowly, she stepped forward to check his pulse and then she looked up.

'You killed him, Edvard.'

The old man lowered the heavy candlestick and sighed.

'I had to do it. He would have killed you.'

'I always carry a knife in my boot since the land went feral. I would have killed him.'

'Then I have taken the guilt of murder from you, my child.'

Maarja sighed and then looked up in fear. 'Were there others?'

'I saw him arrive he was alone.'

'When it is darker, I will get his vehicle and bring it closer to the house. Then I will dump his body in the forest.'

Edvard nodded and stared with dismay at the bloodstained rug. 'Yes, the wolves will feed on him. Where will you go now?'

Maarja closed her eyes and her lips trembled. 'I will go home.'

'Why not go back to those who need you?'

For a while she could not speak, the emotion was too great, then she whispered.

'I betrayed them.'

'You redeemed yourself today, my child.'

'It is not enough.'

'Those who love you are there.'

'I cannot... too much has passed. I cannot look at Märt, without seeing my beloved Huw. I cannot look at Juhan now, after this.'

'You cannot live in the past, Maarja.'

She swallowed hard and wiped the tears from her face.

'I cannot live in the present.'

Edvard nodded sadly. 'So it seems, but there is the future. It can change.'

'Come, let us wrap up Schulz in this rug and get him ready.'

Later, when it was nearly dark and the village was silent and still, she got into the car and brought it closer to the house. She glanced at the house opposite and once again saw the face in the window. It looked back with a half smile, which Maarja hoped was satisfaction, then it disappeared.

CHAPTER TWENTY-EIGHT

Metsavennad

P eeter tossed the stone forward over his head and down towards the waiting man, who hit it away with a club.

'Like this?'

The man lying on the floor behind him nodded.

'Yes, and if it gets caught without hitting the ground or hits the sticks behind him, he is out.'

'A strange game,' Peeter muttered.

'Strange indeed,' came a voice from the tree above him. Märt jumped down to face them. 'Strange that you spend more time playing games than defending the camp. I would have killed you all by now and with Juhan in cover also.'

He nodded to his left and Juhan stood up and waved from a small ridge.

'You should show them your gun, Juhan.'

Juhan shrugged with open hands. 'If I could, but Raio has my weapon.'

The burly sergeant stood up holding two guns. 'A good point made, but we are not totally without guile.'

Then he laughed and Märt was mobbed by his friends.

'Alright everyone, back as you were,' Raio called. 'And Märt is right, be sharper.'

Peeter moved away, leaving Raio to sit with Märt and Harry. Märt found a stick and began to whittle it with his knife as he looked around.

'It is a good setting you have here, Raio. The problem is that it is too easy to find. People walking through the forest are too clumsy and the guards aren't sharp. We walked past one who was happily asleep. You need some early warning snares and sharper guards. How are you, Harry?'

'I have my moments, Märt. I have not much energy still, but...'

'But you are still here, which says that you either have not been sent a boat, or you are too sick to travel. Or they do not wish to see you.'

'Still straight to the point, I see.'

'There is no other point,' Märt said bluntly. 'If you went in a boat at this time of year, the wet from the spray and the wind would kill you off before you were in sight of Helsinki. Yet, if you are still this ill after two months, then I think we need to get you to Finland soon.'

'How will we do this?' Raio asked.

'Sledge.'

Raio gasped. 'Are you mad? You will have to wait until mid December at the earliest. It will be minus twenty or thirty – without the wind chilling you. And this is better than a boat?'

'We can get Harry wrapped up on the sledge like a parcel, that will shelter him from the frozen wind.'

'You will need three, maybe four people and what if the sea does not freeze all the way?'

'We turn back if we have to do so.'

'Why not wait here anyway?' Raio asked.

'Raio,' Harry whispered. 'Märt is right. I need to get the proof of this German plan across as soon as I can and... Well, let's be honest, I am not getting any better. If a boat comes in the next few weeks, I will take it. If not, we will have to try Märt's plan. I won't last the winter in the forest.'

'Who will go?' Raio asked. 'I have skill with skis.'

'You have built this camp and the men trust your leadership,' Märt said. 'I will go and take Juhan with me.'

'I will come also,' Liisbet's voice sounded out and she

came out of a dugout to join them. 'You will not take him from me. I am fit. I have experience of skiing. You will not take him away from me.'

'Then that is settled. We need to get a sledge, clothing, skis, goggles and a compass. I know it sounds a lot, but if we look around and ask the farms perhaps we will get it all. Juhan acquired some medicine, from our last German base. I hope it helps you, Harry.'

'I hope it does too. Make sure he doesn't poison me.'

Märt urged Raio to walk away and carried on the conversation in lower tones.

'How goes it here?'

'It is fine,' Raio replied. 'We are not disturbed by Germans. There is good hunting and the farms around help us and we help them. Peeter was good in that.'

Märt nodded and Raio took a deep breath. 'I want you to head this camp. All the men served under you and it will look bad otherwise.'

'Okay, while I am here, but we do need some changes. I chanced on some Germans at Damned Island and they are billeted in the manor houses, like Sagadi nearby.'

'I know, but they leave us alone.'

They stood in silence, watching those in the camp who had returned to their game. Then Raio shuffled his feet uncomfortable on what he had to say.

'Your woman, will she tell the spy hunter?'

'I don't think so. She has a new mind after reading Harry's papers.'

'It is as well she did not come here. There are a few who see her as traitor.'

'I do not,' Märt replied firmly. 'And I will happily fight anyone who wishes to dispute that.'

There was a cry from ahead. Peeter was looking across and beckoning.

'We will talk more later,' Raio said. 'But for now, re-acquaint yourself with your men. They want to teach you a game called cricket.'

*****

An owl hoot sounded in the night. For a long while, the echo hung eerily in the forest and then it sounded again. There was a faint hoot further out, almost lost to the rustle of branches in the buffeting wind.

Märt gave a long sigh of relief, before sticking two fingers in his mouth and giving three short whistles. He waited and eventually the owl hoot returned.

'That's good, I think,' he muttered.

'Either that or there is a horny owl out there,' Raio muttered. 'We cannot do this too often. It exposes us to our guests and night drops are very problematic at best. We learnt that when we landed with the Finnish Boys.'

'It steers any patrols towards us and gives us unwanted attention,' Märt replied. 'I understand this, but there was some things that needed getting from outside.'

'Well, at least we have tightened up security now, Märt. If anyone came over, we would shoot them before they got within sight of our shelters.'

'You disguised the place well. It blends in, as if part of the land.'

'Ah, but the rat-run out the back of the camp, that was a great idea. Listen!'

Raio stopped as a branch could be heard swishing close by. It was too loud and firm for simple wind movement. Märt crouched down and brought his pistol up ready to bear.

A scrabbling sound came from in front of them and heart in mouth, Märt gently rested his pistol flat on his thigh and gave an owl hoot.

The return hoot was close. Märt relaxed and put the safety catch back on his pistol, although he still held it. Vague shadows turned into the fuzzy forms of men in the dim light of the night. Then they nearly fell over him in their haste.

'You found it?' Märt asked.

'That is why we sound like elephants,' Toomas replied. 'It is so heavy.'

'I feared it had dropped onto Sagadi manor house,' Märt replied.

'It had, or as close as. In the grounds and snagged high up a tree. That was fun, retrieving it.'

'What of the parachute?'

'I took that also,' Juhan chipped in. 'Now Liisbet can make herself some nice undergarments.'

They moved quickly back to the camp, to find Peeter on the floor of one of the shelters with the contents of other canisters on the floor.

'You have done well, Märt. Four winter suits. Four pairs of goggles. Two compasses. Gloves, socks and hats. What's in the new one?'

Juhan clicked open the canister and reeled off a list as he prodded around.

'Ski poles, small skis, charts, pistols, very pistol.'

Peeter went across. 'The skis are halved, you fit them together at the boot. The very pistol fires flares.' He sent a withering look at Juhan.

'Okay,' Juhan replied with a grin.

'You and me,' Peeter replied. 'I don't think we will last two months. There's medicine also, I think, I am hoping it will help Harry's fever. He's drifted in and out of it this last week. Is this enough for us to go, do you think, Raio?'

'With all this now, yes. But is the ice safe? I don't know.'

'The Finns have not said otherwise. Look, we cannot wait any longer. Harry needs to go now or we'll be digging him a grave. He could get hospital treatment in Finland, it might save him. We have to go now.'

'Then go,' Raio said with a shrug. 'The sledge is ready. I have made a harness for each of you. They link to the sledge by a metal loop attached to one thick rope. You will be huskies.'

'Peeter, what do you think?'

'That you should go, before I kill Juhan. I'm joking, Märt, it's just sometimes...'

'*Ja, ja*,' came the reply.

The outer door opened and shut, then the inner flap to catch the light of the bunker, swept across and Liisbet appeared.

'Märt. Harry is awake. He needs to talk.'

'Can it not wait until morning?' Raio asked.

'It's fine,' Märt replied. 'We must talk when we can. Prepare yourself, Liisbet. We will go tomorrow evening.'

Harry looked pale and grey. Liisbet went to his side to clutch his hand and mop his clammy brow. He tried to raise a smile for Märt, but it was now no more than a tremble on his lips. His voice was now no more than a whisper.

'Märt. Perhaps it isn't going so well.'

'Stay rested Harry, we go tomorrow night.'

'Liisbet told me, but why the night?'

'We will be unseen.'

'We will be unable to see unless the sky is clear. What will the weather be like?'

'I don't know.'

'Then I think you are inviting trouble, Märt. What if it is a cloudy night? They are quite common this time of year. What if there is a blizzard? You won't see it coming.'

'We will do our best.'

Harry sighed and his head fell back.

'How will you know where to go?'

'The compass.'

'And you read it by how?'

'The dials are luminous.'

Harry became agitated and he muttered something inaudible before continuing.

'Märt, you are a good leader, but you do not have all the answers. Let me suggest something. Leave at first light, camp at nightfall. Don't make it more difficult than you wish.

I have spoken to men who have done this trek, they say the ice is treacherous, especially in the middle. You need to know where the danger spots are.'

Märt tapped his teeth in annoyance.

'What if we are seen leaving?'

'Make a diversion? The further away, the less chance of them catching. What will they do? Send a plane to find you? It's a lot of area to look for 3 people dressed in white with a sledge.'

'They could alert the Finns.'

'Yes and when they find you, this is what you tell them...'

CHAPTER TWENTY-NINE

Crossing the Baltic

Märt postponed the trip on the next morning. He was loathe to do this for fear of Harry's fitness, but he wanted to be sure everyone was fully rested and fit for the task. They dressed in their white winter gear, boots and goggles. Then they placed Harry on the sledge and secured him to it. He did not look in pain, but when asked about his health, just smiled and gave a casual nod to Juhan. The small sandy beach was now covered in snow and they moved onto it quite easily. Raio soon arrived to join them.

'The boys have searched around and there is no German for miles. They do not patrol the sea when it is frozen.'

'Thanks,' Märt replied. 'Keep them all safe whilst we are gone.'

'I will and you do the same. Do you have everything you need?'

'You're not my mother, Raio.'

The sergeant chuckled. 'I suggest you take the middle harness. The other two are younger and faster.'

'So if I am too slow, the sledge goes up my arse and I can take a ride on it?'

'God speed and good hunting my friend.'

Märt reached out to clasp the other's arm. 'I hope we meet again. You have been a great friend.'

They set off slowly, Raio and Toomas pushing the sledge out to help them start to get a rhythm. Then with a clunk and a shudder, they were on the ice. At first the going was very slippery. The ice was solid and the poles had difficulty in finding purchase. They slowed down to stop the sledge moving from side to side. The snow began to thicken, but the ground underfoot was now smoother and they were making faster progress. He wondered if it could last like this for the whole seventy kilometres.

The wind blew harshly in their faces. Märt knew that he would have been blind without the goggles. Any exposed flesh was numbed like a block of ice and needed to be covered straight away. Harry looked almost mummified by the way they had wrapped him up. Only his goggles gave any hint that there was a human on the sledge at all.

Märt felt as if a load had been taken off his shoulders. They were finally doing something positive. Something he was convinced that would help his country to survive. As he settled into the rhythm of each ski, his mind reflected on what had happened in the last six months.

Once he was a poor bakers boy, socially awkward and shy. Then he found friendship. Then he found love – deep, honest, true love. One by one, they were all lost to him and he had to begin again.

He had toughened up in *Kaitseliit*, from the callow youth of old. He had forged his path at the bakery in Rapla. Then the Reds had taken it away overnight and the past six months had been enough for a lifetime.

He looked across to Juhan, confidently skiing by his side. The young man looked back and Märt knew that underneath the swathe of cladding, he would be grinning.

Märt decided to leave it until as late as possible before they stopped for food. The wind was blowing a bit harder and they tried to use the sledge as shelter, whilst the loose snow swirled around them. As they continued, the snow in the air formed mesmerising patterns of distraction around them. Märt stumbled for a moment, as the ice protruded from the snow. He realised the ice was now different, more undulating and no longer smooth. Certainly not linear, more like a wave. The compass still showed he was pointing north. He prayed to God it wasn't a lie.

He could dimly make out a shape on the horizon, or at least the line between the sea and the sky was no longer straight. Staring at it, he felt almost snow-blind, but he couldn't help feeling that ahead, the ice was jagged.

They had not even gone halfway, there was no way it could be land. Perhaps a ship stuck in the ice? The short burst of daylight was now giving way to an ever-encompassing gloom and Märt had to strain to see what the feature was.

After half an hour, he knew and called them to a halt. The words he feared to say now came from him to the others.

'We should make camp. I think we need to rest and eat and the light is fading quickly. We will need our strength and our wits tomorrow, especially at the start.'

'Why is this?' Juhan said

'Those ridges ahead? It's ice. A jumble of blocks that we will need to manhandle the sledge over.'

'Why is it like that?' Liisbet asked.

'A ship has been through and churned up the ice,' Juhan replied.

'It is difficult to say if it is recent or not,' Märt said. 'Only by daylight will we see if this is old, if the ice has refrozen or if it was ever frozen at all.'

'Maybe we should pitch in the shelter of those blocks?' Juhan said.

'We should do it here,' Märt said. 'We don't know how thick the ice is or anything. Can't you feel the way the ice moves slightly, even here? I say, I would prefer to see my hazards in daylight.'

'Well, I for one need the rest,' Juhan said.

They pitched the tent quickly and Harry was lifted off the

sledge and inside.

'How are we doing?' he whispered to Märt

'I'd like to think we are halfway. We certainly hit one of the shipping channels. How long ago it was last used is difficult to say, so we will explore it at first light.'

'Wind is picking up,' Juhan said. 'I will have food ready soon. Toomas made some Forest Brothers sausage.'

'Hopefully, the paraffin cooker will heat the tent also,' Märt said. 'Are you well, Liisbet?'

Her face was ashen, but she gave a tight smile and nod in reply.

'Exhausted, but I will be ready for morning.'

'I know you will, Liisbet. Let's eat and sleep. The wind may die overnight and with luck, we will be in Finland tomorrow.'

Märt woke as the wind howled its complaint of their presence. The central tent pole rattled in the assault. The howling was all encompassing, but he could see that Juhan was talking to Harry. Märt could not hear the words and was too tired to care. He drifted back to sleep.

In the morning, they found that the snow had piled up against the tent. They ate quickly and packed up for the hazard ahead.

'There will be enough for two meals left,' Märt said. 'After that, we have to get to Finland.'

'Or we cut a hole in the ice and fish,' Juhan said. 'There will be plenty under there.'

'How many fishing parties have you seen?' Harry's muffled voice came from the sledge.

Märt began to hook up to his harness. Liisbet still looked weary, as she struggled with hers. Märt came to help and offer words of comfort.

'We are all tired, but we will all complete this journey. The new snow will give us more leverage for our ski poles.'

'The ice is thinner here,' Juhan said.

'Why do you say this?' Märt replied.

'Because the ice is not just moving, it is springy to the step. It's like being on a boat.'

Märt stopped and tested the ice below him.

'You are right, we must move.'

They made for the nearest block and scaled up to the top to look at what they faced. The ridges of ice were erratically placed slabs that formed a barrier to direct movement across. The blocks lay on the surface in a haphazard way. The different angles of the faces they would have to scale. The crossing would be like scaling a mountain range to them.

'We're going to have to go over many of these blocks, what do you think?' Märt said and Juhan sighed.

'There is about a hundred metres of this before you get past and there looks like a smaller field further on also. I can't see an easy path through.'

'No? The easy path would probably be one of thinner ice anyway, how about you, Liisbet?'

'I can see water. There and there. Grey circles. We will have to go carefully.'

Juhan shielded his eyes and looked further down.

'It looks better further down. There may be a path through some of this.'

They moved down to where a gap gave the impression of a mountain pass. It gave them some distance, but quite soon they had to remove their skis and wade through the snow. The hauling of the sledge across the blocks was bumpy and on more than one occasion, Harry cried out in pain. After an hour they were exhausted and had only a few tens of metres to show for their trouble.

'We can go around this one,' Juhan shouted. 'A few more and then we are halfway.'

They came across a murky pool that they steered far away from. The dark liquid had an air of menace. Märt tried not to think about the consequences of straying into such thin ice, as he looked for a way through the solid boulder field.

The next blocks seemed to form a ridge and there wasn't a way through that was wide enough for a sledge. One of the blocks was not too high and had a slope like a ski jump. They moved towards this, pulling the sledge behind them. Märt was worried about the weather front ahead. The horizon was blurring and the grey clouds darkening. The slight snow was swept up in a stiffening breeze to dance around them like fireflies. They were already panting with the exertion and Märt knew they would need another night's rest on the ice. He started to plan the rationing of their food.

There was a sharp cracking sound. Liisbet screamed as the ropes tensed and they were pulled backwards.

'Harry! The sledge is sinking!'

Reality hit Märt and he grabbed the rope to pull with all his strength. The back of the sledge was slightly lower than the surface level and the area around it appeared dark and rippling. The sledge appeared stuck at the base of the block

'Liisbet! Get Harry off the sledge!'

Liisbet let go of the rope and it slipped further into the pool. Harry's ankles were now in water. Liisbet quickly grabbed the rope again and started to pull. The sledge lurched forward only to stick again.

'We'll have to pull it clear,' Juhan said, trying desperately to dig his feet into the slippery ice block. There was a louder sound of the ice breaking and the whole sledge began to dip into the water.

Harry looked around him quickly as the sledge began to settle and the dark waters neared him. He uncovered his face and gave his friends a strange sad smile.

'Liisbet,' was all he said. Märt looked on in horror, as he saw the glint of a knife in Harry's hand, as he brought it up and started to saw at the harness rope.

'No!' Märt screamed, but Harry's eyes were now closed.

Then the world turned upside down as the tension on the rope broke, sending the three backwards and over the edge of the boulder to the ice below.

'NO, NO, NO, NO, NO, NO!'

Liisbet's shout crescendoed as Märt scrambled back to look over the block of ice. Where Harry had been, a grey pool had appeared, with small pieces of ice floating on it. The sledge had disappeared. Märt pulled himself over the block and lay on the ice panting. The dream had ended. He could hear Liisbet screaming for Juhan to let her go. Nothing needed to be said. He looked around the horizon for anything in the vast grey wilderness that would explain it all. The wind blew snow in his face, all around them the ice stood like statues. What hell had he brought them into?

They had sat there for what seemed like an hour and Märt began to shiver in the wind. With great reluctance he stood up and went to the other two. Juhan and Liisbet were still in each others arms, although Liisbet seemed focused on the ice and oblivious to all around her.

'We should start back for camp,' Märt said. Juhan looked up in surprise.

'Back? Why?'

'What is there left?' the bitter taste ran through Märt's mouth. ''The documents are lost, they went with...' He could not finish the sentence.

Juhan gave a strange smile and patted his breast pocket. 'The documents are safe. Harry gave them to me last night. I think he knew his wound would kill him.'

For a brief moment, Märt covered his eyes and his jaw trembled. Then he wiped the moisture away and the hunter's look was back in his eyes.

'Then we carry on and we reach Finland by dark today. I

will give them these documents and I will make them listen and believe if I have to ram them down their throats. It's the least I can do.'

'Well, we can lose the harnesses,' Juhan said but Märt shook his head.

'Look at the sky, there is a snowfall coming. Looks a bad one and visibility may be bad. Keep linked, I don't want to lose anybody.'

Juhan looked at Liisbet, who still looked grey and distant.

'Maybe Liisbet should be in the middle of us. Liisbet?'

The answer was a shrug of disinterest.

'We must see this through,' Juhan said.

Her eyes flared with a mixture of hurt and anger, but the emotion waned as she locked gazes with Juhan. The compassion in his face made her look away biting her lip, she gave a curt nod.

The second line of ice blocks proved to be less of a problem. It was a combination of being older and having a deeper covering of snow to iron out the undulations.

That and the loss of the sledge, Märt thought miserably, though he desperately tried not to bring up the still raw memories. Yet again he checked the horizon.

'Let's get going. That snow is coming in. No tent or spare food, it went down with Har... so we have to make land.'

He pushed the pace as soon as he saw the first snowflakes begin to fall. The grey clouds ahead felt like a funnel, sucking away the light. Was that land on the horizon? Märt was no longer sure if his mind was not playing tricks. He moved his hat down to cover the nagging pain above his nose. Head down, he hoped his bearing were still good, as he focused on moving one leg in front of another.

CHAPTER THIRTY

Endings

'M oi moi!'
There were a few calls before Märt recognised the words of welcome in Finnish. In the distance, he could see the fuzzy outline of a figure and a sledge.

Märt steered towards him and looked to shout to the others. His dry throat failed him, but a tug on the rope was enough for them to follow.

'Are you fishing?' Märt asked.

'You are Estonian,' the man replied. 'I have heard your language before.'

'Yes, we have come across to Finland on an urgent matter.'

'You have no provisions or tent?'

'We lost them to the sea,' Märt said, not wishing to speak any more on the matter.

'You had better come with me. That storm will swallow us up. Soon we won't be able to see in front of our faces or know left from right.'

'I would be very thankful for the help. We are tired.'

They followed the fisherman for a while before he slowed down.

'Your woman has weakened. She is not able to keep up.'

'She is not weak,' Juhan replied. 'She lost her man in the ice on the way.'

Märt could hear the edge in his words.

'Can we put her on the sledge and then harness up and the three of us pull?'

The man looked at the sledge then Liisbet, then he finally

nodded. Juhan quickly put Liisbet on the sledge and then they moved off. The man was right about the weather, Märt thought. The clouds were becoming almost black with menace.

'We keep going,' the Finn said. 'Thirty minutes or not much more. We get to shore and then I take you to shelter.'

By the time they had reached land, the weather had closed in and the grey torrent of snow had made it difficult for Märt to make out Juhan on the other side of the sledge.

'Here! Here,' the fisherman shouted and set off at an angle. 'Not far.'

Märt looked below his skis and saw the branches of a bush protruding from the snow. He mouthed a prayer of thanks and followed. There was a small boathouse about a kilometre away and they manhandled the sledge up and into it.

There was a room at the back and the fisherman began to place wood in the hearth of a chimney. Juhan joined him and he grunted his thanks.

'Keep stacking boy and I will go out and open the chimney. We will have to stay here until morning, but at least we are warm and there is fish also.'

Märt drew Liisbet towards the fire. She still looked dazed, but slowly her eyes moved to look at him.

'Märt? Where are we?'

'Finland, Liisbet. We made it.'

'He's gone, hasn't he?'

With a nod, he sat her down and put his arm around her.

'Yes, but in the end he sacrificed himself to save us.'

She did not say any more but moved closer to Märt. They ate roasted pike fish and drank warm water from melted snow. Märt hadn't realised how hungry he was and the increase in rations and warmth made him drowsy.

'So, why are you escaping Estonia?' The fisherman asked.

'I need to get to some people. Here, I have a list.' Märt

handed a paper over. The first is government, the second part of JG200 unit – the Finnish Boys, the third is a Navy man. You know nothing about us and I am sure you have suspicions that we may be spies. These men would prove that we are not.'

'Are you Red spies?' The man asked.

'No. I spent a lot of the summer running from them.'

'To be honest, the fisherman replied. 'I don't care, as long as I am able to fish. I will go to the nearest military post to-morrow and they can help you. Until then, make use of what you can find to keep warm.

There are chairs and boxes to keep you off the floor. Leave other problems until tomorrow.'

'Thank you,' Märt said. The fisherman waved his hand in dismissal.

'Tomorrow.'

Märt slept late, as if the temporary haven had given them the first security for months. He woke to the sound of a vehicle approaching and wrapped up to go outside to see what was happening.

The fisherman had disappeared. He noticed the storm had passed also and the sky was clear. The sun shone on the white land, making the snow crisp underfoot. The approaching ve-hicle was the only thing that broke the silence of a world frozen to a standstill.

There was a commotion with the lorry pulling up and soldiers jumping out of the back. From their appearance and age, Märt had them down for home guard. He acknowledged the officer with a '*Tere*'. The man nodded and indicated to the truck.

'You are to come with us.'

'That is fine,' Märt said. 'But do you have blankets? One of my party is in shock.'

The officer turned and shouted orders to the soldiers. Two men rushed inside and carried Liisbet out. Juhan followed them to the truck. When all were on board, the truck moved off slowly back up the track.

Märt reflected on the thought that he had not managed to thank the fisherman. Neither did he know the man's name.

They were taken to an army base and left in a room where a small fire warmed the room as welcome. Someone had thoughtfully placed chairs by the fire and a table had a plate of meats with bread, water and schnapps.

'My God, what do they do for the people they know are friends,' Märt said. Juhan just laughed and set to making up for lost time with his stomach. He approached Liisbet with a plate of food.

'Come on, you need to eat.'

'I'm not hungry.' Liisbet's voice was still dull and soulless.

'Please.'

She screwed her eyes shut, before nodding. 'Juhan, I will share with you.'

'In that case, I will get more.'

After about an hour, the door opened and a bearded man walked in followed by the officer.

'There is no problem, I know this man,' the bearded man said. 'He saved my life.'

Relief flooded through Märt. 'Good to see you again, Sven. How goes it'

'Where is Harry?' Sven said. There was no response and Sven grunted.

'It is a long drive to Helsinki. There is time to talk then.'

The streets of Helsinki were in stark contrast to the ruins of Tallinn. The city still held its charm and bustle. People still moved about their business in a direct manner. The trams still ran, even though in some places there were signs of temporary repair. Märt had never travelled on a tram, so the opportunity was one of interest for him. He sat on the cramped benches of the dimly lit lower deck. The smell of electricity and damp was mixed with that of the passengers. One or two of their coats smelt of the damp. The day was wet, all of the winter had been wet or white, but the plants knew their time was coming. On many of the trees, buds of anticipation stood ready to launch a new bloom. They spoke of the new life therein, Märt couldn't help wishing it was an analogy for Estonia.

Märt found the park and walked down the road. Snow still lined either side, covering the benches, icing the tops of the low hedges and decorating the lamp posts.

There were a few visitors to this haven, surrounded by the bustle of city life. They moved rapidly in deference to the peace. Ahead lay a statue of a man clutching the tunic of his breast.

On this day his head was decorated with snow, but below stood Liisbet, dressed in a long coat and wearing a muffler. She saw him and moved very quickly to hug him, making him wish that the moment would linger somehow.

'That was so un-Estonian,' he said, his awkwardness returning.

'I am just pleased to see you. Where is Juhan?'

'Back at the barracks. They are training us and I was the only one who got a pass, being the officer. I was lucky, it has been a busy time.'

'Well it is good to see you. Can we walk? I am cold.'

She linked arms and they set off on a slow walk. Nearby a group of children had begun a snow fight, amidst squeals of delight and dismay.

'It is good to hear laughter,' Liisbet said. 'I have missed it for so long.'

'Liisbet, we are going back to the forest camp in Estonia. I can't just leave them.'

She nodded and looked across at the children.

'You wish I was Harry instead,' Märt said and she sighed and nodded.

'I don't mean it badly, but I still miss him. I always will. He was a kind man and loyal. As you are.'

'Does the camp look after you?'

'Yes, they have given me help and shelter. There are a lot of good Estonians there and we are allowed to find work.'

'What will you do?'

'I will stay here, if they will let me. They treat us well, for now. I couldn't go back, Märt. For one thing, I would find it hard not to kill your woman.'

'She is not my woman, Liisbet. I did a terrible thing to her a long time ago and it can never be the same.'

She pursed her lips and seemed to be watching the steam of her breath before she said.

'Perhaps the greatest forgiveness has to be to yourself first. There is always time for redemption, if you are ready to give yourself to it.'

They carried on walking and moved out to the long street that paralleled the park, passing the small shops with their yellowing electric lights, displaying their wares. She sighed.

'Was it worth it?'

The change of question threw Märt for a while, before he sighed.

'I think so. The Finns know of the German plans and that means they are cautious.'

'What will they do?'

'What can they do? Try and keep talking secretly to the Western Allies to get a chance of digging them out of this mess. Maybe they could help the Finns and persuade Stalin to do away with his ambitions to take over this land. For now, I am sure they will do nothing, but keep one eye on the horizon and wait for a fair wind.'

'Was it worth a man's life?'

He could see that she still lived the pain and he stopped and gently took her arms.

'Harry believed this was a cause worth fighting for, enough to sacrifice his life for it. He would have thought it was worth it.'

She hugged him again and this time the awkwardness vanished from him.

'Märt, I wish you could stay.'

'As do I, Liisbet, but we can have this afternoon together and hope. Perhaps one day fate will allow us more.'

Maarja walked the remaining kilometres from Märjamaa without any incident. There was nobody on the road; neither civilian nor military. The fields looked deserted, the houses without life. A couple of storks grazing in the grass would have made her feel more at home, but even they had migrated away for the winter. Each step seemed to build up her tension as she got closer and closer to home.

There were plenty of opportunities to move elsewhere and start afresh, but her mind was made up. She had to go back. She had to be part of the farm once more. She had to see the land worked and owed it to others to keep the farm going.

Maarja knew she could not do it all alone, but at least there would be a smaller part that she could begin with and then in time, hire labour to till the land. There would be enough for her to keep busy and stop her dwelling on the past.

The path slipped off from the road and became a gateway through a small stretch of forest. That hadn't changed and Maarja welcomed the shelter. All she wanted now was to disappear from the world.

For a moment, doubt gripped her. How could she survive on her own? It had been scary when Riki had tried to rape her, but she had survived and would again. The revolver she had taken from Schulz had a small supply of bullets. She would just have to make each one count.

The farm was closer now. Maarja could see that the door was not shut, otherwise it looked as it had been left, what seemed like a lifetime ago. It was almost like a clockwork toy, just waiting to be wound up and spring into action. She looked at the house entrance and made a mental note to clear the weeds from the summer away. They were long dead, but the brown strands made a displeasing image in her mind. She wondered how the fruit bushes had fared.

Until spring began, Maarja knew she would need to go hunting and fishing, as her uncle had taught her. It would be the supplement of food that would keep her alive. The cellar may have been raided. The store of grain looked surprisingly intact and locked. Yes, there was a chance that it would be all possible.

With hope restored in her heart, Maarja stepped into the farmhouse and looked around. There was some broken crockery on the floor, but she noted at least one plate was whole. It would be a start. Just a general tidy and clean, that's all it needed and it would be home once more.

Then a whirl of memories flashed through her mind. Of her uncle and aunt, her two great loves and Juhan.

All happy memories from times past, all now gone from her. She looked around the dark and cold house, suddenly it felt so empty.

Her legs collapsed and she fell to her knees, bursting into

tears. Maarja wept uncontrollably for what had been in the past and could never be recovered.

CHAPTER THIRTY-ONE

Return to the forest?

T he boat sped into the small bay. The light of the moon allowing the man at the tiller to expertly weave his way through the boulders that pockmarked the shallows. He bumped the prow against the shore. It allowed a young man to jump out and stagger back to hold the boat in place, using his body weight and that of his pack as counterbalance.

The other passenger turned to the boatman and held out his hand.

'Again, I am in your debt, Sven.'

'No, Märt. You saved my life and besides, I have begun to like you. we will meet again.'

'This war is unpredictable, so anything is possible.'

'Märt, I cannot hold this for ever,' Juhan said.

Märt jumped off with his pack and Juhan let go. Sven immediately turned the boat round and set off back to the empty sea. Märt and Juhan made for the forest edge and then sat waiting as the noise of the boat receded into the night. Nothing was present in its place, just a hollow silence.

'It seems there is no welcome, Märt.'

'That's fine, I didn't expect one. Let's go. I am at least happy to be on Estonian soil once again.'

'Yes, it feels good.'

They moved back up a sandy track and found a gravel road.

'It has seen a few lorries in the past few months,' Juhan said.

Märt did not reply, as he looked around for landmarks.

Then he found a small boulder by the roadside and pointed to it. They made for the track behind and back onto the forest floor.

'Here we stop talking,' Märt said. 'Signs only.'

They reached an overgrown area, around a clump of boulders. Märt signalled they should crouch and he began to approach moving from tree to tree as cover. He flattened himself down on the ground when he thought he saw a moving shadow ahead of him. Märt could see a fallen tree trunk and crawled to it to get a better view. There was a click of a rifle bolt being loaded and Märt froze to the spot, not daring to move.

'Just move very slowly to stand, friend,' a voice said in a harsh whisper. 'And keep your hands where I can see them. No nonsense now.'

'You are getting better, Toomas,' Märt said as he rose. 'It is probably why you are still alive.'

'Märt? You are back?'

'Yes and did you not notice Juhan behind you?'

'Oh, Peeter has him covered. Come let's go to camp, you can tell us all what happened.'

'I hope you have vodka,' Märt replied. 'It's a long tale.'

CHAPTER THIRTY-TWO

Why Me?

T wo years had passed and to Märt it was a lifetime. He wondered how they had all survived in the forest. He knew it was because everyone with him were good men – good, true and resourceful. He had yet to lose a man, even if Peeter was still in danger of murdering Juhan. Märt smiled at the mere thought of it. Juhan's easy-going innocent nature really riled the big farmer. At least Märt knew Juhan now and was aware that beneath the simplistic nature was a far more complex and intelligent mind.

Having warned Finland, Märt had not been surprised when they made their peace. Germany had suffered from the drain of resources and bases and now they were on the verge of being pushed out of the Baltic. It was a frightening time for Estonians. Märt knew the old enemy who would return in their place. He could never forget what they had done before. The memories of Kautla still burned in his mind and he knew he would never be safe from now on.

Had he done the right thing all those years ago? Märt hoped so.

It had turned him into a contact for the West. Now that the Finns were sympathetic to the Allies and not the Axis, he had been happy to help them and report back what he could find out.

Even though he had been doing it for a while, this latest request had been a surprise.

Why Me?

Märt rested high up in a tree and looked out across the

Baltic night. The sea breeze blew in his face, making it uncomfortable to look. Through binoculars, he had made out the dark silhouette of the submarine and further scrutiny found a small kayak paddling to shore.

They were too close to the German gun emplacement and Märt hoped the man would paddle away from Damned Island. He wondered what the hell they were doing dropping him off there. He would need to keep alert.

Would the man be Estonian or Finnish? Maybe a Brit, like Harry. Märt smiled at the thought of the man and the whole adventure came back to him. He hadn't thought of Maarja for a while and the pain returned like a war wound.

No, it was a waste of time lying to himself. Not a day went past without him thinking of her and the highs and lows of that relationship. Maybe one day things would change and he could make amends. Maybe it could start now.

The gun emplacement was now being fired on by the submarine, Märt cursed at the obvious lack of planning.

The kayak was paddling too close and he would have a job getting the man to shore and away from under the noses of the occupiers. He watched the man make for the boulders. There was a feeling of familiarity about his movements, which made Märt smile.

Some of the Germans had begun to run along the shore and then they were past, the man had found a large boulder and appeared to be clinging to it. The swell of the wave meant that he would not be able to do it for too long.

Waiting for the beach to settle once again into silence, Märt quickly descended and ran down lightly to sit on the shore and look out to the boulders. The irony was not lost on him.

'Perhaps you should think about coming ashore?' he said.

GLOSSARY (WITH ENGLISH LANGUAGE PHONETICS WHERE APPLICABLE)

Ardu – (Ardoo) A Central estonian village

Aufstehen – (Owf-shtay-hen) German for stand up

Eestirand – (Eh-stee rand) The largest fishing trawler in the Baltic Sea. Captured by the Soviet forces and used as a troop-ship for Estonian conscripts.

Ema – (Emma) mother

Erna – The name for the JG200 Finnish Army unit, otherwise called the Finnish Boys

F ü hrer – German word meaning leader. Sadly, forever sullied by the association with Hitler.

Günter – (Goonter) German man's name

Hiiumaa – (Hee-you-maa) Large island west of the mainland

Homikust – (Hommikoost) Morning

Isa – (Eessa) father

Jägala – (Yegalah) A river in central Estonia

Juhan – (Yoohan) Male protagonist

Kaitseliit – (Kite-sell-eet)A voluntary organisation involved in and supporting national defence.

Kallis – A term of endearment

Kari – (Carrie) A woman's name

Kautla – (Cowtla) A central area, the forest became a holdout for the Finnish Boys

Kommen Sie Hier – German 'come here' (Come you, here)

Konstantin Päts – (Konstantin Pets) Estonian Prime Minister who took control of the country and ran as a dictatorship until the Soviet advance.

Kõrvemaa – (Kurrvemaah) A central part of Estonia, where Kautla is situated.

Kristiine – (Kristeen-eh) A district of Tallinn

Kübelwagen – (Koo-bell-vag-en) German small multi purpose army vehicle

Laidoner – (Lie-donner)Estonian Commander in chief of armed forces in the 1921 war of independence

League of Veterans – Fascist Estonian political organisation in the 1930s, quashed when Konstantin Päts had all members imprisoned.

Leib – (Layb) Bread

Leppneeme – (Lepp-neh-meh) A small port near Tallinn

Liise – (Leess-eh) Estonian version of Lisa

Liisbet – (Leesbet) one of the female protagonists, Estonian version of Elizabeth

Maarja – (Mahrya) Female protagonist

Märjamaa – (Merryamaa) small town in central Estonia

Märt – (Merrt) The main protagonist in the novel.

Nicht Wahr – (Nicht Vaar, using ch as in loch) German for 'is it not?'

Oberleutnant – (Oberloytenant) German first lieutenant

Pärnu – (Pehrnoo) the summer capital and town on the coast. The area surrounding is known as **Pärnumaa**

Peeter – (Payter) Male protagonist in this story

Piik Hermann – (Peek Hairmann) An iconic tall tower in the medieval walls of Tallinn

Pirita – A suburb east of Tallinn, site of medieval abbey

Raio – (Rye-o) Male protagonist in this story

Saaremaa – (Sah-rem-aa) largest Estonian island, west of the mainland

Schmeisser – (Shmice-er) A type of German semi-automatic gun

Schulz – (Shultss) German surname

Siim – (Seem) A man's name

Tartu – (Tartoo) The winter capital and home of Estonia's university.

Tere – (terreh) Hello

Tervist – (Tare vist) Hello

Toomas – (Tormass) Estonian man's name

Urmas – (Oormass) Male name

Viimsi – (Veemsee) A peninsula east of Tallinn port

Winter war – In November 1939, the Soviet Union invaded Finland, a former part of the Russian empire. The Finns successfully held back the larger Russian army, but in the end were forced to sue for peace in March 1940. They ceded 11% of their land (including the site of the base of the British forces in 1920 and the second largest city) The Soviet's poor performance in the conflict emboldened Hitler to attack Stalin. It also meant Finland sided with Germany by virtue of a common enemy.

Printed in Great Britain
by Amazon

58225452R00180